Operation Chainbreak

– JOHN MYLES –

An environmentally friendly book printed and bound in England by
www.printondemand-worldwide.com

Mixed Sources
Product group from well-managed forests, and other controlled sources
www.fsc.org Cert no. TT-COC-002641
© 1996 Forest Stewardship Council

PEFC Certified
This product is from sustainably managed forests and controlled sources
www.pefc.org
PEFC/16-33-415

This book is made entirely of chain-of-custody materials

www.fast-print.net/store.php

Operation Chainbreak

A catalogue record for this book is available from the British Library

ISBN 978-178035-617-4

First published 2013 by
FASTPRINT PUBLISHING
Peterborough, England.

Chapter 1

The upstairs room was bare and unwelcoming. It smelt faintly of soot and damp upholstery. A sulky little fire burning in the small grate barely touched the chilly atmosphere. The furniture consisted of some shabby armchairs and a battered old desk. In the centre of the room there was a worn carpet and, standing on this, facing the window, stood a young man, his feet a little apart and his back very upright. He was of medium build and had neatly trimmed dark hair. Brown eyes gazed out across the empty quadrangle towards the Chapel on the far side. Ian's thoughts were far away. Outside the sky was dark and menacing. Miniature snow drifts were accumulating on the steps of the Chapel, while over to the left flurries of powdery snow whirled playfully around the buttresses of the ancient School Hall.

Despite its bleakness, use of this room, the prefects' study, was considered to be a great privilege. Nevertheless the young man seemed very much at home. Turning away from the window Ian Maxwell noticed, for the first time, that there was a well-used cane resting on the head prefect's desk - the desk which he himself had occupied not so long ago. He frowned. In his opinion some prefects resorted to use of the cane far too readily. He himself had always reserved it for really bad offences such as bullying. His thoughts were interrupted by a timid knock on the door. Forgetting for a moment that he was a mere visitor, Ian responded with a brisk "Come" in his best prefectorial manner. A small boy entered. "Dr. Heron would be glad to see you in his study, sir," the child announced. Ian relaxed and smiled, remembering that he need no longer play the part of the stern senior. "Thank you. I will go up right away." "Good luck, Sir", said the youngster. This was 1917 and the boy guessed from the other's new-looking uniform, that of a Second Lieutenant in the North Thames regiment, that its owner must be an "old boy" come to take a last look at the school and his ordered past before France and an unknown, and perhaps brief, future swallowed him up.

As the Headmaster shook hands, Ian realised with surprise that the aloof austere man he had remembered now seemed frail and tired. Dr. Heron was older, too, than Ian had recalled. It struck him then that saying goodbye to yet another of his pupils, who was only too likely to be killed or maimed within a few months, must tax any schoolmaster sorely. Perhaps it would have been kinder not to come - still it was the "done thing" - and, like most people, Ian was accustomed to conform. It was a duty that both had to carry out to the best of their ability. "I hear you did very well at Sandhurst, Maxwell", said Dr. Heron. "Thank you, Sir," replied Ian, "but I think my grounding in the Officers Training Corps at School must take the credit for that." "What posting will you get now you have passed out and been commissioned?" asked the Head. "I leave for France tonight and should be with the first battalion of the North Thames within the next couple of days".

When he left the Headmaster's study Ian slipped quietly out of the school by a side entrance. He set off down the deserted road, now sprinkled with clean white snow: then, spotting a tram about to leave the terminus, he sprinted a few dozen yards and swung on board.

The first battalion of the North Thames regiment was part of General Cough's Fifth Army which, in the winter of 1917-1918, was stretched out, very thinly, over a very long front. In the opinion of the General Staff this was fully justified. They believed that the Germans were most unlikely to attack on this sector. In any case they had devised a system of "defence in depth", utilising a variety of strong points. They considered this to be a great step forward in defensive tactics. The strong points differed in size from tiny dugouts under the command of a lance-corporal or corporal to miniature forts with a field officer in charge. This new system replaced part of the continuous line of trenches which until recently had stretched from the Swiss frontier to the sea. There had been some muttering by old soldiers and experienced NCOs about breaking away from the long-standing tradition that the British Army "fights in line," but orders had to be obeyed.

Ian's battalion commander, Colonel May, was less optimistic than his superiors about the possibility of a German attack. His concerns were shared by many other senior front-line officers. Because of their misgivings they organised a number of small raids into “no man’s land” during the early weeks of January 1918. The objective was to try to find out what the enemy was up to. Ian Maxwell was too inexperienced to take charge of a raiding party himself but was appointed second in command of a raid led by Captain Douglas, his company commander. As he climbed out over the parapet for the first time Ian felt a tingle of fear and excitement run down his spine. Behind him came the solidly reassuring bulk of Corporal Jones, followed by three privates chosen for their coolness and their ability to move silently and to "freeze" dead still if a star-shell went up. One after the other they crept out, stopping every so often, crouched in a shell crater, to listen and to peer out into the darkness.

After half an hour of cautious exploration, moving ever closer to the German trenches, they rested briefly in a good sized shell hole which was, as usual, half full of ice cold muddy water. Ian felt a touch on his sleeve. Captain Douglas pointed over to their right. Through the gloom Ian caught a glimpse of two men not far away. Surprisingly they appeared to be upright and in the open. There was a distant flash and explosion as some gunners further up the line fired a single shell at an imagined enemy movement. The brief flash allowed the raiding party to see that the men they were watching wore German "coal-scuttle" helmets. They seemed to be examining something on the ground. Captain Douglas signalled that he and two of the men would approach from one side while Ian, Corporal Jones and the third private cut off the Germans' retreat. Apart from sporadic rifle fire all seemed quiet. Their quarry appeared to be unused to the dangers of no man's land and were easily and silently overpowered. The party was returning to the British lines when Ian overheard an urgent whisper in German. The older of the two prisoners was desperately impressing on the younger man that he must say nothing of the "Kaiserkamph" to his captors.

Once they were below the parapet and in comparative safety Ian turned suddenly to the younger German and said quietly, in the man's own language, "no need to be anxious about giving away any secrets of the Kaiserkamph - we know all about it anyway!" By this time the main party had passed further on and were entering a dugout. The young German seemed horrified. "But even our own front line troops know nothing of the battle of 21st March! My under officer and I have only been told because we are engineers and have to survey the ground ready to bring the guns forward when the main attack has broken through." "Nevertheless," said Ian, "have no doubt that the British army is well aware of your generals' plans". The young prisoner was obviously very shaken. He said nothing further and they proceeded to the dugout in silence.

Once the prisoners had been escorted away to battalion headquarters for formal questioning the two officers relaxed alone in the dugout over a strong coffee. Captain Douglas turned to Ian. "What was going just after we got back to our lines? I thought I heard you talking to one of those prisoners in German. I didn't know you could speak their language." Ian explained. "My father teaches modern languages at Oxford. Before the war we always spent the long vac' in France or Germany. I was lucky enough to pick up both languages at a very early age and without much effort." He then went on to detail what he had learned. "The colonel will be most interested," said Duncan. "This backs his hunch that the Germans are planning a major offensive in this sector - despite the official line from the General Staff". The information gleaned from the young prisoner was duly passed on to Fifth Army headquarters, but as with other items conflicting with the preconceived notions of the "brass hats", it was conveniently ignored.

When the battalion was out of the line on "rest", much of the time was spent training and digging support trenches, so that "rest" was often more exhausting than being at the front! Ian reflected that tomorrow they would face the long march forward again, which would add to the general fatigue. Once back in position officers and men would then have to adjust yet again to the sniping and the mortar fire - and to the artillery shells which mostly whistled overhead but which, occasionally, demolished their defences. This was actually quite rare on their particular part of the front but when it did happen there was the grim task of digging out the survivors – to the accompaniment of the cries and the groaning of wounded and dying men. Then there would be stretcher parties slithering past in the mud as they struggled to get the casualties back to the regimental aid post. Despite these horrors Ian wondered if, given the option, he might not really prefer to remain at the front indefinitely! Most of the time life there had a simplicity that was not unattractive, once one had adjusted to it. It was the adjusting that Ian found difficult!

Today the battalion was in relative safety and, although their “resting” quarters were pretty basic, they were at least dry. One could enjoy a warm-up at a good fire in the evenings - and the food in the rest lines was fairly good. Tomorrow all that would change yet again! They would be back to corned beef and dry biscuits, lubricated with water from cans dragged up through the slime and mud of the communication trenches with much effort and more bad language by the stalwarts of the Army Service Corps. Days and nights would be spent in cold damp excavations and probably it would rain about 70% of the time!

"Mr Maxwell!" - Ian was roused abruptly from his musings by the stentorian voice of the orderly corporal, who had appeared at the door of the battered old farmhouse which served as officers' mess when the battalion was out of the line. "Lieutenant Maxwell. Adjutant would like to see you in his office at once, sir." "Thank you, corporal", replied Ian, wondering what he had done to incur the wrath of the authorities. When he reached the converted byre which served as the unit's headquarters he found Captain Dykes, immaculate as ever, sitting at his makeshift desk, but looking slightly ill at ease. This surprised Ian. The adjutant was meticulous in his duties and was normally very confident and very correct. "Sorry about this, Maxwell", said Dykes, "but it just can't be avoided. You're the only regular officer the Colonel feels he can spare. We can't risk sending anyone with a temporary commission. That might give quite the wrong impression of the regiment, you know." Captain Dykes was a pre-war regular, and very conscious of that fact and of the reputation of the North Thames. He regarded Maxwell and the very few other regular officers left as fellow professionals amongst too many amateurs. "I know you won't want to be away from the battalion, and I entirely sympathize. However the Colonel and I have considered the problem from every angle and there's no other solution". Ian wished Dykes would get to the point and explain what this was all about but Dykes went on talking about the virtues of the regiment not being dispersed and the value of "esprit de corps". When, after some minutes, he paused, Ian seized the opportunity. "Where am I to be posted, Captain Dykes?" he asked bluntly. "Detached, not posted!" corrected the adjutant hastily. Then he added, "To the RFC, of course. One of their squadrons is being allocated for contact patrol work with the 18th Division.

Each battalion has been ordered to detach one officer for liaison duties. Of course I don't suppose you will be required to take part in flying or any nonsense of that sort, but I am afraid you'll have to mess with a very mixed bunch".

The adjutant of 132 squadron, Royal Flying Corps, to whom Ian reported the next day, was, like Captain Dykes, a regular, but he was different in every other way. Lieutenant Bridges was father figure to a very young squadron - even the CO, Major Hunt, was only 26. Bridges had served in the Boer War as a Corporal in the balloon battalion of the Royal Engineers. By 1914 he had risen to the rank of Sergeant. At the outbreak of war that August there were very few officers with the slightest knowledge of aeronautics. Bridges had been hastily commissioned. By 1918 he was a highly competent administrator with an extensive knowledge of aerial warfare. When Ian entered the adjutant's tented office, on his arrival at the RFC station, he was pleasantly surprised to be welcomed with an invitation to sit down and have a cup of tea! The tea having been produced very promptly by an orderly, Bridges proceeded to brief the new member of the squadron.

"You will find life here quite a contrast to your regiment, but I am afraid the casualty rate is just about as high", he said. "If I may offer a bit of advice, though, I suggest you get involved with our sort of work as soon and as fully as you can. There will be plenty of chances to fly as an observer and the RFC lads will co-operate better with a man who can talk their language! Find out for yourself what it's like up there. Take my word for it, it may seem very peaceful at first, but you'd better not relax for a moment or you may pay for it with your life - or your pilot's - or both." After this little pep talk he paused for a moment. Then he continued. "Report now to Colonel Bryant, the station commander, and after that to Major Hunt our squadron commander. Then you can get settled in to your quarters. All the junior officers here are in tented accommodation. Tomorrow at 0800 hours you and the other regimental officers joining us are to report to the Chateau. There you will start with introductory lectures and discussions. The day after that there will be practical training. The pilots of B flight will fly their planes in late tomorrow and after that you will be told to which aircraft you have been allotted." Ian reflected wryly that Captain Dykes comments about there being "no flying or nonsense of that sort" had been somewhat misleading, but he did not mind in the least. Instead he rather looked forward to a new and exciting experience.

Punctually at 8am on the morning of 12th March 1918 Ian Maxwell stood beside a two-seater biplane waiting for his pilot to emerge from the battered khaki bell tent which served as flight office. To Ian's untutored eye the plane looked vaguely reminiscent of a rather disorganised daddy-longlegs, though smelling somewhat of petrol! Three RFC officers appeared abruptly and one, a very tall young man, strode straight over to the plane. He was in full flying gear, but Ian could see that he had a rather long hooked nose, cold hard blue eyes and a tight mouth. "Who the devil are you?" was his greeting. "Second Lieutenant Ian Maxwell on detachment from the first battalion, North Thames Regiment", replied Ian as formally as possible, much annoyed and surprised by such a hostile greeting. The other grunted and swung himself into the front cockpit while Ian, assisted by a silent mechanic, climbed into the rear one and strapped himself in. The pilot and the corporal in charge of the ground crew exchanged a formal ritual of checks then "contact." The mechanic swung the propeller and the engine burst into life. The pilot shouted "chocks away" and moments later the plane taxied over the grass, swung into the light headwind and roared across the airfield. Ian felt the tail lift, then the bumping of the wheels over the grass suddenly ceased and he was airborne for the first time in his life. It was an exhilarating experience and one which would never fail to cause him a thrill of excitement, even though it would be repeated it many times over during the next few months.

Looking around, Ian saw to his horror that they were still only about ten feet above the ground and were heading straight for a line of trees beyond the edge of the airfield. He bit his lip but, just as disaster seemed inevitable, the plane tilted suddenly to the right and, with the engine at full throttle, they cleared the last of the trees by inches. Evidently the pilot had his own method of testing his new observer's nerve.

For three days B flight practised dropping messages, spotting ground markers and interpreting signals from the ground by flags, Very pistol and lamps. During this time Ian and his pilot barely exchanged a dozen words. The latter, meanwhile, carried out every known aerobatic manoeuvre in as violent a manner as possible. On 15th March sleet was falling at 8am and flying was cancelled. The trainee observers were taken by tender to a firing range and spent the morning firing Lewis guns. During Ian's four years of OTC training he had specialised in the use and maintenance of machine guns and this stood him in good stead. He scored very well and by the end of the morning he felt he had enjoyed himself. Life was much better in the absence of his objectionable pilot! "Well done, Maxwell," said the officer in charge of the range as they were preparing to return to the airfield, "but remember that firing from a moving aircraft is a very different proposition." "What's the best way of coping?" asked Ian. "Never take your eye off the target whatever your own plane is doing", replied the other, "but tomorrow you should get in some air to ground firing, and that will at least be a start".

The practice firing was a dismal failure. Ian found that each time he had lined up his sights on the target his pilot would bank the plane sharply to one side or the other, so that by the end of the morning he had only fired off half of his ammunition and had scored no hits. The other two trainees on the exercise did considerably better, but this was hardly surprising as their pilots were doing their best to be helpful. Ian settled miserably into his cold cramped cockpit, wishing heartily that he was back with his regiment. However, self-discipline and training soon re-asserted themselves and as the biplane, an RE8, climbed for the flight back to the airfield he began scanning the sky for other aircraft. This he did almost automatically at first but then a tiny speck high above caught his eye. It was hard to make out anything against the sun but the speck was undoubtedly getting larger and then he suddenly realised that there was more than one speck. Ian grabbed the speaking tube - hardly used up to now as he and the obnoxious Lieutenant Guy Huskett barely communicated - "three strange aircraft high right and astern", he said. His unwilling partner looked up and to the right and, after a moment, corrected tersely. "Three triplanes 2000 above, 120 starboard and closing fast".

Huskett's voice changed. "Any ammunition left?". "Two full drums and one half used". "Put on a full drum on and keep your sights on the leader - don't fire till he's within 200yards. I'm going to stall just before he gets in range and he'll overshoot us. That's your chance. When I stall I'll bank hard to starboard and we'll drop like a stone! They won't dare follow us at low altitude." Ian's confidence, which had fallen to zero during the firing practice, lifted. Swiftly he fitted the full drum of ammunition onto the Lewis gun and swung it up to engage the leading triplane, now enlarging in his sights at an alarming rate. His judgment of range had always been good and at 400 yards his finger started to press gently against the trigger. When he opened fire moments later he saw, to his delight, that fragments of debris were leaping from the cowling of the other plane. He strove to keep his sights on the engine and cockpit, but he had only been firing for what seemed like a couple of seconds when he heard the engine of his own plane suddenly cut back to a mere tick over. Almost at once he felt the nose lift. The whole aircraft started to judder. He saw the damaged triplane shoot past close above them and then disappear out of sight. He looked for the following triplanes but before he could bring his gun to bear, his own plane's nose dropped and they swung to the right in a sickening lurch. Now the engine burst into life again and they were diving almost vertically towards the fields of France under full power.

Ian tried to spot the three enemy triplanes that had attacked them but truthfully this was mainly to divert his mind from the crash that he confidently expected must come at any moment. To his amazement that crash never came! He felt tremendous pressure against his seat and a sinking feeling in his stomach and suddenly the biplane was horizontal again and flying fast only a few feet above the ground. They lifted to clear a small wood and then continued back to base at low level. Huskett landed the plane smoothly and taxied over to the aircraft park. As they climbed down he turned to Ian and said, "What about a drink?" They set off towards the mess and he added, "I think you got that first Fokker, you know - pity we couldn't hang around to make sure". After this relations between them improved steadily and Ian began to realise that he was fortunate to be flying with a cool and exceptionally skilful pilot

Not long after the Fokker incident Ian was surprised to be greeted by an unfamiliar pilot when he reported for flying one morning. "You've to put up with me today" said Second Lieutenant Bob Brown cheerily as he introduced himself. They took off and spent the morning training with an infantry unit from the division's slim reserves. At lunch time Bob and Ian sat together and Bob explained that he was just back from leave. He said he was "the squadron dogs body" - the most junior pilot. He had to stand in for anyone who was away. Ian was surprised. "Guy never mentioned that he was due for leave". "He isn't" said Bob, "but the CO fixed it for him to fly over to Croydon today so that he could attend the memorial service for his younger brother". Ian was puzzled. "What happened to his brother. I didn't even know he had a brother?" Bob looked serious. "Guy probably wouldn't mention it to you as you were a newcomer and he was very cut up. His younger brother was midshipman on a destroyer. Just before we were transferred here he heard that that it had been sunk with all hands".

Ian Maxwell woke at 4.30am on the 21st of March, the first day of the spring of 1918. To start with he wondered why he was awake. Then he realised that the growling, rumbling sound that filled the darkness must be the cause. As consciousness returned he remembered the German prisoner he had talked to in the trenches months previously. The man had spoken of the "battle of 21st March"! Was this it? Sleep was impossible. He looked out of the tent and saw that the airfield was shrouded in a mist so dense that even the next tent was only barely visible. Thirty miles further forward at the front line the same mist was providing perfect cover for the well-rehearsed advance of the German infantry. As they moved forward, an intensive and perfectly coordinated artillery barrage crept on ahead of them, destroying the British defences and shattering the defenders. On the airfield Ian could hear the sound of officers and men, woken by the distant gunfire, starting to move around. Ian's first thought was to dress and join the others but then he remembered that if there is nothing useful he can do, a good soldier rests, even if he cannot sleep. It seemed certain that once the mist lifted the squadron, and probably every other element of the RFC, would be in action. He would rest in preparation for what was to come.

The mist did not clear until well after mid-day. By then the Germans had penetrated deep into the front line defences of the British Fifth Army. Those who survived the most intense artillery barrage of the war were dazed and bemused. Many were captured before they realised exactly what was happening. The thick mist had allowed the attackers to bypass the chain of strong-points inaugurated by General Gough and his staff. Helped by that mist the Germans had been able to infiltrate the defences, often unseen by the defenders. The strongpoints were surrounded and then dealt with by second line infantry following on behind the highly trained "Storm Troops" who spearheaded the attack. The initial barrage had severed most of the British field telephone lines and by noon many commanders had lost all contact with their forward units.

Towards mid-day urgent messages began to come in to the airfield. Battalion commanders and divisional staff officers were desperate for information about their own troops as well as for news of the enemy advance. Major Hunt called together his pilots and liaison officer/observers and explained the situation. Each flight was allocated a sector of the front to cover. The flight commanders then allocated individual aircraft to specific areas. Fortunately, at this stage of the war, the RFC had strong fighter forces available, and these were quickly mobilised to protect the two seater observation planes cruising above the battle area. Once the mist had cleared, Guy Huskett and Ian Maxwell were sent to investigate the area where the Crozat canal joins the river Oise. Here the right wing of the British Fifth Army should have been linked to the left wing of the French Sixth Army. It was soon apparent that the German break-through had been planned to split the two allied armies. The attack was on a massive scale. It had penetrated deeply, completely separating the British and French forces. Ian and Guy returned to make their report but were soon sent out over the battle zone again, to try to obtain more detailed information and to attempt to contact individual units.

Well behind the original front line they spotted a company of British infantry obviously gathering for an attempt at a counter-attack. Most of the British troops they had seen before this had appeared disorganised, with individuals and small groups heading away from the enemy in a haphazard fashion. Up to now there had been little sign of any resistance to the German advance. This was the first organised group they had seen. They flew low over the advancing soldiers and attacked the enemy with machine gun fire in an effort to assist the British counter attack. The attack soon faltered, however, and came to a halt in the face of the overwhelming numbers of the enemy. There were many British casualties. Guy and Ian returned to the airfield dispirited and with their plane splattered with bullet holes from German ground fire.

Others in the squadron had had similar experiences. There was general despondency about the situation. Over the next few days there were innumerable flights to reconnoitre the ever deepening German advance. Aircrews and ground staff alike became weary. Patrols were out over the battle area whenever visibility allowed. The task of servicing and repairing the aircraft was a never ending one for the ground crews. Casualties started to mount too, as tired pilots made errors of judgment and when German single-seaters managed to slip through the fighter cover and attack the slow cumbersome RE8 reconnaissance planes. As the situation on the ground got steadily worse, Generals who had previously had little faith in the air arm began, in desperation, to demand more and more of such units of the RFC and Royal Naval Air Service as were available. Attacks from the air on German ground forces were urged and the planes of the ground contact patrol started to carry bombs.

By March 27th Guy and Ian were the only original crew in 13 flight still fully operational. That morning they were ordered up to locate and support an artillery battery which was attempting to withdraw to a new position under heavy attack from enemy infantry. The airmen located the gunner unit with some difficulty and the RE8 then circled while the situation was sized up by pilot and observer. The artillerymen were almost surrounded. Their only route of escape by was being swept by fire from an advanced German machine gun post. "Better drop a couple of eggs and then spray Jerry with the Lewis-gun while the gunners make a dash for it", said Guy. Ian assented and they dropped a message to let the battery commander know their plan. As the biplane swept low over the battery Ian saw an officer wave in acknowledgement. The horses were already being hitched up to the guns and limbers. "Nothing to wait for, Guy", said Ian. Guy banked the plane steeply and they made a run at low level heading directly at the

German machine gun post. Their two bombs appeared to land close to the target, but smoke and dust concealed the airmen's view for a couple of minutes.

The gunners wasted no time and as the plane turned back towards the battery Ian could see the leading gun moving off at a gallop. "Now for some covering fire", said Guy bringing the plane round so as to pass low behind the German post, giving Ian a chance to distract the enemy by attacking from their rear. As the biplane banked round ready for the attack Ian glanced down towards the artillery battery and saw that the first gun and limber were well clear of the encroaching German infantry. The second team was not so fortunate. A stray German shell had blown a wheel off the limber Limber and gun had jack-knifed, throwing the crew to the ground. Several were lying very still. Others were struggling with injured and terrified horses. The rest of the battery, marshalled by their commander, were almost ready to move off. Ian had no time to take in any more. As they neared the machine gun post it was soon apparent that the Germans were ready for them. One machine gun was out of action - destroyed by the bombs they had dropped - but the other had been righted and swung upwards. The approaching RE8 was met by steady and accurate fire. Ian concentrated on directing the fire of his own Lewis gun in return, but was aware of holes appearing in the fabric of the fuselage unpleasantly close to him. Then he felt as if something had knocked hard against his hip and he noticed that his right leg felt numb.

A moment later black oil was spraying back over the cockpit. The engine began to stutter. Guy's cool voice came over the speaking tube. "I'm going to try and climb to gain a bit of height. I don't know how much longer the engine will keep going!" The plane lurched erratically but under Guy's skilled nursing it headed back towards the safety of the British second line defences. By this time their ammunition was exhausted and Ian realised there was little more they could have done to help the gunners. He felt rather faint but sat back in the rear cockpit trying to keep a good lookout. After a few minutes of very unsteady flight Guy called out, "There's a small airstrip over to our starboard side. I'm going to try and put down there". The landing was horrible. Ian felt the plane veer suddenly to the left as it touched down. It came to rest with the remains of the port wing on the ground. Guy shouted "Get out quick Ian - she may catch fire!" The jarring had done something to Ian's injured leg and he was in agony. He managed to pull himself up out of the cockpit and with a tremendous and agonising effort swung himself clear of the plane, only to collapse semi-conscious on the ground beside it.

The airstrip was about to be abandoned. It was now within range of the advancing German guns! An RFC sergeant, who had been left in charge, came running over to the plane. With his help Guy Huskett lifted Ian and the two men carried him as gently as circumstances allowed away from the wreck of the faithful RE8. "We're just about to pull out from here, sir," the sergeant said once they had got Ian settled on a couple of blankets. "Must get my observer to a medical post as soon as possible," said Guy. "Can you take us on your lorry as far as is necessary?" The sergeant explained his orders. "We've to report to Montidier and set up a new airstrip as quickly as possible. You're welcome to come on the lorry with us but it's pretty heavily loaded. It will be a slow journey, and I'm afraid it won't be very comfortable for the wounded officer." After about an hour of grinding slowly along atrocious roads they came to a point where a fresh unit was digging in to prepare a new line of defence. "Stop here", ordered Guy. "This is the first properly organised outfit we've come across so far. They're likely to have an MO. with them." The RFC lorry ground to a halt and Guy jumped down. "What unit are you?" he asked a corporal who was supervising the digging of a trench close to the road. "Dismounted 16th Lancers, sir", was the reply." "Have you got a medical officer with you?" asked Guy. "Yes, sir, Captain Humphries is our MO." At Guy's request the obliging corporal sent a runner to fetch the doctor and a stretcher party.

Fortunately for Ian the doctor was an unusually experienced and mature man for a front line Regimental Medical Officer. Before the war he had run a fashionable London practice and had held an honorary appointment at the Royal North London Hospital. A medical orderly swiftly slit the seam of Ian's flying suit and the doctor examined the wound carefully. By this time Ian was conscious but still in great pain. He told the MO. that at first he had thought he had just knocked his hip on something in the cockpit but that his leg had then gone a bit numb. After the crash-landing the pain had suddenly become excruciating. Now every jolt or jar sent a sort of shock wave right down the back of his leg and into his foot.

"I'm pretty sure there's a bullet lodged against the pelvis, “said Dr. Humphries. "As a result of the crash it's now compressing your sciatic nerve." "Despite the pain, I don't think your life's in immediate danger. Removing the bullet without damaging the nerve will be a very delicate job - one for an expert. I know that the field hospital near Amiens is over-run with severely injured men. In my opinion the best course is to have my motor ambulance take you direct to the railway station for immediate evacuation to Britain by hospital train and ship. I can put in a recommendation for you to be taken to the Royal North London Hospital. I know a surgeon there who is a specialist in nerve repair work." Ian looked at the doctor and then at Guy. "If you take my advice, old man, you'll do exactly what the MO. says," Guy responded to the unasked question. "It sounds to me like very good sense. From what we've seen in the last few days the medical units round here must be almost swamped. It will help them, and the more urgent casualties too, if chaps like you, who can wait a day or two for their operation are evacuated to a hospital in Blighty." "You're right Guy," Ian replied. He turned to the MO. "Thanks doctor, please carry on". The medical orderly produced a syringe and rolled up Ian's sleeve. Captain Humphries drew up a solution of morphia and injected it very slowly into a vein. "This will ease the pain for now", he said, "and I'll send a note to the MO. on the hospital train to give you another dose in a few hours". Ian was grateful for some relief, but despite the morphia his pain never really left him, but only fluctuated in intensity. The long journey that ended in hospital in London was a blurred nightmare of confused images and bouts of searing pain.

Chapter Two

Ian Maxwell opened his eyes then hastily closed them again. It was too bright. There seemed to be a white glare everywhere. There was a strange unpleasant smell too - rubber and something else - something vaguely familiar and yet at the same time unknown. He slept again. When he opened his eyes for the second time he saw a pair of steady grey eyes looking directly into his own eyes. He was aware of a deep-set ache in his right hip, but the agonising pains like electric shocks that had burned his leg from the back of the hip to the ends of his toes had gone. It seemed to him that he had endured these for so long that their absence was almost sinister. Perhaps they had taken off his leg. Perhaps his life was over!

Now a firm but gentle voice was speaking. "You are awake, Lieutenant Maxwell. Your operation is over.

The bullet has been removed. Does your leg feel better?" He registered, gradually, that the owner of the voice was also the owner of the grey eyes. "Yes, thank you, Sister. I feel completely different." He was talking to a young nurse in a pale grey dress and dazzling white apron. A neat cap almost concealed her fair hair. He noted that there was no red cross on the bib of the apron. She must be a "proper" nurse, not a VAD. He realised, with a shock, that this was the first thing outside himself and his closed world of pain, and of enduring pain, that he had registered for many days. It was somehow reassuring to feel that he could think of something beyond the inner world of his damaged body once again. "Who are you, Sister? Have I seen you before?" "I am Nurse Saunders and I have been on this ward for three weeks now. I had to stay with you until you recovered from the anaesthetic. Now you are awake I must report to Sister and tell her that the operation has succeeded. She will want to pass on the good news to your surgeon, Mr Handley. We all knew it was a very delicate op." Maxwell drifted off into a natural sleep that was the first stage of a remarkable recovery.

Mr Handley, coming round the ward subsequently, felt that, in an era of ghastly injuries and of mutilating surgery - necessary to preserve life - here was at least one man who really had benefited from the patient delicate skill he had all too few opportunities to practise these days.

Two weeks after the operation Grace Saunders removed Ian Maxwell's stitches under Sister Graves' watchful eye. By this time he had been up and about in the ward for several days, and able to chat sympathetically with other patients. "I'll leave you to tidy up and finish the dressing, Saunders," said Sister. "Make sure you get the bandage firm. We don't want the dressing slipping and exposing that long wound. Mr Maxwell must rest after that." When Sister had left the screened off bed and returned to her desk at the top of the ward Ian, greatly daring, turned his head and looking directly at his nurse said, "Miss Saunders, I hope to leave hospital for convalescence soon. When I do, will you allow me to take you to tea, if you have a free afternoon." He was quite shy and the effort had cost him a good deal. The fear of rejection was very close. The grey eyes met his. "That would be very nice, Mr Maxwell. I get a free afternoon most Wednesdays." Ian grinned with pleasure and relief. No "put-down", no hesitation, just a quiet acceptance with that intriguing half smile that he suddenly realized had been in and out of his thoughts much of the time for the past couple of weeks.

The little group of white coats, accompanied by the authoritative figure of Sister Graves in her tall cap and dark blue dress, moved slowly up the ward. At each bed there was a discussion as Mr Handley's assistants reported on patients' progress and as decisions were made. An arm amputation for one man, a high thigh amputation for another, a change of plaster, mobilization on crutches and then - Ian Maxwell. Sister spoke to Mr Handley. "Mr Maxwell had done remarkably well, sir. I think we could transfer him to the Banstead convalescent unit. They have a vacancy on Tuesday." Poor Ian's heart sank. If he was sent so far away it would put paid to his outing with Grace Saunders. "All right with you, Maxwell"? said Mr Handley, and Ian had little alternative but to say "Yes, sir." Then he added, "thank you for what you have done for me. I feel a different man since that operation". He was very quiet for the rest of the day. “A visitor for you, Lieutenant Maxwell," said the VAD the following afternoon. Ian looked up from his book and there, to his astonishment, was Guy Huskett, tall and debonair in immaculate RFC uniform. "Thought I would pop in to see how you were faring after our little adventure," he said. "I hear you've had a very successful op." "Great to see you, old chap", replied Ian, "and yes, thanks. I'm really feeling fine now; had my stitches out yesterday. Anyway, how are things with B flight?" "It's been brisk work", answered Guy, "but the tide may be turning now. We’ve had to move to an airfield south of Amiens, but the German advance has petered out to some extent and our chaps are consolidating. We have had quite an influx of new aircrew on the station - mostly pretty raw! By the way our friend, Bob Brown, has been posted to 212 squadron. He's flying a Sopwith Camel now. I rather envy him!"

After some further professional exchanges about the work of the contact patrol flight in particular and the RFC in general, Guy Huskett asked, "What are your prospects for getting out of hospital, and what are your plans when they let you go? If you want a billet within striking distance of the hospital, my folks would be delighted to have you stay with them out at Highcrest. Father's in the city all day and mother is tied up a lot of the time with her Red Cross work, but there are two old retainers who would just love to have a wounded officer to look after! My parents would be glad of your company in the evenings and will want to hear your views on the war and about your experiences in the trenches. Since my brother Jack's ship was sunk they have longed to have a bit more contact with people who've been actively engaged in the war. For the rest of the time you would have the run of the place and could come and go as you pleased".

This sounded like a big improvement on the convalescent home in Surrey, and so it came about that on the Wednesday of the following week Ian was waiting, rather impatiently, outside the door of the nurses' home of the Royal North London Hospital. Grace emerged at exactly 2.15pm - a slim fair-haired girl with smiling grey eyes. She was wearing a mid- blue costume and a white hat and carrying white gloves and a white handbag. The sight of her was enough to make Ian's heart beat faster.

The late April sun was pleasantly warm as they walked to the end of the road to catch a tram up to Highcrest, where Ian knew of a little tea-room, reached by a walk through a well-kept park. After the ride in the half-empty tram they strolled leisurely through Stanhope Park. Swans moved serenely on the ornamental lake and ducks poked about in the shallows looking for food. One or two prim nursemaids passed, wheeling high perambulators along the broad path at a genteel pace. They met an elderly lady exercising a small podgy dog and were amused by her many breathless exhortations as to good behaviour in the park. Mostly they walked in silence, enjoying each other's company, but each rather shy of starting a conversation. In such peaceful surroundings it was hard to realise that Britain had been embroiled in a terrible war for four long years and that at this moment the battle in France was going pretty badly for the allies.

At length they reached the "Copper Kettle" and found a table. Ian ordered tea, sandwiches and cakes. "You've made tremendous progress", Grace said as they waited for their tea to arrive, but what will happen once your convalescence is over". "I will have to go before a medical board and, with luck, I can get back to my regiment", replied Ian, "though what I would really like best of all would be to return to my attachment to the aerial reconnaissance unit. I've got rather hooked on flying!" "Wouldn't you prefer something a bit safer and more peaceful now," asked Grace. "Certainly not", replied Ian. "I decided to join the army as a regular and I want to continue my career. I grew up with the war! I joined the Officers Training Corps at school in 1914. When I left school the war looked like going on for ever, so I decided to do things properly and apply for a regular army commission." Grace laughed. "That's exactly why I decided to do a full nursing training and not just enrol as a VAD." "Tell me –about yourself," said Ian. "It's not very exciting," said Grace. "I grew up in Cincombe in Gloucestershire where my father is rector. I went to boarding school at Malvern when I was twelve. When we were sixteen Marion, my best friend, and I decided we ought to do something to help the war effort. She is very independently minded and, despite all that the headmistress and her parents could think of to dissuade her, she went off to work in a munitions factory in Swindon. I'm much more timid, and after talking to Miss Horton, our headmistress, and mother it was eventually agreed that I should stay on at school until I was old enough to start to train as a state registered nurse. Eventually, a few months ago, Marion's mother persuaded her that she would be more useful working at the Ministry of Munitions, where she could make use of her education as well as her practical experience in the factory. Now she shares a flat in central London with another school friend. I meet them quite often." Do you like nursing?" asked Ian. "It's very hard work," replied Grace, "but most interesting, especially when they let me help in the operating theatre. We don't get very much time off but when my training is finished I should have a job for life! I think it's much more satisfying than just being a VAD and I think I'll probably be more use as a trained nurse too." Time flew by but Ian managed to get Grace to agree to go to the theatre with him one evening the following week.

Towards the end of May 1918 Ian appeared before a medical board and was passed as fit for restricted overseas service. Two days later he was summoned to the War Office where - to his surprise - he was interviewed by his old company commander from the North Thames regiment, now on staff duties after three years in France. An officer from the newly-formed Royal Air Force took the leading role in the interview. Captain, now Major, Douglas had remembered Ian's perfect command of German and French and had recommended him as a candidate for the Air Intelligence Branch now being formed. The rather unusual combination of experience both in the trenches and in the air, together with his language skills, made Ian an excellent candidate. Within a few days he had been commissioned as a Flying Officer in the RAF and given a posting to a large airfield in northern France. Before he left, there was time for a farewell dinner with Grace Saunders and her friend Marion. Guy Huskett, now seconded - much to his disgust - to instruct trainee pilots in aerial combat tactics at Northolt, made up a foursome. At the end of the evening Ian walked Grace back from the tram stop at the end of the road. They said "Goodnight", then Grace suddenly kissed him lightly on the cheek, whispered "come back safe to me," and ran up the steps and disappeared into the Nurses' Home before Ian had time to draw breath.

When Ian joined his new unit, he found that the German offensive was finally over. The Allies were starting to counter-attack in force. His station commander, Group. Captain Bluett, received Flying Officer Maxwell without much evidence of enthusiasm. "The Air Ministry has laid down that we must have an intelligence officer, but I doubt if there will be much work for you," he said when Ian reported, to the CO on his arrival. Ian seized the opportunity. "May I have your permission, sir, to fly as observer from time to time to familiarize myself with the battlefield area and with the work of the flying wing?" Bluett looked at the file on his desk and reflected before replying. "I see you were wounded in action flying as an observer and were recommended for "mention in dispatches". You may fly if you can get one of the flight commanders to agree and if you can find a pilot who'll risk having you!" Ian saluted and withdrew, quite pleased with the outcome of the interview. He was even more pleased when, in the officers' mess that evening, he met Pilot Officer Bob Brown and learned that he and the rest of 212 squadron were based on the station.

RAF St. Pol was situated in a rather bleak flat part of northern France between Paris and the Channel coast. It was well sited for air operations in support of the advancing Allied armies. There were three squadrons, two of Sopwith Camel single seater scouts and one of RE8 reconnaissance planes. Ian made every effort to get to know aircrew from the latter squadron in the hope of getting a chance to fly again. He was soon on good terms with a number of pilots and observers and also made friends with the young medical officer and one or two of the engineer officers, as well as the station chaplain. This was a large cheerful Welshman. who went out of his way to make Ian feel welcome when he first arrived. Ian and the chaplain found they had something in common. Unlike the other officers neither had any very specific duties laid down and so they were free, to some extent, to plan their own work.

After lunch one day, when Ian was sitting with the padre and the MO, the Reverend Jones said to the doctor, " I'm worried about young Hunt, Doc. He's in the bar far too much and I think he's developing a sort of tremor. Could it be shell shock? Do you remember that six weeks ago he and Armitage had to make a forced landing in no man's land in the middle of a pretty hellish barrage. They were jolly lucky to survive. The very next day they were out over the battlefield again in a replacement aircraft and they've flown practically every day since." "I'll get them both in for routine aircrew medicals," said the doctor. "Who knows but what Hunt may need a few investigations - X-rays and so forth. It might even mean a short spell at the base hospital and then a medical review. "Good," said the padre, "I'm grateful to you George. If I went to his flight commander it could stir up a hornet's nest. The last thing we want is any suggestion of "lack of moral fibre". He's a brave lad but personally I think he's reached the limit of his endurance." "Armitage 'll be fed up if he gets grounded for lack of an observer," grimaced the MO. "They're a scarce commodity just now." Ian had been following the conversation with mild interest, wondering vaguely what Grace would make of a doctor who was prepared to take such an unorthodox approach to solving a very human problem. On the whole he thought she would probably approve. Now he pricked up his ears. "Do you think Armitage would take me on as temporary observer?" he asked. The MO looked hard at him. "Sure you want to get involved when you don't have to? The casualty rate for reconnaissance crews is pretty high." "I know," said Ian. "That's how I got into intelligence. I got a bullet in the backside while I was on ground contact patrol back in March. I was lucky, though, and once they had taken it out and stopped it pressing on my sciatic nerve I was soon fit again. Now I'm really missing flying."

A couple of days later there was a knock on the door of Ian's small office and a short, stocky and rather scruffy Pilot Officer came in. Ian Maxwell gave no indication that he knew the purpose of the visit. "Come and have a seat, Neil," he said, indicating the shabby armchair which was the only comfortable seat in the room. "Just been for my medical with the MO," said Armitage. "How did it go?" asked Ian. "Passed Al," was the reply. "That's great," said Maxwell. "The trouble is, Max," replied Armitage, "the Doc. wants some tests done on Jim Hunt, my observer. Until they're completed he's grounded and without an observer I'm as good as grounded myself!" Ian looked sympathetic and Armitage continued, "The Doc. said something about you having had observer experience. If you're not too busy with intelligence work I wondered if you would consider flying with me, providing Jack Hayes, my flight commander agrees." "What sort of hours will it involve, Neil?" asked Max. "Normally we do two or three 90 minute flights a day, when it's clear enough for photographic work," said Neil, "but of course there are quite a few times when conditions aren't good enough, and then you could catch up with your other work. " "Right", said Ian, "I'll be pleased to fly with you, if Jack Hayes agrees. By the way, you can tell him the CO has cleared me for flying, as and when any opportunities arise."

For the next six weeks Ian Maxwell and Neil Armitage flew quite a number of missions together and Neil was more than once grateful to have an observer who was able to handle a Lewis gun with confidence and accuracy. German pilots had orders to prevent reconnaissance flights at all costs, and despite the presence of many British and French fighters, Neil and Ian were attacked several times.

As the Allied offensive built up from August 1918 onwards, Ian became increasingly involved in questioning German prisoners, especially those from the enemy air service. He wrote to Grace fairly regularly. Though his letters were a little dull, partly owing to the needs of censorship but mainly due to his deficiencies as a letter writer, Grace was always cheered to see his now familiar writing when she went to her pigeon hole in the Nurses' Home. She herself wrote chatty interesting letters, so that Ian soon had an excellent mental picture of her life as a nurse, and also gained quite a good idea of her home and of her family, even though he had never met any of them.

Early one morning in September 1918 Ian was shaving when he heard the clatter of the crash alarm, a huge gong operated by an airman turning a handle. He hurried to the door of the Nissen hut in which he was billeted and saw a triplane, with smoke pouring from its engine, staggering down towards the grass landing field. Behind and a little above was a Sopwith Camel. As the triplane touched down it slewed round and came to an abrupt halt. Ian could see little tongues of flame starting to break out from the engine cowling. The airfield crash tender was alongside in seconds and airmen in protective clothing attacked the fire with a cloud of foam. An ambulance pulled up near the tender and a limp form was extracted from the cockpit. The rescued German pilot was carried to the ambulance and rushed to the station medical post. Ian finished shaving and went over to the mess in a thoughtful mood.

He was about to leave the table after his usual light breakfast when one of the pilots came over to him. It was Bob Brown. "Max," he said, "I think you might be interested in a new arrival here. I managed to shoot up a Fokker when I was on early patrol this morning. I trailed him in and forced him down on the airfield. He was on fire but managed to land and does not seem much the worse for his adventures." "Thanks Bob," said Ian,

"I'll see what I can get out of him." "This chap could know a bit," said Bob. "He's young but seems to be an Oberleutnant of sorts - and surprisingly confident despite his narrow escape." Ian thought for a minute. "Would you be willing to invite him to lunch in the mess and let me join you? I know it's sometimes done. He's much more likely to give something useful away after a decent meal and a brandy! I think it'll be all right with the CO if your prisoner gives you his parole for the time he is on the station." "Right," said Bob, "you're on. We'll give him a really good tuck-in before we send him off to the prisoner of war camp."

Bob Brown and his prisoner, now cleaned up and having discarded his filthy flying jacket in favour of the well-cut uniform he had been wearing under it, turned up at the bar punctually as arranged. Ian Maxwell joined them as if by chance and was introduced to Oberleutnant Maximillian von Straussen. The latter spoke to the two British officers in a mixture of broken English and schoolboy French, but Ian suspected that von Straussen's command of English and French was a great deal better than he admitted to. Ian noticed that as he relaxed his pronunciation improved considerably! He would not be drawn on military matters, but from casual comments about the food, the running of the airfield and other topics Ian gleaned some background information which he felt sure would be useful to Air Intelligence. At length von Straussen said he would like to visit the toilet and they all got up. Ian excused himself, leaving Bob with his prisoner. Soon the Oberleutnant would be in the hands of the Military Police. He would be taken to the railway station at Lille and then escorted on the journey to one of the big prisoner of war camps in southern France.

While he was passing through the cloakroom on his way to the toilet von Straussen managed to acquire an RAF forage cap from a rack near the door! Folded flat, this slipped quite conveniently inside the tunic of his uniform. Nobody noticed his slick movement. Bob had happened to meet another pilot who asked him about weather conditions over the front line. A few minutes later, when Bob Brown and his prisoner reached the main door of the mess they were met by a medical orderly carrying the German's leather flying jacket which he had cleaned up. Von Straussen was touched by the man's kindness. He unfastened the Swiss watch on his left wrist and gave it to the orderly as a keepsake. He then put the jacket on over his uniform. He and Bob walked to the guardroom at the entrance to the airfield, where they were to meet the Military Police escort. As they walked, Bob noticed that his prisoner seemed to develop a hunch and a slouching gait. He imagined that the sudden realization of his situation as a prisoner proper, rather than as "temporary guest", had had a depressing effect on the young man. He supposed that he would have felt much the same had the situation been reversed, but hoped he would have been able to conceal his feelings better. When they reached the guardroom they found that the escort consisted of a large, red-faced Captain of the Military Police and a driver. The Captain exchanged a curt greeting with Bob and then barked a few words of indifferent German at von Straussen, ordering him into the back of the car which stood waiting to take them off to the railway station. The prisoner complied without comment, becoming even more hunched and looking even more depressed. He seemed to Bob to have shrunk!

At the station von Straussen again asked to go to the toilet, groaning a little and rubbing his stomach to indicate his acute discomfort and the urgency of the situation. The Military Police Captain looked disgusted. He muttered to his driver, cursing the stupidity of RAF officers who fed their prisoners with rich food! Leaving the car and driver he marched von Straussen off to the extensive men's toilet inside the station. Having ascertained that the windows were barred and that there was only one door he left the prisoner in a cubicle and waited on the main concourse outside. After about three minutes a tall, smart looking officer emerged. "M. Le Capitaine," he said, with a strong French accent, "I think your prisoner has become rather ill." The MP officer swore and entered. In one of the cubicles he saw a hunched figure in a flying jacket slumped on the floor. He grabbed a shoulder and shook. The man groaned but took no further notice. Realising he would need help, he ordered a passing Army Service Corps lance-corporal to watch the prisoner and went to the RTO in charge of the movements of military personnel at Lille railway station. A stretcher party was summoned and the man was taken to the nearest aid post. The doctor there pronounced that he was concussed, and a military ambulance took him to the nearest army hospital. Here he was stripped for a full examination and it was found that the uniform under the flying jacket was that of a French infantryman!

By this time von Straussen, who never went anywhere without an ample supply of gold coinage, was on his way to the Swiss frontier by a suitably circuitous route. His authoritative bearing, uncertainty as to the precise nature of his uniform, there being in France at that time Belgian, Italian, Portuguese and American officers as well as those from numerous French and British formations, made detection relatively unlikely. His command of language was good and the British he encountered tended to think he was French or Belgian while the French thought he was British or American.

After the armistice of 11th November 1918 the objective of most British servicemen was to get home to "Blighty" as soon as possible. Ian Maxwell was as keen as any. Unfortunately for him this was a particularly busy time for the intelligence services. Information from their own and their allies' sources had to be sifted and evaluated. Prisoners had to be cross-examined before their release. Despite his pleas to his superiors for a brief spell of leave it was not until early February 1919 that he found himself walking up Hereford Road towards the nurses' home of the Royal North London Hospital in the comfortable knowledge that, according to her latest letter, Grace Saunders was free for the afternoon and evening and very happy to spend the time with him for their own private celebration of the end of the war.

Chapter Three

Hereford Road, which ran from High Road, where there was a tram stop, to the Nurses' Home of the Royal North London Hospital, was a long road. It was quiet in the early afternoon and as Ian Maxwell strode on towards the Nurse's Home he noticed, with some surprise, a distant but vaguely familiar figure walking slowly towards him. As he got closer he recognised Grace's friend Marion. He was a little put out by her presence. He had expected to have Grace to himself for their first reunion after so many months. Then he saw that Marion was dressed in black and, as they got closer, he noticed how red her eyes were. When they met she said, "Oh Ian, I am so very, very sorry." "What on earth is the matter?" he demanded, in growing anxiety. "It's Grace," said Marion, "she went down with this awful 'flu two days ago. She died last night!" Ian could hardly believe his ears and could barely take in what she was saying. "When Grace went off duty on Monday she was feeling awful," continued Marion. "She phoned to tell me because she was worried about being well enough to go out with you today. They looked after her in the nurses' sick bay along with several others, but she just got worse and worse. She collapsed early yesterday morning. Her parents were sent for but she never really came round. She died late last night with her mother and father at her bedside"

Marion laid a gentle hand on Ian's arm. "I'm going to take you to stay with Guy Huskett's parents until tomorrow," she said, "then Guy will motor you down to Oxford to your own parents' home. He's going to stay with you there till the funeral. It is to be on Tuesday at Grace's father's church. I shall come down to Cincombe by train early on Tuesday morning." Ian was so numbed and bewildered that he allowed himself to be led back down the road towards the tram stop and escorted out to Highcrest without protest, and saying hardly a word. Guy's parents were full of sympathy, but as soon as possible Ian excused himself to go to his room where, at last, he could break down quietly and alone. In the evening they insisted on his having a little to eat. After that he went to bed, but slept only fitfully, waking very early with a sense of loss which was deeper than any emotion he had ever felt in his life.

The next few days passed in a blur, though with odd moments of clarity such as his meeting with Grace's elderly parents for the first time and the point in the funeral service, when the Bishop, in his address, spoke of Grace with the intimacy and affection of one who had known her from early childhood. After the funeral Ian returned to Oxford for the few remaining days of his leave. His parents were concerned and sympathetic but they had never met Grace and it was difficult for him to talk about her with them. In the end Ian was glad to return to France, where he threw himself into his intelligence work with a hectic energy that was, he felt, a better alternative to numbing his misery with drink.

In the long, lonely, years that followed Ian always attended the Armistice Day Remembrance Service wherever he happened to be. He had many to remember - boys from school - young soldiers he had known in the trenches and numerous airmen. However when, each year, he heard the familiar words

"They shall not grow old as we that are left grow old,

Age shall not weary them, nor the years condemn,"

one face alone, that of a fair-haired young nurse, was before him. In the early years when he saw her thus, it was with a deep sorrow, tinged with bitterness over what might have been, but time heals over the raw surface of the most terrible scar so that, while the scar remains, the acuteness of its pain is tempered. Ian's love, too, had been true and, at least in part, unselfish and in later years he could find it within him to be grateful that, in her short life, Grace had always been loved. She would never know the loneliness of old age nor the indignity of dependence on others nor the pain and weariness of chronic illness.

In 1920 Flying Officer Maxwell was posted to an RAF station in southern England. He began to hear rumours of squadrons being sent to the Middle East and of others being disbanded. At the end of the war Britain had the largest air force in the world. Its' peacetime role, however, was limited. There were policing duties in various parts of the Empire and training activities at home but otherwise there was little requirement for so big a force. Cuts would have to be made. He wondered at times if there was much future for him in the RAF. Air Intelligence, like the rest of the service, must surely be due for extensive pruning. The crunch came one wet April morning when an orderly appeared with a message that the Station Commander wished to see him at 11.30am. A couple of hours later, as he entered the office in response to the CO's gruff "come in", he noticed that the latter was not alone. The visitor was Squadron Leader Avon, the Senior Intelligence Officer from Group Headquarters. "Sit down, Maxwell," said the CO, quite kindly. "Squadron Leader Avon has some bad news for you, I'm afraid." Avon wasted no time. "You must be aware, Maxwell, that the Service is being cut down drastically. As you have never been considered, officially, as being fully fit since you were wounded in 1918, I have no choice in the matter. I'm afraid I have had to put your name down for a "bowler hat". However, if you are applying for a civilian job I can give you an excellent reference. You've been one of the most effective and hard-working intelligence officers in the Group. I'd keep you if I could but the Air Ministry has laid down that only fully fit officers and men can be retained."

At this point the CO spoke. "Maxwell", he said, "I don't know if you've any ideas about what you might do in civilian life, but I think you would make an excellent detective officer with the Police! I happen to know that your old Colonel from the North Thames Regiment is now Chief Constable of Midhamptonshire. I'd be more than happy to recommend you!" Ian pondered for a few moments. He had never thought of serving in the Police as a career but the idea quite appealed to him. Since Grace's death, life had seemed pretty drab. He had no real commitments and a fresh start in life might be just what he needed. Had it not been for the war, he might well have followed his father in an academic career but, after the turmoil of the last two years, he knew that he could never settle to an ordered way of life. "Thank you, gentlemen," he said. "I had been half expecting the chop," and then, turning to the CO, he added, "I'd be most grateful, sir, if you can help me to get into the Police. I think it might be just the right sort of job for me at this stage." He stood up, saluted, and then returned to his own small office to think things over quietly.

Three months later Ian Maxwell was enrolled as a probationary Constable with the Midhamptonshire Constabulary, a largely rural force. His first two years were to be spent on the beat, as a uniformed officer. For three months he and several other probationary constables were attached to the force's main station in the cathedral city of Queensbury. This was quite an interesting period. He shared "digs" with one of the other probationers and they enjoyed learning the basics of police work from the Inspectors and Sergeants to whom they were attached at various times. At the end of each day they would return to the lodgings and spend the evening discussing the day's work over a pint of beer and a pipe. After the initial three months the probationers were paraded before the Chief Constable and the Queensbury Superintendent gave a report on each officer. One had made poor progress and received a warning and was ordered to remain at Queensbury for a further period of probation. "Max", as he was now known to one and all, and three other probationers were told that they were accepted for the full two years. They were then given postings to smaller stations around the county for further practical experience. Max was to go to Market Braxtead where the small station was under the charge of a Sergeant Gear. Afterwards they all repaired to the canteen. While they were chatting one of the older Constables, who had been particularly friendly to the youngsters, came over to ask them about their postings. Max noticed that, although he did not say anything, he made a face when Sergeant Gear's name cropped up.

Punctually at 7.30am on the following Monday, his uniform brushed and pressed and his boots shining, Max reported to the desk at Market Braxtead police station. The elderly constable behind the desk was expecting him. "You must be the new probationary lad," he said. "Best wait in the back office till Sergeant Gear arrives to take over the station. I'm on night duty and I'll be off shortly." "Is there anything I ought to be doing meanwhile," asked Max. The other looked doubtful. "Best wait till 'sergeant gets in," he replied. Max lifted the barrier and went behind the desk and through the door into the back office. This was a bleak little room containing four wooden chairs and decorated with one or two official notices and posters. The window looked out onto a rather bare backyard. Ten minutes later there was a stir outside, then the door was flung open and a tall, moustached, rather gaunt looking man in police sergeant's uniform swept in. "So you're our new recruit," he said looking Max up and down with an offensive stare. "Nothing to do, I see, but we'll soon remedy that. See that yard out there? I want it swept and tidied right away. I know you're an ex-officer and supposed to be going into the CID, but you'll get no favours here." "I don't expect any favours, sergeant," replied Max. "That's another thing," said Gear, "don't answer back while you're here. I 'm not likely to ask your opinion but, in the unlikely event that I do, you can speak, otherwise I'll expect you to restrict yourself to "yes sergeant" and carrying out my orders. Now get outside and sweep that yard."

There followed one of the most depressing periods of Max's life. Sergeant Gear was undoubtedly a tyrant and life for his subordinates was a misery. Max realised how fortunate he had been in never encountering anybody of this calibre during his military career. Of course there had been a few officers and NCOs of a bullying disposition, but there had always been the influence of some more senior man to keep situation in hand. Here the sergeant was virtually his own master. The Inspector from the next town, 15 miles away, had nominal supervision of Market Braxtead but he was nearing retirement and was only too happy to leave things to Gear as long as there were no complaints from anybody influential. The other constables usually said very little to each other or to Max, although Taylor, the oldest of the constables occasionally made some friendly remark when the sergeant was out of the way.

One warm September day Max and two of the others were eating their lunchtime sandwiches in the back office when sergeant Gear abruptly opened the door and addressed Max. "Maxwell, go at once to the Weston Arms. They've sent word that there's some trouble and the police are needed." Max jumped up and put on his helmet. PC Taylor also started to get up. "Shall I go with him, sergeant," he said, "they can be a pretty rough crowd to deal with down there when they've been drinking on a market day." "No," said Gear, "Maxwell must learn to stand on his own feet - it's no good you trying to wet-nurse him. In any case I've got a job; for you this afternoon. You're to cycle over to Stratton Hall and tell the butler that there have been several burglaries at big houses in the next county so to be extra careful when he's locking up at nights. You can say we will send an officer to look around each night for the next week or two. I want Lord Brownlow to know we're on the alert. Come on Maxwell, get moving!" In front of the counter stood a frightened lad of about eleven. "Come quick, gents," he said as Max and the sergeant appeared, "my Dad says there'll be murder done if the police don't come soon." "That'll do, boy," said the sergeant, "you take this, officer right back with you. He'll sort it all out, no doubt," he added with a sneer directed at Max.

When they reached the square in front of the Weston Arms there was a good deal of noise and quite a crowd was milling about. With some difficulty, Max forced his way to the front. Two biggish men were engaged in a furious battle and the crowd was egging them on with much enthusiasm. "What's going on here" shouted Max stepping forward to try and part the two. The men took no notice of him and the crowd was hostile: angry at the prospect of having their entertainment cut short. It was obvious that both men had taken quite a lot of punishment and Max guessed that one of the more responsible men in the crowd had sent his son for the police, so as to prevent any really serious consequences. Max grabbed the bigger of the two men by the arm and tried to hold him, but got punched in the mouth for his pains. At this point his helmet was knocked over his eyes by somebody behind and for a short time he could see nothing. While Max's vision was temporarily obscured, the man who had hit him turned back on his opponent and managed to fell him. By the time Max had tilted his helmet back into position and could see what was going on the man on the ground was being kicked in the most brutal manner. At this stage unexpected help arrived. A hefty labourer emerged from the crowd and shouted to the mob, "don't be bloody fools. There's going to be murder done here. Give the Copper a chance can't you." Then he turned to Max and said, "You grab one arm, mate, and I'll get the other and we'll pull him off before he kills the bloke."

They were successful and the man, a big swarthy fellow in his late twenties, calmed down surprisingly quickly. "What was that all about?" asked the labourer. The swarthy man looked angrily at the man on the ground. "Bloody stuck-up airman - what would he know about the Midhants Regiment? I was in from 1914 to the end and I lost more good mates than he'll ever have. What right has he got to lead off about us running away on the Somme in 1918." "Well," said the other, "that's bad, but not worth getting yourself hung for, which you certainly would be if you killed him!" "Your right said the ex-infantryman. He's not worth bothering about but he'd been drinking and was taunting me and I'd had a drop or two as well." He turned rather anxiously towards Max who was now kneeling beside the man on the pavement.

"Is he going to be OK, mate," he asked. Max did not reply at once. He was coming to terms with his own astonishment. The man groaning on the cobbles was someone he knew very well! It was a very battered Guy Huskett, smelling strongly of whisky, who lay sprawled there! He remembered from his own experience a few years back that Guy could be difficult even when sober, but to get involved in a street brawl like this was extraordinary! "He'll live," he answered tersely, "but you'll have to come up to the station with me." By this time most of the crowd had slunk away, but the landlady of the Weston Arms had come out, anxious to try and avert trouble for her husband, the licensee "Can I do anything, officer", she said. "Yes," replied Max. "You can help this man inside and get somebody to go for the doctor. He needs attention. After that keep him under your eye till I get back. He'll have some questions to answer. I'll hold you and your husband responsible for looking after him and making sure he doesn't leave here." He turned to the labourer who was still holding the assailant by the arm. "I'm more than grateful for your help. Will you join me for a pint when I'm off duty on Thursday evening?" The man grinned and nodded. "See you Thursday, then," he said, and went on his way leaving the prisoner to Max. The two walked silently up to the Police station where charges of "common assault" and "breach of the peace" were prepared by sergeant Gear. After that a much sobered farm hand was released to make a belated return from the market. He knew that he would receive a severe reprimand from the farmer. Much worse would be the tongue lashing he would get from his wife when he returned home at the end of his day's work.

Guy Huskett had been too dazed and too drunk to recognise the policeman who had attended to him as he lay on the ground, but by the time Max returned to the pub Guy was more himself and was astonished to see his ex-observer in such an unfamiliar role. Max dealt with him very formally, cautioning him and telling him that he was to report to the Police station to be charged with "breach of the peace" as soon as the doctor had seen him Then, dropping his official tone when the landlady had left the room, he invited Guy to a late supper at his lodgings and gave him a note with the address.

When they met Guy was rather subdued. "What the dickens was all that row about," Max demanded. Guy was obviously rather ashamed and, at first, reluctant to go into details. "Oh, the fellow was at the bar and we got talking and he was boasting about his war service and the Midhants regiment and I got fed up and told him about all the infantry we saw heading back after the German attack in March 1918 and one thing led to another and it ended up in a fight." "But what were you doing in the first place, drinking far too much in a disreputable pub in a little place like Market Braxtead?"

asked Max. "Oh well," said Guy, "I suppose I had better tell you the whole story. You know that I was friendly with Marion Standish. Well after I was posted to that air combat training unit, I could get up to town quite easily and we began to see quite a lot of each other. She seemed to enjoy our outings and I gradually got into the way of thinking she was the girl I would like to marry. I rather thought she felt the same way. Anyway I eventually got sick of instructing conceited young fools, who thought they knew it all before they started, and eventually I resigned my RAF commission. I have quite a good allowance from the old man and I decided to set up in an apartment in London and enjoy life. Marion seemed a bit surprised when I told her I was leaving the RAF but we went on seeing each other pretty often. Then last week I decided the time had come to propose to her. She listened quietly enough, but when I had finished she said she enjoyed being friends with me but was not going to marry a chap who had no proper job and lived off his father! I was furious and we had a frightful row. In the end she told me to take her home and not to expect to see her again in any capacity. By the next day I felt rotten about the whole thing and phoned, hoping to make things up, but she wouldn't speak to me. Since then I am afraid I have made a fool of myself with drink and some "not very nice" girls up in town. Today I decided I would go up to north Wales, where I can get some fishing. I thought I might try to meet up with a rather decent chap I knew at school and who farms over in Anglesey now. Anyway, I stopped off at that god-forsaken pub for some lunch and started drinking again. The rest you know! Now tell me how life is treating you and how you come to be the local bobby in this backwater!"

Max explained briefly that he had been compulsorily retired from the RAF and was training for the police and hoped to join the CID. Then he asked, "well Guy, and how do you see your own future?" "I haven't really thought much about it," answered Guy. "Well," said Max, "If you want my opinion, this is the time to start thinking about it - very hard! I remember Grace telling me that Marion is pretty headstrong but I think she's got it right this time. You're fit, you've got a good brain, you've got a bit of money and you're good at practical things and it's a combination most fellows would be grateful for. You could do something really useful with your life!" Guy made a grimace. "If I'd known you were going to lecture me I wouldn't have given you the benefit of my company," he said with a laugh. Max smiled, "If I didn't know you better," he said, "I wouldn't have wasted my words of wisdom on you!" After that no more was said on the subject. In the Magistrate's Court the next day both the "disturbers of the King's peace" were fined and admonished by the Justices. Guy paid both fines and apologised for his offensive remarks. The two men shook hands outside the Court.

It had cheered Max to meet his old friend, even if the circumstances had been rather unusual, but after this episode life at Market Braxtead returned to its depressing norm. Sergeant Gear was impossible to please however conscientiously Max tried to carry out his duties, The other constables remained as distant as ever, apart from Taylor, who was rarely on the same turn of duty as Max. Then, suddenly, with that curious idiosyncrasy which occurs in all bureaucracies from time to time, the Midhamptonshire Constabulary administrative office notified Market Braxtead police station that Probationary Constable Maxwell was posted to Down Sutton with immediate effect. The change was a profound one. At Down Sutton he was under the supervision of the sole officer for that station, one Constable Dobson. Max's whole concept of police work was changed within a few months. Dobson had been at Down Sutton for as long as most people in the force could remember. Once he had served in the Birmingham City Police but being a countryman at heart and a keen gardener he had later transferred to Midhamptonshire's rural force. Dobson was a bachelor and was thought of by his superiors as being slow of wit but reliable. Why they decided to send Max to serve under him nobody ever discovered.

On Max's arrival Dobson invited him into a little office, which was really more like a cosy sitting room than a police station. It was now November and a bright fire was burning in the grate. There was a teapot on the trivet by the fire. Dobson poured a mug of strong tea for each of them. There was a faint but pleasant smell of pine logs and toast about the room. They sat comfortably in easy chairs on either side of the fire and Dobson began. "Well lad, I'm right glad of some company but I'm surprised they sent you here! We don't get a lot of crime round these parts. Did the Superintendent say what he expected you to learn working with me?" "Nobody said a thing," replied Max. "Yesterday, when I came in off the beat at mid-day, Sergeant Gear told me to get my things packed and be over here first thing this morning." "Ah," said Dobson, "so you've been with Gear have you. He's got the reputation of being a very efficient man! More prosecutions in his patch than in any other of the same size in the whole County. Keeps the Market Braxtead magistrates very busy, I hear! I'm afraid you'll find it pretty dull here in Down Sutton, not but what there aren't some interesting folks round about, and when the spring comes I can maybe teach you a bit about gardening. Sweet peas are my favourites, but I grow quite a few flowers and some decent veg, though I say it myself."

P.C. Dobson was as good as his word and Max learnt a good deal about plants and gardening over the next eighteen months. He also learnt far more about policing than he had ever expected when the bus dropped him off in that sleepy little village. Dobson had his own philosophy on the subject of law and order. He knew everyone for miles around and had acquired detailed knowledge of the background of any person he considered likely to run foul of the law. It was his policy to prevent offences before they happened. Over one of their leisurely meal breaks he explained how he had come to work in this way. "When I first came here old Admiral Dunham was the senior magistrate. He sent for me and said, "young man", for I WAS quite young then, "I know that you've come from the Birmingham City Police and that they're a fine force but we don't do things here the way they do in big towns. As far as I and the other magistrates are concerned the less we see of you the better. We don't like sending local lads off to jail, though we will if we have to. We prefer to have peace and quiet and good relations all round. See to it you do your job by stopping trouble before it ever happens - not by waiting till afterwards and then arresting folks!" Well it seemed a strange idea to me at first. I'd been in a force that set a lot of store by catching villains and bringing them to justice. Still what the old boy had said set me thinking."

The results of Dobson's thinking became apparent as the months went by. He insisted that they did a regular patrol through the village every morning and every afternoon. "It reassures the older folks to see their policeman," he said," and because I go at the same times every day anyone who wants a word knows when to catch me. I've come by a lot of useful bits of information that way." He also did a very different sort of patrol using his cycle. "The bike's quiet and quite quick," he explained. "It lets me cover a lot of ground. I never go at regular times when I use it. Anyone who might be up to no good knows that I may pop quietly round the corner at any time of the day or night. It makes them a bit uneasy, which is just the way I want it!" Max found that the system worked pretty well. Even when there was more serious trouble, as happened from time to time on a Saturday night, Dobson could usually sort things out fairly easily. A drunken labourer or farm hand usually sobered up pretty quickly when threatened with his wife or mother being told he had been misbehaving and was in trouble with the police! It was very rare for reinforcements to be needed at Down Sutton. The Inspector from the nearest town, who had charge over several villages as part of his remit, was happy to leave Dobson very much to his own devices, making an occasional visit for the sake of appearances.

Max settled easily into the rhythm of country life. Down Sutton was a pleasant little place and with such an interesting and unusual mentor as PC Dobson time passed quickly. As spring turned to early summer he was almost alarmed to find how absorbed in local activities, like the cricket club and village dramatic society, he had become. To his chagrin he found himself thinking of his transfer to the CID as something of a nuisance: - an interruption to a variety of pleasant activities! Dobson was a constant source of interesting snippets of local history from pre-war days and of the hierarchical life which, up to 1914, was accepted by country people of all classes as the normal and proper way of things. Dobson had noticed a profound change since men had come back from the horrors of France to return once again to the hard life of agricultural work, with its long hours and low pay. Girls too were unsettled by the excitement of factory work in big towns or the novelty of taking over from men on the railway or working as a conductress on the busses. After such experiences and the freedom and independence they brought, it was difficult to adjust to being a servant in a farm kitchen or even in the "Big House". People were less predictable and a lot of understanding was required when dealing with them. This was where Dobson's policy of knowing everyone and about everyone was so useful. Such knowledge, applied by him judiciously and with understanding, often prevented problems from escalating and leading to serious trouble.

Sometimes Dobson would talk about life in Birmingham at the turn of the century when he had been a young man and a proud member of an elite police force. In those days he had seen real hardship and deprivation amongst the urban unemployed - dreadful housing conditions and the constant anxiety of debts and the heartbreak of hungry children. He amused Max with his account of Lloyd George's speeches against the Boer War which had enraged the populace at that time. On one occasion Dobson and his colleagues had saved the great man from an angry mob by removing him from the City Hall in a dustcart! It seemed that the Boer war had brought work to many so that, quite apart from any patriotism, there were strong practical reasons for disliking Lloyd George's pacifist ideas.

There was a smell of dust and a faint hint of thunder in the heat of the Berlin afternoon that day in the summer of 1923. Detective Constable "Max" Maxwell climbed wearily down from the train that had brought him from Hamburg and the Harwich ferry to that great city. Professor and Mrs Maxwell had resumed their pre-war habit of long continental holidays and had written urging Max to join them in East Prussia at the little house they had rented. To Max's surprise the Superintendent had readily agreed to Max's belated and rather diffident request for leave. Now, here he was, nearing the final stage of the journey.

His parents had been fascinated and shocked by the state into which Germany had fallen by that summer. Professor Maxwell thought his son would find the visit intensely interesting - Mrs Maxwell thought that a complete change would do him a lot of good. Since leaving Down Sutton Ian Maxwell had been working much harder and had become more and more absorbed in the work of the Midhamptonshire CID.

Max discovered that the local train he would use for the last stage of his journey did not leave for two and a half hours. He decided to wander out into the city and have something to eat. The delicious smell of freshly ground coffee drew him towards a large, rather expensive looking cafe a little way down the broad street on which he had found himself after leaving the station. Soon he was seated at a table near an open window and was giving his order to the attractive young waitress, who assured him that payment with British money would be no problem, adding that, being so near the station, the cafe had many foreign visitors. Before he had been in Germany much longer he would have learned that the rate of inflation was so high that his cup of coffee would have cost a quarter of a million German Marks! The country was in dire straits. French soldiers occupied the Ruhr and French and Belgian officials controlled the main industries. The government was weak and indecisive. The middle classes were bankrupt and the workers were in a state of despair. There was constant unrest.

After his coffee and apple strudel Max felt revived. He started to relax and take an interest in his surroundings. The cafe was crowded but through the open window he saw that many of the passers-by, especially the older ones, looked thin and anxious. Many wore clothes that were shabby and threadbare, though usually well brushed. There was a constant buzz of conversation in the cafe, but he suddenly caught the sound of a voice that was vaguely familiar. Looking round he saw a table not far away at which several men about his own age were seated. The man who was speaking had his back to Max. On an impulse Max got up and went across. "Oberleutnant von Straussen, I believe!" he said with a slight bow. The other rose to his feet with an astonishment which, however, he quickly concealed. "Gentlemen," he said to his companions, "allow me to introduce one of my erstwhile captors." Turning to Max he said, "Please let us dispense with formalities! My friends call me Max - my first name is Maximillian, but that's overlong for everyday use! Pardon me that I have forgotten your name, but that of your friend Pilot Officer Brown is etched on my heart! One does not forget the man who shoots one down before breakfast and then entertains one to a most excellent lunch!"

After introductions had been made, von Straussen asked what Max was doing in Berlin and then enquired after Bob Brown. Max said, "Brown never looked back after his encounter with you! He has done well in the RAF and is now second in command of a squadron out in India." "Alas," replied von Straussen, "we poor German airmen are in a very different situation. As you may see our country is ruined financially and there are no prospects for us here. I myself leave for South America in a couple of weeks' time to start work as a mining engineer. My father still has his estate but there is no money to run it. In any case my elder brother, who lost a leg serving in the army during the war, will inherit. I am trying to persuade one of these gentlemen to join me when I leave to seek my fortune abroad!"

Ten years after Max's encounter with Maximillian von Straussen, Adolf Hitler came to power in Germany. Five years after that, in 1938, his army marched into Czechoslovakia, and householders in southern England dug trenches in their gardens to provide protection in the event of air raids. Detective Inspector "Max" Maxwell offered his services to the RAF but his offer was politely declined. Later that year Neville Chamberlain returned from Munich with a piece of paper in his hand and a promise of "peace in our time". The trenches were filled in again.

By now Max was established as a confirmed bachelor with a comfortable cottage on the edge of the little Midhamptonshire town of King's Aston. His housekeeper, Mrs Green, came in each morning to clean and cook. Max himself came and went, at any time of the day or night that suited him, without arousing undue interest locally. He maintained good but not intimate terms with his elderly neighbours, who were pleased to have a policeman living next door but whose knowledge of his duties and of his activities in general was very vague.

In 1939 the German army swept into Poland, and then Britain and Germany were at war. Max contacted Air Intelligence. He was granted an interview on this occasion but was told that, for the present at least, he was more useful to his country where he was, a pronouncement which he privately regarded as rather patronising!

By the autumn of 1940 he had become very frustrated. He saw the work which he had previously enjoyed as almost irrelevant while the country was fighting for survival. Britain now stood alone, against the apparently overwhelming might of the German war machine. There were those who felt that this was madness and that the government should be seeking terms to end the war.

One morning in late November Ian Maxwell was feeling particularly depressed. As he looked out onto the gently sloping fields behind his cottage he reflected that police officers in the Channel Islands were already having to co-operate with the German occupying forces. Would this would soon be his own fate? Usually the view of small neat fields, surrounded by their autumn-brown hedges, pleased him. Today he wondered, sadly, what would happen to those fields under Nazi control. Even in Midhamptonshire there were, as he knew from his police work, Fascist sympathisers who would be very happy to take over the running of affairs. Why wouldn't the authorities give him some job to do which would help directly in the defence of Britain? His mood of depression and dissatisfaction lingered on through the morning. Then, as he sat at his desk trying to concentrate on a lengthy report from the detective branch of a neighbouring force, the phone rang. He picked up the receiver.

Chapter Four

A chill wind blew along the broad avenue. It tore at the few leaves still clinging precariously to the trees lining the roadway. It raced the many dead leaves already fallen, along the street like a flock of merry children rushing home from school. It probed inquisitively at the doors and windows of the handsome buildings on either side of the avenue. The few stray Berliners walking on the wide pavements turned up their collars and hurried about their various affairs. Had any of them paused to look up at the first-floor windows of the most impressive building of all, he or she might have caught a glimpse of a tall, stern-looking, man pacing to and fro. The Grand Admiral was restless. Earlier that week, late in October 1940, he had been greatly relieved to be informed by the Fuehrer that operation "Sealion" was postponed. The prospect of being responsible for conveying a large contingent of the Wehrmacht across the English Channel, with the RAF still undefeated and the British Home Fleet waiting in the wings at Scapa Flo, had been giving him nightmares! In recent weeks the deteriorating weather had done nothing to lessen his anxieties. Now a new, less immediate, but equally profound cause for disquiet had come to his notice.

Twenty-three paces up the room and twenty-three paces back. He had counted them a hundred times before he summoned his junior staff officer from the outer office. "Oberleutnant, be so good as to order my car." The Admiral's mind was made up. He would return home and put his problem to the back of his mind for a little. He now remembered that Rosa would be home. His wife had specially asked him to be punctual and for once he would be able to please her! The Admiral and his wife had not seen Rosa, their only child, for many weeks and the pleasure of having her at home would be all the greater because there were to be no other guests - only Rosa, and Rudi, her husband of six months. Rudi was a brilliant young pilot and had just been promoted Meyer. Of course he was a Nazi, like all the other young Luftwaffe officers, but Rudi was not a fanatic. The Admiral liked him and on their relatively few meetings had been pleasantly surprised by his common sense.

As the big car bore him swiftly out of central Berlin towards his substantial home in a prosperous suburb, the

Admiral forgot his resolve. His mind returned to the events of the day. The morning conference with senior officers of the submarine service had been mere routine. The really interesting, and worrying, events of the day had occurred at the formal luncheon, held in honour of a visiting Italian Admiral. As neither guest nor host spoke the other's language, a few halting remarks in French had satisfied courtesy. Both men had then settled down to enjoy an excellent meal, faultlessly served. Their silence had made it easy to overhear conversation further along the table. A naval Captain, newly appointed to the Admiral's staff, had been talking to a young General of the Wehrmacht whom he appeared to know very well. The Admiral had listened, casually at first, but then with increasing interest. Both men had clearly been enjoying the fine wines provided with the meal and were speaking more freely than they should have been. "Tell me, Herr General," said the naval man, "are you not somewhat bored now that your remarkable triumphs in Poland, the Low Countries and France are complete?" "Ah," replied the General, "you forget, my friend, how professional we are in the Wehrmacht. As soon as one campaign is under way we start to plan for the next! I can assure you that we are very far from being idle at this time!" "Would it be indiscrete to enquire where your plans are leading you at present?" enquired the Naval Captain. "It would," answered the General with a smile, "but in this select company and within the security of your most excellent admiralty I could venture to say that we are looking East once more and that we are unlikely to require the assistance of your service in connection with our plans!"

This conversation alone might not have caused the Admiral too much concern had he not chanced later to overhear a Senior Gestapo Officer speaking to a more junior colleague. "You will ensure," said the former, "that the list of those to be present at the Fuehrer's meeting next week is on my desk tomorrow morning. I must be absolutely certain that no hint of the new plans reaches any unreliable element. As you know it is not long since the Fuehrer signed a pact with the Soviets. At present everything points to their being off guard, in so far as Germany is concerned, and entirely preoccupied with affairs in Finland." The implication of all this, reflected the Grand Admiral, was that certain of the Feurher's current advisers and favourites were urging a surprise attack on the Soviet Union. He knew that amongst the army staff there were many who rated the military capabilities of Soviet Russia fairly low. Men who had been involved in the final stages of the war on the Eastern Front in 1917 had witnessed the collapse of Russia's vast army at that time. The Admiral had read extensively. He believed that such a collapse was unlikely to occur again. Stalin's hold over the Russian people was exceedingly powerful - and the KGB were certainly far more effective than the old Czarist secret police! It was the Admiral's view that to open such a huge campaign as would be needed to defeat the USSR would be to court disaster, especially with Britain still undefeated and defiant.

Now the car was turning into the drive of his house. It might be a lesser evil, decided the Grand Admiral, to reinstate operation "Sealion" next spring and divert the energies of the Wehrmacht to an invasion of England. This would at least postpone the awful risks of war on a huge front against an enemy whose military potential might be much greater than that of any nation conquered by Herr Hitler so far! The key to the problem of attacking England successfully must be air power! If the RAF were eliminated then the combined efforts of the Luftwaffe and the German navy should surely be enough to maintain a clear passage of twenty-one miles across the Channel! Given that, he could easily transport large numbers of soldiers from France to England, just as the British had done in the reverse direction from 1914 to 1918. Why had Goering's airmen failed to defeat the British in the air during August and September? As the car pulled up at the front door he made a sudden decision. He would talk to Rudi tonight! Who better to give an insight into the problem? Rudi had been involved in the campaign from the start and was intelligent enough to form his own views as to what had gone wrong.

Dinner was over. Rosa and her mother had retired to the drawing room, and the Admiral and his son-in-law were relaxing over their port. "Tell me Rudi," asked his father-in-law, "what was your impression of the air attacks on England in the late summer, and what did you think of the British air defences?" "Ah," said Rudi, "I've had a bit of time to think about that lately. The weather has been too bad for much fighter activity in the past few weeks and we have been fairly idle." "If," said the Admiral, "you had the job of tackling the RAF a second time, how would you go about it." "Well," said Rudi, "the British have some disadvantages. For a start many of their pilots are inexperienced and although their Spitfires are pretty much of a match for our Me 109's, the Hurricanes are not quite so good and their new turret fighters, the Defiants, are easy meat for us, provided we identify them and remember to attack from below and astern! Where the British score, however, is that they always know when we are coming! I understand that technically their radiolocation system is quite crude, but it is so well co-ordinated that there are always enemy fighters waiting for us when we cross the coast! The other great advantage the British have over us is that when one of their pilots bales out he can be flying again next day. Any of our pilots who survive being shot down are likely to end up in a POW camp!"

The Admiral puffed meditatively at his cigar. After a couple of minutes he turned to Rudi again. "What about destroying the British radiolocation units first so that the enemy have no warning of impending attacks?" "This was tried early in the campaign," said Rudi. "The installation on the Isle of Wight was heavily attacked by dive bombers and was put out of action. Unfortunately there were very heavy losses by the "Stukagruppen" involved. Also, we discovered that the detection units overlap the zones they cover, so that knocking out one station alone is no use. Our reconnaissance flights showed, too, that the British had repaired the damaged site within a few days." "Would I be correct in supposing," asked the Admiral, "that there is a chain of these radiolocation units, all overlapping with each other all round the British coast." "They certainly cover all the south coast and probably much of the east coast as well," replied Rudi. "Do you think that they could be destroyed by simultaneous attacks from the sea? That would leave the British without their early warning system for a few days. Then the Luftwaffe could strike hard and without warning and could perhaps destroy the British fighters before they got off the ground." "Simultaneous destruction of all the units over a wide area would be ideal and would give us the chance we need," said Rudi, "but I doubt if many of the units could be reached by naval forces and I think such an attack would be suicidal, even where the sites are close to the sea. They will almost certainly be protected by minefields and shore batteries." The Admiral glanced at the clock. "Rudi," he said, "this is most interesting, but it is time that we joined Rosa and her mother! Would you be free to call in at my office tomorrow to continue our talk?" "Rosa wants to do some shopping, I know," said Rudi, "and I suspect she will get on far better with her mother for company than with me! I feel fairly sure that I can make my excuses without getting into too much trouble!"

When "Herr Meyer Rudi Muller" was announced and shown into the Grand Admiral's office next morning, he was quite surprised to see a large table spread with maps of southern England, together with a collection of aerial photographs. He was introduced to the Chief of Naval Intelligence, who was already in deep discussion with the Grand-Admiral. Clearly these Naval men were taking things pretty seriously! Rudi wondered if he had spoken too freely to his father-in-law the previous evening! He would not like to get into trouble with his own superiors in the Luftwaffe, especially as his career seemed to be going rather well at present. "Rudi," said the Admiral, "Captain Heimgarten tells me that we have an exceedingly reliable naval intelligence agent based, rather surprisingly, in Birmingham. He has two other men working with him and they collate information from agents in other parts of Britain and transmit it direct to us here at the Kriegsmarine headquarters by radio. Captain Heimgarten has heard from me your comments about the British radiolocation units, of which he already knew something. He has made a remarkable suggestion! He thinks that, by using our existing agents and recruiting extra personnel from disaffected Britishers, the IRA and others, we could organise teams to sabotage the radiolocation sites without any German regular forces being involved."

Rudi, forgetting for a moment of the presence of the two very senior officers, whistled! "That's quite an idea, Captain," he said, "but do you think it would be possible to co-ordinate the sabotage attacks to a precise time. Then, of course it would be necessary to immediately notify the attacking aircraft that the approach was clear for them." The Captain spoke for the first time since their formal introduction. "Given a really good leader to set up and supervise the operation, I think this could be achieved," he said. "I know that I can rely on you not say anything of our arrangements outside this room, and therefore I can let you into the secret of our communications with our agent in Birmingham. One of his men is a Britisher who owns a commercial barge. This barge plies the canals around the English midlands.

The owner was a sergeant in the British army and served in the trenches from 1915 to the end of the war. Early in 1918 his younger brother, who was a little simple, was called up and sent out to France. While in the front line he panicked and disobeyed an order. His commanding officer sent him for Court-martial. Eventually he was sentenced for desertion and shot. Sometime after the war the elder brother learned what had happened and, without a word to anyone, sought out the German consul in Birmingham and volunteered for our intelligence service. His barge carries sophisticated radio equipment, carefully concealed. By means of this he can communicate with us here in this building! As the barge is constantly on the move detection by British counter-intelligence is most unlikely!"

The Grand-Admiral looked at the other two. "What type of man would be suitable to act as leader of such an operation were we to set it up? I imagine it would have to be somebody with excellent English, a knowledge of the Luftwaffe and a rather daring disposition!" The others laughed. Captain Heimgarten said, "Well sir, I most certainly agree with your last requirement. We should have to find somebody quite exceptional to carry off a coup of this sort." At this point Rudi spoke. "Might I be permitted to make a suggestion, sir?" he said. "Carry on, Rudi," replied the Admiral, "but I hope you are not offering to take on the job on yourself. Much as I appreciate your knowledge of the Luftwaffe and your daring, I am quite sure your English wouldn't deceive anyone on the other side of the channel!" "Sir," said Rudi, "I am being completely serious. I really believe I know the ideal man for such a job. He is the adjutant of our Staffel, Meyer von Straussen. He was a fighter pilot in the last war, but was born and brought up in England. His father was a diplomat at our London embassy up until 1914. Von Straussen went to English schools and speaks English which, I am assured, would deceive anyone into thinking that he really was an Englishman. As for daring, his plane was shot down in 1918 and he had to make a forced landing on a British airfield. They took him prisoner, of course, but he escaped within hours. He then made his way to Switzerland and reported back to his unit within days! He's an exceptional man and quite a legend in our fighter Gruppe."

The two naval officers looked at each other. "What an extraordinary stroke of luck, Admiral," said Captain Heimgarten, "that your son-in-law should know of such a man. Will it be possible to persuade the Luftwaffe to release him for special duties." "I shall have to visit the Reichsluftfahrtministeriumium later today," said the Grand Admiral. "There will be much to discuss and I shall have to arrange an appointment with Reichmarshall Goering. I will broach the question of Meyer von Straussen with the Reichmarshall himself. The

Reichmarshall might even have met Meyer von Straussen during the last war. I will need to talk with you again later today, Captain Heimgarten, but I will release you for the present. You will have much to do."

When they were alone, Rudi asked his father-in-law, "do you think that Reichmarshall Goering will be willing to co-operate with this plan? It is rumoured in the Luftwaffe that he is in bad favour with the Fuehrer because of our failure destroy the RAF once and for all during the air battles of the summer, and that he is still in a very fractious state of mind!" The Admiral looked at his companion for a moment. A slight smile played about his lips. "Rudi," he said, "how do you think I became head of the Kriegsmarine? Do you think it was because I was a fine navigator or a good gunnery officer or a brilliant tactician? There are plenty of naval officers who are all of these things. I happen to have a much more important qualification! I have learned how to manage other men and how to use their talents to the best advantage of the service and the Fatherland. By the time the Reichmarshall and I have discussed this plan once or twice he will be convinced that it is his own! When we go together to put our case to the Fuehrer, I shall congratulate him in front of the Fuehrer on the brilliance of his plan and express my pleasure that the Kriegsmarine is able to assist the Luftwaffe by sharing our intelligence network. You may think that I am cynical, but if it is in the interests of the Fatherland for such a promising plan to be put into action, what does it matter who gets the credit? I know Goering of old and I know that he craves publicity and praise. Personally I am quite content to work behind the scenes to achieve results."

Within the week Meyer Maximillian von Straussen had been summoned to the Reichsluftfahrtministerium and had expressed himself enthusiastic at the prospect of playing a much more vital role in the German war effort than that of an administrative officer in the Luftwaffe. His taste for adventure had not lessened with the passing of the years. The prospect of having charge of the organisation and execution of a daring plan to break the current stalemate was very much to his liking! After initial scepticism, Goering had become an enthusiast. He had personally visited many of the fighter units stationed in northern France and, after talking informally to the pilots, he had added to the plan an element entirely of his own devising. It was obvious that as soon as the chain of radiolocation sites had been destroyed, the Luftwaffe should concentrate their attacks on the British fighter stations. Goering reasoned that in the hour before dawn British night fighter pilots would be nearing the end of their patrols and would be tired and less than fully alert. The pilots of the day fighters would still be comfortably ensconced in their quarters. Past experience would make them confident of receiving early warning of any impending attack. The radio-location system had always proved reliable. Goering decreed that German attacks were to be concentrated on the officers' mess at every fighter station in south-east England. The objective would be to kill as many fighter pilots as possible. A secondary objective would be the airmen's barracks, where NCO aircrew might be quartered. The British policy of using a standard layout for all RAF stations would make this fairly easy! The airfields themselves would be left relatively undamaged. They would soon be needed by advanced units of the Luftwaffe as the invasion got under way. Experienced Luftwaffe officers endorsed the concept of eliminating as many British pilots as possible. They had already come to the conclusion that the British were able to replace aircraft much more easily than had been expected. They also knew that replacing pilots was a slow process.

Once the mercurial chief of the Luftwaffe had endorsed, and largely taken over, the naval scheme for sabotaging the British radiolocation system as an immediate preliminary to an invasion, detailed plans evolved with great rapidity. Reconnaissance flights were made and photographs of sample radiolocation sites were taken. These were carefully examined by radio experts and engineers. Using the information obtained, a mock unit, with towers exactly similar to the British ones was constructed. This work was carried out far away in East Prussia so as to avoid the prying cameras of the RAF and the sharp eyes of resistance workers in the occupied countries. Experts in demolition and in the use of explosives examined the towers and set about devising a special pack of explosives designed for their destruction. This was to be suitable for use by amateurs who would probably be working in the dark with very limited time at their disposal and who might well be under attack by the RAF guards!

Meanwhile, Meyer von Straussen was packed off to a parachute training unit. On arrival he was introduced to Hauptscharfuhrer Clauser, a very correct and military figure, who saluted the Meyer with punctilious correctness. The commandant of the training unit indicated that Clauser had been allocated to instruct him personally. Once the commandant had left them, von Straussen, sensing the instructor's dislike for the task he had been allotted, addressed the warrant officer. "Hauptscharfuhrer, I know well that it is almost impossible to train a man in a week, let alone a man of my age and one who is your senior in rank! In this case, however, something far more than my life is at stake. If you can make me into a reasonably competent parachutist in the time available you will be doing a service to the Reich, the importance of which you may understand one day in the future! I will work as long and hard as you direct and for instructional purposes you will treat me exactly as you would treat one of the men under you!"

The instructor was considerably taken aback but responded promptly enough. "Then Meyer we will proceed at the double to the preliminary training hanger where we will practise falls for the next two hours!" Maximillian von Straussen was an apt and very hard-working pupil and at the end of his week's training was able to jump confidently from a low or high flying aircraft and make a decent landing on any reasonably suitable sort of territory. The Meyer's instructor was, by now, proud of his pupil and anxious that he should learn everything that he, Clauser, could teach him. On the last day he said, almost shyly, "Meyer, there is one little trick of my own which is not in the official course, but which might be useful to you. I have found that I can steer my parachute to some extent by pulling the cords on one or other side during the descent!" They practised the technique on their last two jumps. Some weeks later von Straussen had reason to be very grateful for the tip!

The naval staff car carrying the Grand Admiral and Captain Heimgarten moved slowly towards the main entrance of the Chancellery. The ensign of the Kriegsmarine fluttered proudly from a miniature flagpole on the radiator. A glint of wintery sunshine reflected the restless flag on the highly polished bonnet of the black car. The November afternoon was cold. There was a light breeze. Today was the great day on which staff officers of the German army, navy and air force would present the results of the last few weeks of feverish planning activity to the Fuehrer for his consideration! It was known that other, and very different, plans had already been submitted by rival experts and that they had received favourable consideration. This team, however, was headed by Reichmarshall Goering, commander-in-chief of the Luftwaffe, backed by Field-Marshal Brauchitsch of the Wehrmacht and the Grand Admiral, commanding the Kriegsmarine. Hopes of obtaining Hitler's approval were high.

From the car ahead there emerged a Wehrmacht general, followed by a quite elderly man in civilian clothes and a young officer of the engineer corps. Captain Heimgarten was puzzled. "Tell me, Admiral," he said, "who is that old fellow and how does he come to be attending such an important conference?" The Grand Admiral smiled. "Where were you, Heimgarten," he enquired, "in the spring of 1918?" "On a U- boat in the mid-Atlantic," was the reply. "Ah," said the Admiral, "that explains why you don't recognise him. That man is Brauchenmuller. He was the architect of the break-through on the Western front in March 1918. He was the perfecter of the technique of the "hurricane barrage". He became famous at that time. No doubt his advice has been sought by the army. His presence, also, may impress the Fuehrer, who, of course served on the Western Front himself! He is known to favour men from the army of 1914-18." "Unless," interposed Heimgarten, with a sardonic smile, "they happen to be Jews!" He immediately regretted his unguarded remark. The Grand Admiral made no response and Heimgarten hoped that the chauffeur had not been listening. Nowadays so many men in that sort of position were Gestapo agents!

The meeting took place in a vast room. To Maximillian von Straussen, the assembled company seemed to be quite lost in so large a space. It was more suitable, he felt, for a concert or even a political rally! He was very curious see the Fuehrer close to. He had often heard Hitler's voice on the radio but had previously only seen the Fuehrer in the distance. This had been at a couple of open air meetings which von Straussen had attended since his return to the Fatherland. He had left South America in 1938, during the Czechoslovakia crisis. Von

Straussen had done well abroad and, as a result of his various business activities, had accumulated sufficient capital to live comfortably without needing to work. However, he had been getting weary of the rather limited life he led as an exile, even though a voluntary and quite prosperous exile! His patriotism was just the spark needed to prompt him to return to Germany. Once home he had many contacts and had had little difficulty in obtaining a commission in the rapidly expanding Luftwaffe.

Now he was in close proximity to Herr Hitler! - the man who in a few years had transformed Germany from a state of near chaos to one of order and purpose! Goering was explaining the outline of their plan. He said that by the spring the British people would be demoralised due to a winter of night-time air raids and by food shortages resulting from the U-boat blockade. Next the Grand Admiral explained the present position of the German intelligence service in Britain and the ways in which it could be expanded and how the espionage teams needed could be set up. "What about the actual destruction of the radio-location equipment?" enquired the Fuehrer. "How is THAT to be achieved?" At this point Field Marshal Brauchitsch stepped forward. "Mein Fuehrer, might I be permitted to present Herr Brauchenmuller, one of our foremost experts on explosives!" As the rather nondescript elderly man in civilian clothes stepped forward, von Straussen suddenly realised that here was the only man in the room who was not to some degree afraid of Hitler - and that included himself! There was something indefinable about the Fuehrer which inspired awe. He had a curious air of an authority above that of rank. He somehow gave the impression of knowing things without being told - of being able to read one's innermost thoughts without effort. Von Straussen sensed that almost all the others in the room, despite their high rank and distinguished careers, felt themselves to be in Hitler's power.

Herr Brauchenmuller, however, spoke gently and in a perfectly natural way, rather as if he were explaining a new game to a friend over coffee. "We have calculated the exact quantity of explosive required to demolish one of the British pylons. This is all that is necessary. If one pylon falls the ariel will be destroyed. Without an ariel either the transmission of the radio waves, or the reception of the return waves, reflected from our aircraft, or both, will be impossible. It does not really matter which function is affected. The result will be the same. We have produced a special pack which will cause an explosion big enough to destroy about half a metre of one of the four supports of the pylon. This will be followed by two smaller explosions to weaken the supports on either side. Finally there is a really big charge which will sever the remaining support and topple the whole structure. Our device has been tested on an exact copy of a British radio- location mast. It worked perfectly. We have designed it in such a way that it can be packed like a life jacket, and so can be worn by the agent from the time he leaves on his mission until he is ready to undo the pack and position the explosives. It is quite safe until the two protective safety fuses are removed and the 30 second timer device switched on. This gives the agent just time to get clear before the pylon falls." Von Straussen could see that Hitler was impressed both by the man and by his lucid exposition. The Fuehrer was not, however, completely satisfied. "I assume that at least twenty of these devices will be required. How is it proposed that they be delivered to the agents in England?" The Grand Admiral now spoke. "Fuehrer, we have very reliable agents in Britain. We shall transport the explosive devices by U-boat to a remote point on the west coast of Scotland. This will be done shortly before the explosives are required. One of our agents will then be responsible for moving them to a place from where they can be distributed, ready for use."

Hitler nodded. He turned to Goering. "Now tell me who you intend shall be in charge of this ambitious project - on the spot - in England?" The Reichmarshall beckoned to von Straussen. "Fuehrer, may I present Meyer Maximillian von Straussen. He was a pilot in our air force in 1918 and, though captured by the British, escaped within hours and rejoined his unit. He speaks perfect English and has just completed a parachute course. He has also been fully briefed by Herr Brauchenmuller on the use of the special explosive charges." Von Straussen felt those frighteningly penetrating eyes assessing him, but giving away nothing of the Fuehrer's own thoughts! "Tell me, Meyer, how does it come about that you speak English so well?" "My father was a diplomat, Fuehrer. When I was two years old he was posted to our embassy in London. I went to school in England until 1914, when we returned to Berlin. Up to that time my father had intended that I should follow him in the diplomatic service and for that reason felt it advisable for me to be educated in England. He also thought it important that I should speak good French. Accordingly I spent the summer vacations in France for several years. My ability to speak English and French greatly aided my escape when I was taken prisoner." Hitler seemed satisfied by this reply and proceeded to ask von Straussen, "Who will you work with when you arrive in England?" "I am to report to the principal agent of the Kriegsmarine in Britain, who is to work under my direction in this matter," replied the latter. "This man was once naval attache to the German embassy in the Argentine, but has been practising as a solicitor in Birmingham for some years. He passes as an Englishman as does his clerk, who is also one of our agents." "And how will you make contact?" enquired the Fuehrer, who surprised von Straussen by his interest in the details of the plan. "I am to be dropped by parachute in open country near an isolated house. This is owned by a wealthy South American who is sympathetic to the German cause," answered von Straussen. "I shall find a large summer house in the grounds, well away from the main residence. There I will change out of my flying suit and conceal it, together with my parachute. I will rest until the next morning and then, dressed as an English business man, I will walk 4 kilometres to the local railway station and take a train to Birmingham. When I arrive at the office of our agent I will introduce myself as "Max". This code name has been selected as Captain Heimgarten, who has instructed me on the intelligence aspects of the operation, advised that I should use a code name which is similar to my first name. It will come to mind instantly in an emergency situation or under interrogation. Mr Pattenson has been fully briefed to expect me and ordered to give full co-operation." "Well, Meyer, you, at least, appear to have a clear-cut and workable plan", said the Fuehrer and, to von Straussen's relief, he was dismissed with a curt nod.

Hitler now turned his attention to the Wehrmacht! "Field Marshal," he said, "supposing that the sabotage of this chain of English radio stations, on which the Luftwaffe places such importance, is successful, and if, on this occasion, the Luftwaffe manages to destroy the English fighter command, as they promised to do in July, and in August and in September," with a meaning look at Goering, "how do you intend to exploit the situation." "Mein Fuehrer", said Brauchitsch, "as you know, I made detailed plans for the invasion of England, should operation Sealion have proceeded. These I have now completely revised with a view to an invasion in the late spring of 1941, when we may expect to have weather suitable for the crossing. A large force will, by then, have been thoroughly trained and fully practised in landings from the sea on a variety of coastlines. My plan envisages two main landings: one on the beaches beside the Romney Marshes and the other on the north Kent coast near Whitstable. At the same time parachutists will be dropped along the old "military canal". They will secure this as a barrier to protect our forces assembling on the Romney Marshes. The canal will prevent counter-attacks by enemy tanks. A further strong force of parachutists will be dropped on the high ground along the line of an old Roman road running between Hythe and Canterbury. These men will immediately sever all road and rail links between East Kent and the rest of England. The two main forces will advance rapidly to take Dover from the rear. Once Dover is in our hands, a rapid build-up of our forces will be possible. We have two of the Cross-Channel rail ferries, used before the war to transport the fast London to Paris trains from Dover to Calais. These we shall employ to ferry our panzer divisions. We shall capture the airfields at Lymphe and Hawkinge to provide advanced bases for the Luftwaffe. With complete control of the air throughout the south of England, and with submarines, reinforced by aircraft from Denmark and Cherbourg, guarding the North Sea and the western approaches to the Channel from interference by the British navy, a shuttle service from France to Dover and other British harbours will be able to supply and reinforce our armies. In order to confuse the enemy a number of small groups of highly trained shock troops will be landed simultaneously at places widely dispersed along the southern and eastern coasts of England.

"Thank you, Field Marshal," said the Fuehrer. "As usual the plans of the Wehrmacht are clearly thought out and confidently presented. I shall now consider the various proposals that you have put to me. Suitable refreshments await you in the ante-room. You will all withdraw there until I call for you again." All present came to attention and raised their right arms in the Nazi salute. As they filed out into the ante-room von Straussen could feel the sense of relief around him. It was extraordinary, but there was no doubt that these men - some of the most senior commanders of the German armed forces - were in awe of the lonely figure whose presence they had just left. He himself felt exactly the same. There was an uncanny and, he felt, rather sinister aura of power about Herr Hitler which he could sense but could not understand.

When they were called back into the Fuehrer's presence they lined up facing him to hear his verdict. Hitler's gaze moved slowly along the line of faces, scanning each intently for a moment before moving on to the next. The plan you have put to me," he said eventually, "is accepted. There is one condition. If the invasion has not commenced by the 25th of May 1941 the plan will be completely abandoned and all personnel involved will be released for other duties. The operation depends entirely on the simultaneous destruction of the chain of radio-location stations which protect the English coast. For this reason it will be known by the code word "Chainbreak", which I have personally chosen. Meyer von Straussen is promoted Oberst from this moment. Do not fail me, Oberst, do not fail the Fatherland, do not fail the Third Reich!"

A nondescript truck with Luftwaffe markings bumped along a track at the edge of a military airfield in northern Holland. Away on the main runway eleven Junkers 88 bombers were lining up ready to take off. It was already dark and the airfield was blacked out. The truck made its way towards a twelfth bomber, stationary, but with its engines running, standing close to the perimeter track. Concealed by the canvas canopy of the truck, Oberst von Straussen sat with his parachute pack at his feet and a case on his knee. The driver of the truck was Captain sur Zee Heimgarten, dressed in the overalls of an aircraft mechanic. He pulled up close to the waiting aircraft. "Good luck," he said to von Straussen. "Remember that you will be known only as "Max" to our agents in Britain. They know that you have the authority of the Fuehrer himself and that they must follow your instructions - to the letter! And don't forget that whatever happens your case must not fall into the hands of the British! Although I have taken care that nothing in it should compromise any of our existing agents, it contains the dummy explosive pack for instructing your saboteurs, and also maps and aerial photographs of the radio- location sites. It can be hung well below you during the parachute descent and should not interfere with your landing. It has been designed to look like a commercial traveller's sample case."

They shook hands. Von Straussen scrambled out and, carrying his case and parachute pack, walked to the open hatch of the aircraft. He passed the pack and case to someone inside, and then hoisted himself up and into the plane. The hatch was closed. The truck backed away and drove slowly off along the perimeter track. The engines of the bomber opened up and it rolled towards the runway. Within a couple of minutes it had taken off in the wake of the other eleven Junkers 88's and had disappeared into the night sky.

Chapter 5

"Midhamptonshire CID, Detective Inspector Maxwell speaking," Max's depression lifted momentarily. For the first time that morning he felt almost light-hearted. A call from the RAF! He had a brief vision of being miraculously recalled to his old job with Air Intelligence! His optimism was quickly dispelled. "This is RAF Weston, sir. The duty officer would like to speak to you." "Put him through", said Max, wearily, realising that this could not possibly be the sort of call he was hoping for. "Flight Lieutenant Tweedale here," said a rather languid voice. "I wonder if you can help us. We seem to be having an epidemic of disappearing mail! The RAF police here are totally baffled." In the conversation that followed Max learned that in recent weeks a number of letters posted in the station post box had failed to reach their intended destinations. Wives and mothers were not receiving money posted to them, and one airman who thought he had done rather well in a football pool had learned, to his disgust, that his entry had never arrived! Morale on the station was being affected and, said Tweedale, the Wing Commander, (Admin.), would be grateful if the civil police could assist. Max thought that an early visit to the station would be a good idea - and a welcome break from the rather wordy report he had been struggling to read! "I'll come over this afternoon if that will suit," he said. "Splendid," replied Tweedale. "When you get to the station here, ask the chap at the guardroom for the Admin block. I think the Winco would very much like a word with you, when you arrive. He can give you the full details. I can tell you he's quite worried about the whole business."

About 3pm that afternoon Max's trusty Austin 10, a 1936 model but still going like a bird, pulled up at the gate at RAF Weston. The air force policeman on duty asked him to identify himself. While the man was checking his identity card Max looked around and noted that the guardroom was well-kept but, like every other building around the airfield, it was camouflaged with green and brown paint applied in an irregular wavy pattern. On a rather overcast late autumn afternoon this gave the whole place a sombre appearance which was, Max reflected wryly, pretty much in keeping with his own frame of mind! When his police identity card had been returned to him, the service policeman called a colleague who hopped into the passenger seat and guided Max to the Administration block. The helpful police corporal led him to the door of the Wing Commander's office, knocked, and announced, "civilian police detective officer to see you, sir." "Thank you corporal: show him in," came the reply, in a voice that Max immediately recognised! The Wing Commander was none other than Guy Huskett! "I might have guessed," said Guy as Max entered the room. "Of course, I remember you were planning to go into the Midhamptonshire CID when we last met - it must nearly twenty years ago!" "How did YOU manage to get back into the service,"said Max enviously. "I tried too but got nowhere." "You're in a reserved occupation," said Guy, "but as a director of a house-building firm, and one incidentally with very little work to do, due to the war, I was not. I was lucky enough to be interviewed by a sympathetic sort of chap who'd been in the 14-18 war himself. Anyway I was accepted, so I packed Marion and the family off to stay with my friend in Anglesey. He and his wife have children about the same age as ours - by the way Marion and I did get married after all - probably as result of my taking your good advice! Once I'd got the family settled in Anglesey the RAF sent me on a few refresher courses to get up to date and learn how to fill in forms. After that I was promoted Wing Commander and posted here!"

Some minutes were spent catching up on personal news then Max and Guy got down to the matter of the missing postal orders and other mail: mostly postal orders, though! Clearly whoever was responsible was after money. The RAF police had already checked with nearby post offices but nobody had been cashing abnormal numbers of postal orders locally. The culprit must either be cashing them well away from the area, while on leave, or have an accomplice. While they were talking, Max started to recall one of PC Dobson's stories about his time with Birmingham City police. Suddenly an idea about the thief's probable technique came to him. He asked abruptly, "what time is your post box emptied?" "About 4pm usually," said Guy. Max looked at his watch. It was ten minutes to four. "I'd like to see it emptied," he said. Guy asked if he should come too, but Max said no, it was best to draw as little attention to the matter as possible. He would go himself, but could he borrow a bright torch! At the post box all was quiet. When the mail van pulled up, Max showed the driver his CID identity card. "When you have emptied the box I should like to inspect the inside. This is a confidential police enquiry and I must ask that you do not mention the matter to anyone else," he said. Once the letters were removed and before the postman shut the door Max made a minute inspection of the area on the inner surface of the door around the posting slot. There were a number of tiny scratch marks on either side of the slot.

He looked at them carefully through the pocket lens he always carried. Then he examined the upper and lower edges of the slot and was delighted to find a small piece of grey-blue serge caught on a sharp edged scratch on the inside surface of the door just above the letter-slot. Having completed his inspection he thanked the postman and again reminded him that he must say nothing of the matter to any other person.

When Max returned to Guy's office the latter was very curious to know what he had found. Max outlined his findings but Guy was still puzzled. "I think," said Max, "that one of your airmen has made himself a gadget for catching letters! If you can envisage a sort of net inserted through the slot and then held in place just below the slot by a light wire frame temporarily fixed to the metal of the inner surface of the door by two strong magnets, one at each side of the posting-slot, then you will see how it has been done. Postal orders are most likely to be sent off on a Thursday or Friday evening, after pay parade and ready for the Saturday football pools. I noticed a wooden hut opposite the post box. If you get a reliable chap concealed there and have a small hole made in the wood, he can watch the box without being seen. I suspect he will see somebody come at a quiet time, ostensibly to post a letter, but taking an unusually long time about it. Tell your man to take no action then, but to watch for the same man returning quite late in the evening to remove his catch! Once he has removed the net, arrest him immediately. You should find the letters on him!"

Guy sat back to absorb what he had heard. He was quite impressed by Max's business-like approach to a problem which had completely foxed everyone else. It was so simple and logical once explained. Then he noticed how sad and weary Max looked. He must be really depressed, Guy thought, at failing to get back into the Air Force. His disappointment would be heightened by finding that his friend had succeeded in re-enlisting when he, Max, had failed. Guy began to feel guilty. Max was really the author of Guy's own happy and successful marriage and yet he and Marion had never given Max a thought - had never invited him to their wedding - and had made no effort to keep in touch since. It was worse because they had both known about Grace and should have realised how lonely his life had probably become. Guy thought that at least he could start to make amends now that they had met up again by sheer chance. "Max," he said, "would you be able to stay on and have dinner with me in the mess. It would give us time for a good talk. We have obviously got a lot of news to catch up with!" Max brightened. "Can I use your phone?" he asked. Once he had checked with CID headquarters and been told that there was nothing urgent needing his attention, he told his deputy that he would be at RAF Weston for the rest of the evening. He then accepted Guy's invitation enthusiastically.

RAF Weston was a new station, built in 1938, at the time of the Munich Crisis, when war seemed imminent. Despite its recent origins, the officers' mess was a dignified rather pleasing building. The large dining room was well appointed. When they entered after a preliminary drink at the bar, Max noted with approval the dark oak tables, neatly laid for dinner, and the white coated mess-waiters moving about the room with quiet efficiency. The windows were sealed by removable frames covered with strong lightproof material. This allowed the room to be well lit despite the blackout. Guy led the way to a partly occupied table where there were still had a couple of vacant chairs, explaining to Max as they crossed the room that it was an unwritten rule of the mess that each partly occupied table must be filled before an empty table was used. This made life easier for the waiters but, more importantly, it was a means of ensuring a good mix of officers at meal times. The Station Commander, Guy said, was against the formation of cliques who always did everything together - one table all pilots - another all engineers and so on. The table they had joined was already occupied by a flying officer and a pilot officer, both wearing wings, and a flight-lieutenant; a radio engineer. They greeted the Wing Commander respectfully and Guy introduced Max. The conversation was about night fighters. The young pilot officer had just arrived on the station and seemed disappointed to find that there was no special search equipment fitted to the Defiant night fighters at RAF Weston. "I heard rumours at the operational training unit," he said, "that there was something new being fitted to night fighters to help locate enemy aircraft in the dark."

The engineer smiled at the more senior pilot and said, "Will you tell him or shall I?" "You go ahead, if it won't bore the Wing Commander and his guest. I must get on with my meal. My plane is on first stand-by tonight and I prefer to take off well fed!" The engineer looked at Guy, who nodded encouragingly. "I am sure Mr Maxwell will be quite interested in what you have to say, and you need not worry about any security risk. He's a CID officer and was an RAF intelligence officer in the last war and was my air gunner before that!" The engineer turned to the young Pilot Officer. "What you have heard is quite correct, but is not the whole picture. It is quite true that there is a device, nicknamed "the magic mirrors", which can be mounted on an aircraft and can detect other planes in the dark. There are two snags. Firstly it is bulky and secondly it needs one highly skilled man to do nothing else but operate it. Because of this the only fighter we have at present which is big enough to carry it is the Blenheim which, as you probably know, is barely fast enough to catch up with a modern bomber anyway! Another problem is that, so far, there is no way of telling which aircraft are friendly and which are enemy ones. This means that the Blenheim night fighters equipped with airborne radio-location equipment can only operate singly."

By this time the more senior pilot had finished eating and was toying with a cup of coffee. The smell was good, but it was evidently much too hot! He was now quite happy to join the conversation. "Actually" he said to the younger man, "you've a much better chance of shooting down a Jerry bomber with a Defiant than those Blenheim chaps have. We can slip in underneath. Then the gunner can swing up his four guns and turn his turret almost at leisure till he's right on target. He can afford to wait to fire until he's quite sure of his aim! Once we've located Jerry it's very difficult for him to escape. Quite often they never even see us! With a Blenheim you have to aim the whole aircraft at the target, which is quite difficult in the dark and with only a small margin of extra speed." Mind you, Dick," said the engineer, "you're in a very strong position personally - you've got the best gunner in the squadron, if not in the whole group! And you've been working with him so long that each of you must know exactly what the other is thinking at any given moment!"

Guy explained to Max and young Pilot Officer Tait that Dick Holland and Sergeant Evans, his air gunner, were amongst the very few aircrew who had survived the early days of the Defiants. At that time Defiants had been used as day fighters. They had done rather well over Dunkirk, where they first saw action. Here the Defiants had surprised the Germans by their gunners' ability to fire from almost any direction. Soon, however, the Luftwaffe had discovered that Defiant fighters had a blind spot below and behind. After that there had been very heavy losses. Eventually they had been withdrawn from daytime action, leaving the Hurricanes and Spitfires, which were both faster and more manoeuvrable, to battle with the German's very successful Me109 fighters. Now, however, the Defiants were coming into their own as night fighters.

"Well," said Tait, "But how do you locate an enemy bomber in the dark?" "If you're lucky enough to have really good eyesight, it’s not so hard," replied Dick Holland. "The fighter controller will give you the general area and bearing of the enemy planes from the radio-location plot and then you have to rely on the moon, if it's out, or on searchlights. Sometimes on a very dark night you can spot the glow of the exhaust from their engines. Once you see that, you can manoeuvre to get in a little below and behind. Once you're in that position they usually don't see you and you can close in for the kill." He looked at his watch. I'll be going down to dispersal in twenty minutes. Why don't you come with me and meet some of my flight. You're sure to pick up some useful tips."

After the two pilots had left the engineer excused himself to deal with a problem concerning some new radio equipment. Guy led Max through to the lounge, where their coffee was served at a small table in a corner of the spacious room. They settled themselves in comfortable deep leather-upholstered armchairs. The room was half empty and the lighting was subdued. There was a faint, quite pleasant, aroma of mingled tobacco smoke and coffee. They relaxed and Max described his experiences and progress in the police since the days when he had been a probationary constable at Market Braxtead, explaining that he had enjoyed his work and had found it satisfying up until the outbreak of war. Since then he had felt an urge to be more fully involved in the momentous events which had been unfolding and which had now engulfed all Europe. Guy sympathised. He was, however, particularly interested to hear of Max's holiday experiences in Germany in the years up to 1939. Max and his parents had, at first, been pleased to see the country emerging from the terrible inflation and the many other problems of the early 1920's. Then they had then become increasingly worried by the growth of Fascism from 1933 onwards. They spoke German fluently. They knew Germany very well. They had had a much better insight into the evils of the Nazi regime than most visitors. Thousands of Britishers had flocked to the Olympic games in Berlin in 1936 but most had only seen what they were meant to see. By contrast Max and his parents had heard and seen things that at first worried them, and latterly appalled them.

At 10.30 pm Max decided that it was time to set off for King's Aston and his cottage. He and Guy agreed to meet again as soon as their work allowed. Guy walked him back to the administrative block where the car was parked. As usual the Austin started at the first touch of the self-starter button. Max switched on the lights - side lights shielded by the regulation two layers of tissue paper behind the glass and a single headlight with a slotted cover allowing only very restricted illumination. The car was soon out of sight and Guy took a short walk around the main buildings to get some fresh air before turning in. Shortly before he arrived back at the officers' mess he noticed that the flare path had been illuminated. A couple of minutes later he heard the roar of an aircraft engine. Dick Holland's Defiant, with Sergeant Evans manning the gun turret, was taking off. Enemy aircraft had been detected approaching from due East. They had been reported crossing the coast: coming in from over the North Sea.

As Max, driving slowly through the blacked-out streets of the small cathedral city of Eastborough, approached a crossroads he saw a figure emerge from the shadows and step into the roadway. The man was dressed in a dark cape. The feeble light from the Austin's single shrouded headlight was reflected from the wet roadway and glinted feebly on a black steel helmet. The man raised his hand in an authoritative manner and Max pulled up. "And where might you be going?" His manner was abrupt. Max did not reply. He felt in his jacket pocket and produced a card which he handed to the special constable. There was a pause as the card was scrutinised with the aid of a torch. Then, in a very different tone the constable said, "very sorry to detain you, sir, but there's been an air raid warning and we have orders to stop all vehicles." "I am glad to know of the raid," said Max, "but next time you stop anyone, remember that a little courtesy costs nothing and does a lot to maintain good relations between the police and the public!" The special saluted and Max drove on.

The road to King's Aston ran at first through open country. From time to time there was a break in the clouds and a pale moon shone through, making driving a little easier than it was when one had to rely solely on the car's lights. After about ten miles the King' Aston road crossed the Great North road at a notoriously dangerous junction. Now, with petrol no longer available to civilians, there was virtually no traffic. A few miles further on the road ran through wooded country. It was very dark here but the drizzle, which had come and gone throughout the evening, had cleared and the moon glimmered through the trees. Max felt a little sleepy. He opened the car window for some cool air. At once he caught the note of an aircraft engine. The noise got rapidly louder. The sound was very strange. The engine was racing - screaming as if out of control. He pulled into a gateway and was getting out of the car, when he heard a new sound - louder and louder - a sort of tearing crushing sound. He was out of the car now. The noise was tremendous. Roaring engines and the tearing and crashing of branches. A plane was smashing its way through the treetops. It must come down somewhere very close by and would probably explode! He threw himself into a ditch at the roadside. As he did so there was a mighty rending, tearing noise - then total silence. The plane had crashed somewhere very near and there had been no explosion! There might be survivors! Max scrambled out of his ditch, snatched a torch from the car, heaved himself over the gate and scrambled off up into the wood, slithering on wet leaves and muddy clay soil in his haste to reach the wreck.

The steady rumble of the Junkers Jumo engines made conversation difficult. Conditions were far from comfortable in the glazed cabin of Junkers 88A "4U DA". They were flying at 6000 metres and it was bitterly cold. The observer, Meyer Reinhard, who was captain of the aircraft and the commander of the twelve planes flying that night to bomb factories in Coventry, had made Oberst von Straussen use his own seat and was squatting on the floor. Carrying five men in an aircraft designed for a crew of four was far from ideal. Early in the flight Reinhard had explained that he had delegated his second in command to lead the raid - nominally for experience, but actually so that von Straussen could be picked up without anyone outside the aircraft knowing. His own crew, Reinhard explained proudly, were totally reliable - dedicated Nazis who would say nothing of their passenger to anyone and would never mention the matter again even to each other.

The blanket of cloud beneath them seemed to be breaking up to some extent as they flew westwards and from time to time von Straussen had glimpsed waves far below, sparkling in the light of a moon which was still nearly full. Now the commander was shouting to him. "I regret, Oberst, that I will now have to resume my position. We shall shortly be crossing the English coastline." "What sort of response do you usually get from their defences," asked von Straussen. "Oh," replied Reinhard, "they'll know we're here all right. If it was daylight they would send up fighters, but at night all we are likely to see is a little flak from the coastal anti-aircraft guns." "Don't they have any night fighters?" The commander smiled contemptuously. "If they do, we've never seen them! As a matter of correct procedure, of course, all observers and air gunners in the unit are instructed to maintain observation throughout the flight, and especially when we are over enemy territory, but no one in this unit has ever actually encountered a British fighter during a night raid!"

By now the two men had exchanged places and von Straussen was squatting on his parachute pack on the floor of the aircraft. He checked that the case provided by Captain Heimgarten was safe and conveniently near to him- ready when the time came for him to jump! He noticed that the radio-operator, who had been fiddling with his set throughout the flight, was now more pre-occupied than ever. This seemed odd. He had assumed that radio silence would be maintained for security reasons. The man looked up and turned to his commander. "Thirty minutes to the drop and forty to the target, Meyer," he said. Von Straussen felt a tingle of excitement run down his spine! He made no comment, though. Presumably they were using some sort of radio beam to guide them. The less he knew about that the better! It was rumoured in the Luftwaffe that the British had sophisticated means of interrogating prisoners. He shuddered. Capture was a possibility it was better not the think about. As a spy he would probably be shot but, at least what he did not know about, he could not give away to the enemy - even unintentionally!

"Five minutes to the drop," called the radio operator. "Better be getting you ready, then I'll open the hatch," said Reinhard. Von Straussen noticed a change in the note of the engines and felt the attitude of the aircraft alter slightly. "We're going to come down to 3000 metres for the drop." he was informed. Von Straussen heaved himself up from his perch on the parachute pack and Reinhard helped him to struggle into the harness - no easy feat in the cramped cabin. Once that was done, Reinhard turned his attention to the fastenings of the hatch. He was releasing the final catch when the rear-facing air-gunner, sitting right at the back of the cabin, suddenly shouted, "Achtung!" Almost simultaneously bullets began to tear into the plane, singing through the cabin and smashing into the fuselage. Von Straussen heard the Junkers' own MG machine gun open up in reply. Then it stopped abruptly. The gunner fell back, blood pouring from his head. At the same moment the aircraft lurched into a steep spiralling dive.

Meyer Reinhard, standing in front of von Straussen, lost his footing. The aircraft's dive steepened. As he slid towards the front of the cabin Reinhard grabbed frantically at the back of the pilot's seat in an attempt to save himself. Finally he came to rest, very dazed, at young Schulz's feet. Schulz was a quiet young man, the most junior member of the crew, but he was a skilful pilot - and uninjured! He had responded immediately to the totally unexpected attack and thanks to his avoiding action the Junkers was saved from further damage. Schulz had succeeded in escaping from the attacking Defiant. The dive had carried the bomber into a patch of cloud and temporary safety. Schulz tried to level out. He succeeded but found that the plane's response to the controls was sluggish and a little erratic.

By the time the Junkers was flying straight and level again Reinhard had pulled himself together. He looked around the shattered cabin. Schulz was uninjured and had acquitted himself well. Rottmann the gunner was very obviously dead. Reinhard looked away quickly. Even for a battle-hardened officer of his experience some sights are too dreadful to be contemplated for more than a few seconds. He turned to the pilot. "Can you still fly her?" he asked. "I've got control at present," replied Schulz, "but I'm sure there's something wrong." Kranz the radio operator was at his post but his right arm was hanging limp at his side and Reinhard could see that the sleeve of the man's flying suit was in tatters. Dark blood was dripping from it onto the cabin floor. Reinhard moved towards him. His instinct was to try and stop the bleeding. It was essential to keep his crew functioning as far as possible. Suddenly he remembered their passenger! The hatch was still open but of Oberst Maximillian von Straussen there was no sign! Reinhard's heart sank. He had been entrusted with a delicate and very important mission. The Fuehrer was said to be directly interested in the operation He, Reinhard, had made the classic mistake of underestimating the enemy. He had been complaisant about the risk of an attack by night fighters and now the price was being paid. He had failed miserably! "Head west," he said to Schulz dully. "We will drop our bombs as soon as possible on a railway or any other likely target. Then we'll try to pick up the Knickerbien beam and head back to base. Keep at low altitude for the present." Reinhard then turned his attention to Kranz. He managed to stop the worst of the bleeding and then bound the injured arm across the man's chest. Kranz never spoke but continued to operate his radio equipment with his uninjured hand. "We will be dropping our bomb load shortly," said Reinhard, " after that I want you to get us back on the beam and guide our return to base." "Ja, Herr Meyer," Kranz replied briefly. His arm was increasingly painful. He must reserve all his strength for his task. A few minutes later Schulz reported that he had sighted a railway track. Reinhard ordered him to follow it.

Conditions in the cabin were atrocious. A howling gale of freezing air buffeted the crew through the shattered glazing. It was impossible to close the hatch and with every change in the plane's attitude the obscene body, that had been the gunner Rottmann a few minutes earlier, lurched to and fro spattering blood around it.

The aircraft flew low and erratically above the railway. It was easy to follow the track for they were out of the cloud by now and the moonlight caught the well-used, polished, rails and made them glitter like a bright silver ribbon. Reinhard, looking over to the starboard side suddenly saw a second ribbon getting closer and closer to the one they were following. He indicated the second track to Schulz. "We will drop our bombs where the lines join," he said. Once the two 500 Kg bombs that they carried on racks beneath the wings had been released the plane started to lift. "Turn now and climb and we will try to pick up the beam," said Reinhard to the two surviving members of his crew. He had already looked carefully around and had seen no sign of any other aircraft. The night fighter must have lost contact with them for good.

Schulz opened up the throttles controlling the Junkers Jumo engines. He did this quite gently but, while the port engine responded normally, the starboard one almost immediately erupted into a hideous roar. Gentle closing of the throttle made no difference. Controlling the aircraft had been hard enough up to now but with one engine hauling the plane round to starboard, and the other quite unable to balance it, Schulz had an almost impossible task. He managed somehow to ease the plane into an erratic climb. Suddenly Kranz yelled above the racket of the engines "I have the signal now. We are back on the beam! Level out and hold the course." Schulz eased the control column forward but as he did so he felt something give! The cables running to the tail-plane had been rubbing against a damaged spar. Now they had finally snapped! Under full power the Junkers went into a shallow dive from which there was no escape, nor was there time, at that altitude, for any of them to struggle through the shambles of the cabin and bale out through the open hatch. Schulz stayed at his controls struggling to achieve the crash-landing. It was their only hope of survival.

For some seconds Oberst Maximillian von Straussen was too dazed to know where he was or what had happened to him. Then the biting cold of the night air roused him and the drill he had learned so recently from Hauptscharftfuhrer Clauser came to his aid. He counted to ten, slowly and aloud, to ensure that he was well and truly clear of his own plane and, with luck, the one which had attacked them. The counting helped to steady his nerves and bring him back to the reality of the situation. He pulled the rip cord. Almost immediately he felt the strain on his harness as the canopy of his parachute deployed. Moments before he had been in a wholly German environment - amongst his fellow countrymen and in the apparent security of the cabin of a fair-sized German aircraft. In another five minutes he would be in an enemy country. He had not visited that country for more than a quarter of a century. He would be passing himself off as an Englishman! For the moment, though, he was in limbo - entirely alone. Apart from the bitter cold he felt surprisingly relaxed. He had no idea of the fate of the aircrew who had so recently been his companions In his present state of mind that seemed almost irrelevant. He was on his own. His future survival and the success of his mission depended on him alone. He must try to assess the ground conditions in preparation for his landing.

Obviously he was not over the planned dropping site. He estimated that the aircraft should have travelled on for at least two more minutes before he was due to jump. At the cruising speed of the Junkers that meant he must be eight or twelve kilometers short of the correct area. Below him he could see a gap in the clouds. Through that gap the landscape looked dark and unwelcoming. The area planned for the drop by von Straussen and Heimgarten had been one of open fields and parkland. This looked ominously like a forest! Von Straussen knew that from now on he must concentrate on his landing to the exclusion of everything else. To be caught high in the branches of some great tree deep in the middle of a forest would mean certain death - and the failure of his mission. He would either remain trapped there helpless until he starved or succumbed to exposure, or he would be found by some Britisher, cut down, found to be wearing civilian clothes under his flying suit, and shot as a spy. He knew he must look at the darkest spot he could find so as to accustom his eyes to the blackness below. As he did this the uniform darkness of the wood gradually resolved into a pattern of varying of shades of black and grey. There to his right was a small patch of relative lightness! As he got nearer the ground he could see that this was a small clearing. It looked lighter than the surrounding trees because the lank grass covering it had withered to the colour of hay. He would miss it though - it was too far to his right! Once again Clauser came to his rescue. He tugged at the cords to one side of the 'chute and felt it tilt - agonisingly slowly. Now he was very close to the trees. At the last minute he swung just far enough to the right. Because of his desperate effort to guide his approach away from the trees he hit the ground much faster than he should have, but he was down! The dead grass and the soft damp soil beneath it saved him from serious injury, though he was badly winded. He lay for several minutes before he regained enough strength to release his harness. He was in a little clearing in the middle of the wood. Here there was hardly a breath of wind stirring. His parachute had settled limply, close beside him. As soon as he had recovered sufficiently he gathered it up and looked for somewhere to hide it. At the edge of the clearing there were badger setts. With the aid of a dead branch he forced the rolled up 'chute down one of the wide tunnels then kicked in the loose earth, thrown up by the badgers, on top of it. After this he stripped off his flying suit and disposed of it similarly. Now his appearance was that of a typical British business man - apart from his very muddy shoes and from his presence in such unlikely surroundings.

As he was wondering how to spend the rest of the night and how to get to a railway station and so, on to his destination in Birmingham once morning came, his thoughts were interrupted by the noise of a distant aircraft engine. Could it be the plane that had attacked the Junkers? An unreasoning fear suddenly struck him. Could it be that the crew of the enemy night- fighter had seen him jump and had come to search for him? He quickly withdrew under the cover of the trees. As the noise of the plane got closer and closer and von Straussen realised that there was something very strange about the sound of the engines. Then, with a deafening shrieking roar, a dark shape shot low across the clearing. In that momentary glimpse of its passing he recognised the outline of a Junkers 88: the aircraft which had brought him from Holland! It must have been severely damaged. He guessed that the pilot had turned for home in the hope of making it back across the North sea. That it would not do so was now only too obvious. The plane was losing height at an alarming rate.

With the moment of recognition of the aircraft came the horrifying realisation that the vital case which Heimgarten had given him was still on board! Hardly had he grasped this awful truth than he heard the rending of trees and the tearing of metal and then a final crump as the plane hit the ground a mile or so away. He knew he must retrieve that case at all costs! The sky had cleared by now and the moon was easily visible. If he kept it to his right side it should guide him the direction of the crash. The trees were completely bare. There was no difficulty in keeping the nearly full moon in sight through the canopy of branches overhead. He set off. In places thick undergrowth made progress slow but much of the woodland floor was clear and for a good deal of the time walking was easy, as long as one was wary of the slippery leaves and mud underfoot. Once he heard the crack of a twig and the tail of his eye caught a movement away over to the left. He stood stock still for a full minute but nothing stirred. Perhaps it was some animal: possibly one of the badgers whose setts had proved so useful! He knew that they were often quite active in the early part of the night. When he was satisfied that there was nobody else about he continued on his way, still keeping the moon to his right.

To reach the wrecked aircraft was an urgent priority. No doubt the crew of the night-fighter would report their encounter and a search would be made for the aircraft they had attacked. He must retrieve his case and be well away from the crashed aircraft before English soldiers or police came nosing round. It was possible, too, that one or more of the German aircrew were alive. If so they would help him by distracting the searchers when they appeared, as they surely must before very long. As he got nearer the wreck he saw a small faint light not far from it. He crept closer to investigate. It might be one of the German airmen using a torch but he could take no risks. Then he saw that the light was shining on the very case he had come to retrieve! A shadowy figure was beside it. Whoever it was seemed completely absorbed in what he was doing. The man was trying to open the case! It certainly could not be one of the Junkers' crew. None of them would ever have dreamed of interfering with the property of a German agent. The man might be a thief or he might be some Britisher who suspected something about the case.

Von Straussen knew at once what he must do. Killing a man in cold blood was against all his instincts but in this situation there was no alternative. He would force the man into the wreck of the aircraft at gunpoint and then shoot him several times. After that he would set fire to the remains of the plane and then get out of the area as fast as he could, taking the precious case with him. The fire would occupy the attention of the British authorities for some time and that would improve his chances of escape. It would be difficult to get a fire tender to the site of the crash, so the plane would probably be completely destroyed before they could do much about it. The fear of explosions from the fuel tanks and from bombs which might still be on board would discourage the firemen from venturing too close. This would be an advantage. Later when the bodies were examined it might not be possible to tell that there had been five of them. Even if it was and even if the man's body was still more or less intact after the blaze it might be assumed that he was one of the crew who had been killed by machine gun fire from the night fighter. The British probably knew that a Junkers 88 normally only carried a crew of four, but with luck they might assume that the fifth man had been a passenger of some sort who had "come along for the ride". Von Straussen stepped silently up behind the kneeling figure.

As soon as he entered the wood Detective Inspector Maxwell began to find pieces of broken branch littering the ground. He made his way through the trees, aided by his torch. Soon the bits of broken branch scattered around became larger and then he began to see bits of aircraft debris as well. He knew he must be getting near the scene of the crash. The beam of his torch fell on a sort of hump on the ground. As he got nearer Max saw that it was a man in a flying jacket. The man was lying very still. Max unfastened the jacket and felt for a heartbeat. There was none. Beneath the jacket the man was wearing the uniform of a Luftwaffe Major. Quite a senior officer, Max thought, possibly a squadron commander. He saw that the head was lying in a very odd position and guessed that the Major had been thrown out of the aircraft as it hit the ground and had broken his neck. A few yards further on he caught sight of the plane. It was nose down with its tail plane lodged among the top branches of a clump of young beech trees. He approached cautiously. It was possible there might be survivors still within the fuselage. He clambered in through a gaping hole in the port side and almost at once encountered the horribly mutilated body of the rear gunner still strapped into his seat. His gun, mounted beside him, pointed crazily skywards. Max had not seen such awful head injuries since 1918, and found that time had in no way reduced his horror of such things. He turned his torch hastily towards the front of the cabin and saw that the pilot also was still strapped into his seat. The nose of the plane was partly embedded in the soft earth and the pilot's face was almost buried in soil and debris: there was no sign of life. A little behind the pilot was another member of the crew - the radio operator. He also was fastened to his seat but his face had smashed against the radio panel in front of him and Max's brief examination confirmed that he too was dead.

Max decided it was time to get out but as he started to turn away something caught his eye. It was an attaché case lying on its side close to the pilot's seat. He picked it up rather gingerly and scrambled out. It was such a strange finding that he decided to investigate it further. First, however, he would get well away from the wreck. There was no obvious risk of fire or explosion, but it was stupid to take any unnecessary chances. In any case he was glad to distance himself from the aircraft and its horrifying cargo of death. He wedged his torch in a crack in a tree stump three or four hundred yards from the grim remains and, kneeling on the ground, started to examine the case in detail. It was obviously well made and the leather was of excellent quality. He was just starting to try and test the locks when something hard was thrust abruptly and totally unexpectedly into the small of his back! At the same moment a harsh voice said, "leave the case, raise your hands above your head and stand up - slowly!" Even in the shock of that blood-chilling moment he thought that the voice had something faintly familiar about it! He knew that he had no alternative but to obey. As he started to comply and was cautiously straightening up there was a sudden flurry of movement behind him, then a loud report. Detective Inspector Maxwell lurched forward and landed face down on the moist earth.

Chapter 6

Corporal Christine Turner of the Women's Auxiliary Air Force straightened up and closed the bonnet of the big Humber Super Snipe staff car. Unlike the other cars in the RAF's Central London pool, which were painted Air Force blue, this one was shiny black, just as it had left the factory in 1937. It's mileage had been very low when it was acquired by the RAF and it had been allocated as VIP transport. Across the bonnet of her own car Leading Aircraftswoman Laura Dutton, her blue eyes twinkling and her blonde hair beginning to escape from under her second-best uniform cap, grinned at Christine. "You look after that car as if it was a baby!" she said. "Well," replied Christine, "you must admit that it's a cut above that Austin you have to put up with!" Laura laughed and threw the wet chamois leather she had been using at Christine. Christine dodged easily but in the process her cap fell off, revealing her shiny brown hair, neatly trimmed, but still a little unruly. The colour of her hair set off her large brown eyes rather nicely. Her pleasant oval face was lit up in a cheerful smile. The girls had a fit of the giggles then Christine retrieved the cap and, using the mirror of the staff car, rearranged both hair and cap. Both girls had a healthy tan. Although their hours of duty were long, they had been on the night shift for the past four months and had managed to get out of doors and play quite a bit of tennis during the daytime. The summer of 1940 had been an exceptionally fine one and, in spite of the efforts of the Luftwaffe to spoil things for everyone, Christine and Laura, like many others in the south of England, had taken full advantage of the good weather. They had become firm friends and found that bit of light-hearted horse-play helped to reduce the tension of night-duty now that winter and the "blitz" had arrived.

As drivers, they often had to put up with long hours of boredom when their cars were not required but these quiet spells were interspersed with sudden calls to drive out into the night - and the air raids! The German planes came over at nine o'clock almost every evening. People joked and said that you could set your watch by "Jerry". The raid would start with the eerie wail of the sirens, rising and falling for a couple of minutes or so before finally dying away in a faint mumble. By then a tingle of mixed fear and excitement would be running up and down your spine! Anything could happen before the all clear sounded: your whole life might be completely changed by the time the sirens wailed again with the long blast of the "raiders past" signal. Soon the ack-ack guns would open up. The racket was tremendous but quite heartening. We were hitting back at Jerry! The downside was that shell splinters from the guns came rattling down everywhere - including the streets that the girls had to drive through! Those jagged pieces of red hot steel, weighing several ounces each, caused many casualties. After a big raid there were splinters everywhere. Children collected them on the way to school. There were extra marks for the biggest collection of the month! The copper from the driving bands was especially prized. Everything they collected was sent away to be recycled and used to make more shells. London was so big that one part might be quite peaceful while another area had a terrifyingly bad night. Even in the relative security of the basement depot, where Christine and Laura waited for calls, a "close one" from time to time set the nerves tingling and the building trembling! Christine had filled the petrol tank of her beloved Humber, checked the oil, water and tyres and polished it to gleaming perfection. She was ready for a break. "Come on," she said, "Let's make some coffee before Sergeant Walters appears to chase us about something or other." They retired to the bleak little basement room which served as both air raid shelter and rest room for the drivers. Over coffee, rather to her amusement, Laura was treated to a long dissertation about the Humber. It had only recently arrived at the depot. It had been allocated to Christine a few days previously. Christine explained that although its "split" windscreen might not be to everyone's taste and that its rear was flat, lacking the fashionable bulbous boot of 1939 models, it was a really advanced car. "Automatic choke, built-in jacking system and a one-shot lubrication point on each side," she said. "I don't have to go crawling about underneath to do a bit of greasing like the rest of you!" Laura gave her a quizzical look. "What you need," she said, "is a nice boy-friend to give you something else to think about other than swanking that you've been allocated the latest VIP car!" Christine's usually cheerful face clouded. Laura was not to know that a couple of years previously Christine had met, and been very much attracted to, a young naval officer. She was fairly sure that he had liked her too. But then, just over a year ago, had come the news that the German battleship Graf Spee had been defeated at the battle of the River Plate. This had been a considerable boost to civilian morale but unfortunately many of the crew of the British cruiser, HMS Exeter, had been killed during the battle. Charles Merton had been one of them.

Rather fortunately they were interrupted. A shy young WAAF clerk, recently arrived on her first posting, scurried into the rest room. "Corporal Turner, please can you report to the duty officer at once," she said, breathlessly. Christine jumped up and followed the girl along the corridor to the office. The duty officer, a gentle quite elderly man, smiled as Christine entered the office. She was one of his favourites. He knew her to be calm under pressure and very reliable. "Air Intelligence have asked for a fast car to report to 176 High Holborn immediately and prepared for a long run. Is your car fuelled up and ready?" "Yes, sir, I've just checked it and everything is in good order." "Excellent: then collect your things and get going - and remember that anything you see or hear on this particular trip is forgotten immediately! When you arrive at High Holborn ask for Group Captain Avon."

Within ten minutes the Group Captain, a well-built tallish man in a dark civilian overcoat and bowler hat, was settled in the back of the car, his brief case on his knee. "I want you to head up the Great North Road as fast as you can without killing us or anyone else!" was his greeting. "Do you know the route?" Christine's parents had been keen caravaners. In the years before the war she had picked up a good knowledge of the more important main roads in many parts of Britain. Her knowledge of the geography of southern England was one of the reasons why she had been selected for the "Central London Pool" of WAAF drivers. Once stationed in London she had made it her business to get to know her way about the metropolis as soon as possible. She assured the intelligence officer that she was quite familiar with both the route out of London and the Great North Road itself. "I want you to go as far north as Norman Cross," he said. "After that I will guide you by map. From there on we shall be using minor roads."

London's streets were almost empty and although, as usual, there was an air raid alert there was little sign of activity locally as they left Holborn. They turned into Tottenham Court Road and headed north for Camden Town. Here Christine noticed a couple of Auxiliary fire tenders pulling out from their depot, not far from the Underground station. These fire tenders were really just taxi cabs which had been painted grey and fitted with ladders. Each pulled a trailer pump. They headed off in the direction of Regents Park. Christine guessed that there had probably been an "incident" on the far side of the park. At Kentish town the doors of the regular fire station there were standing open. The engines had already left for the same trouble spot - somewhere over to the west. It was lucky, she thought, that there was no sign of anything happening on their own route so far. Even quite a small bomb or fire could delay them - or worse! At the Archway the Humber had to slow down briefly as a white ambulance ahead of them swung into the big hospital at the foot of the hill. After that the powerful car made light work of the long rise, then under the tall span of the Archway Bridge, and out past the Highgate Woods and through Finchley. On Barnet hill they swept past several heavy lorries grinding slowly up towards the tall church that marks the summit of the hill and the fork of the road. Soon they were out of the built-up area and beyond the hazards of the night's air attack on London. With a clear moon to assist her, Christine was able to open the throttle and let the big car run up to 70 miles an hour on the straighter stretches of road. The dead pallor of the withered grass of the roadside verges contrasted with the black of the Tarmac. This helped to compensate for the rather feeble illumination provided by the hooded headlights.

For many miles they travelled in silence. Christine concentrated on making the most of the Humber's power and road-holding. There were some places where the road was good and the view ahead clear, but here and there were nasty twists, such as the double bend where the road crosses the railway near Welwyn - two abrupt turns on a downward gradient - they might have caught a less experienced driver unawares. Christine knew the bridge. She braked firmly on the straight as she approached and then accelerated progressively out of the second curve. When they reached Baldock the town appeared to be deserted. The road through it includes some sharp, rather blind, corners so they had to slow almost to a snail's pace. Once they were at the far end of the town and beyond the arch of the railway bridge the road straightened again. Christine accelerated firmly. She felt the exhilaration of having a powerful machine under her control. They swept on towards Biggleswade meeting only the occasional lorry.

The Group Captain appeared to be absorbed. He was reading through papers from his briefcase with the aid of the small interior light in the back of the car. It was, he reflected, interesting that luck was sometimes quite as important as skill in time of war. Of course the skill of the crew of that night-fighter had been the initial factor, but luck had decided that the plane they shot down happened to be carrying something much more important than a load of bombs! The documents he had been reading confirmed his recollection that Naval Intelligence were very worried at the apparent ease with which German U-boats seemed able to target ships carrying particularly important cargoes. If the information he had received an hour and a half ago was correct it might be possible to penetrate the German information-gathering network, which he guessed must be responsible for the U-boats' successes. It was possible that even more important matters were at stake but this was just guess-work. In any event his actions within the next few hours would be crucial.

Abruptly he packed his papers away and, looking up, addressed Christine, "you handle this car very well, Corporal. Have you been driving it for very long?" "No, sir," she replied, "but my father had a similar model before the war and I sometimes drove him on business." Her voice was calm and pleasant - respectful without being subservient. The Group Captain was politely interested. "Where does your father have his business," he asked, quite casually. "Our home is in the country, towards Warwick," replied Christine, "but father's business is around the Birmingham area." Avon's interest increased considerably at this piece of information, but he was careful not to let this show. "Father's original business was a bakery," she continued, "but he branched out into catering and now he has quite a chain of shops in Birmingham and the surrounding area. They're called Turners Tearooms and are rather like the ABC in London, but a little bit more up-market, or so we like to think!" "I suppose you know Birmingham pretty well then," said Avon. "Yes, sir," replied Christine, simply.

Avon was silent for a while, apparently lost in thought, then he asked, "have you been in the WAAF long?" "My brother was an RAF pilot - a regular," Christine replied, "so I decided to join up in 1939, when Hitler invaded

Poland." What's your brother doing now?" enquired the Group Captain. There was a brief silence, then she answered in a low voice, "My brother is dead. His Hurricane was shot down over France in April." "I'm sorry," said Avon. It was true. He was sorry, both as a human being and as a fellow airman. As an intelligence officer, however, he realised that this was of great interest and could conceivably be advantageous. This woman not only knew the area in which he hoped to mount a very important operation, but as well as that had a strong incentive to work against the enemy. That the work was likely to be both difficult and dangerous he knew well, but on the face of it she might be willing to face the hazards involved. Also she was probably competent to do the job efficiently.

Nothing more was said during the next quarter of an hour. The car sped on northwards through Sandy and St. Neots. Soon after Buckden there is a long gentle hill leading to the point where the Great North Road merges with the old Roman road to the north. Beyond here the road runs straight for many miles, and the Humber raced on towards Norman Cross. They were well towards Stilton when Group Captain Avon leaned forwards and asked, rather abruptly and in a very formal tone, "Corporal, are you aware of the Official Secrets Act?" Christine was rather startled but replied promptly enough, "Yes sir." Avon then continued, "When we reach our destination it is possible that I may ask you if you are prepared to undertake some special duties. If I do, you may be assured that the work will be of vital importance. Whether or not you agree to undertake what is asked of you, and whether or not you are needed, this conversation must never be mentioned to anyone. Do you understand?" "Yes sir," she replied again, "I understand." "Good!" said Avon, "Would you, then, be willing to take on what may be a dangerous job, and one which will bring you, personally, no particular credit: perhaps the reverse? Before you answer, though, I will explain the situation. Something has occurred which may give us an opportunity to break into the enemy's intelligence network in this country. It is possible that your help could be very valuable." Christine hesitated for a few moments. Then she said, "I'm willing to do anything the RAF needs me to do, if it will help to win the war."

Satisfied with her firm reply, her steady voice and her composure, Avon explained that if she was needed the first step would be to have her released from her unit. This would have to be done in some way that would avoid awkward questions being asked. Perhaps she might have to feign a sudden nervous breakdown. If she did this, she could then be sent home on "medical advice." Once at home she would have to persuade her father to give her a job in one of his tearooms in the centre of

Birmingham. She would rent a "bedsit" and live quietly there, working all day in the tearoom and awaiting contact with Avon's agent who would be working from within the German intelligence service. He would drop in at the tearoom for meals from time to time and they would be able to exchange messages. Christine would then have to relay information back to Air Intelligence without arousing the suspicion of those with whom the agent would be associating. Christine was far from enthusiastic. She very much disliked the idea of deceiving her parents and inflicting extra worry on them. They had already lost their only son. However she realised that the Group Captain was a very senior and responsible officer. She felt instinctively that he was not the sort of man to make a request of this sort unless he considered it absolutely vital. Rather reluctantly she agreed that she would follow the plan if it should turn out that this was necessary.

By the time this was settled they had slowed down and were passing the outlying cottages immediately to the south of Stilton. "When we are through this village and at the top of the next hill", Christine said, "we shall be at Norman Cross." Avon spread a map across his knees. "Just beyond the crossroads at the top of the rise," he said, "is a monument to the prisoners held there during the Napoleonic wars. It has an eagle on top and is quite tall. It should be a good landmark. Exactly a mile beyond the monument there is a tiny lane off to the left. Turn down that lane and then follow it westwards to the village of Warmington, about six miles further on. I will give you fresh directions when we get to Warmington."

In his mind Avon had already decided to use the girl. It was essential that as few people as possible knew of the momentous development that had brought him on this sudden journey. This girl was already involved, even if only peripherally. She knew the area of the operation he hoped to mount and had access to a very suitable job which would provide cover for her part in the work that lay ahead. In the normal way potential agents were vetted with great care and over a period of many months before being recruited for intelligence work. In the present situation there was no time for such well proven but time-consuming procedures. Quite a number of quick decisions were going to be necessary over the next few hours.

Avon was quite prepared to back his judgement of WAAF Corporal Turner. She was undoubtedly reliable and intelligent. Her handling of the car, too, showed both confidence and competence. He struggled to be honest with himself. He knew that he rather enjoyed making quick bold decisions. He went over the case again in his mind several times before he cleared himself of the charge of putting his instincts before his professional judgement. When there is no time for prevarication, one must assess the situation and use the people and resources available, he reassured himself. This was the route to success when a quite exceptional opportunity like the present one is suddenly presented. Even a delay of a few hours to consult with other senior officers would that mean the chance of rounding up the complete German spy network in Britain at one stroke might slip through his fingers! He confirmed to his conscience that the plan he intended to follow, though dangerous for those involved, did not involve any additional risks for Britain. On the contrary the nation stood to gain an enormous advantage. If the flow of information about British shipping could be stemmed, losses should be much reduced! It was possible also that something more than ordinary intelligence gathering by the enemy was involved. That message he had received from Midhamptonshire had carried a hint of something new and sinister. What it might be he could not guess. He was desperately impatient for the car to reach its destination. Hurriedly he turned his attention back to the map. The final details of the route were his responsibility. Any delay from now on would be his fault!

Chapter 7

The morning rush hour was almost over. The stream of office workers pouring out from New Street station in the centre of Birmingham was starting to thin. The railway policeman on duty at the main exit began to think of the cup of coffee he would enjoy once his colleague took over. He was approached by a man dressed in a dark suit and carrying a case. "Can you direct me to Fiveways, please?" the man asked. Evidently a stranger to the city; perhaps a lawyer or an accountant. The officer would have been more than a little surprised to know that the case the man was carrying had arrived by air from Germany only the previous night. "Yes, sir. Walk up Station Street to John Bright Street and turn left. Take the first right into Holloway Head. That leads to Bath Row. Then you'll pass Davenport's brewery and the Accident Hospital on your right and soon after that you'll join Islington Row, and that goes straight up to Fiveways." "Thanks very much," replied the other. "How far is it?" "About a mile and a quarter. You could get a bus or tram at the bottom of Holloway Head if you want." "It's not a bad morning for November - I think I'll walk." Walking, he thought privately, would be quite a useful way of getting his bearings in a strange city.

The brewery, with its red name board, was easily recognised. Shortly after he had passed it he could see the Fiveways Junction. A few yards before Fiveways, at the top of Islington Row, a brass plate beside a doorway indicated that here was the office of Pattenson & Co., Solicitors. The door was open: it led to a flight of stairs. At the top was a glass door and behind this, in a small outer office, a severe- looking middle aged lady sat typing. "Have you an appointment?" she enquired. "It's a personal visit, but Mr Pattenson was expecting me to call sometime today," the visitor replied. "If you want to see him now you'll have to go down to the warehouse office. He and Mr Riddle had to go down there early and expect to be there most of the day. Do you know where it is? They only started using it quite recently." It turned out that he had passed close to the warehouse already. "Go back down Islington Row and look for a door which is at the top of some steps leading down to the canal towpath. The door is on this side of the bridge, just before the Accident Hospital. The warehouse is the first building you'll come to once you're on the towpath." He retraced his steps. On his walk up from the station he had not noticed that a canal ran beneath the road, but now he saw that there was a gap between the buildings. The parapet was high and the canal was not visible from the roadway, but a shabby grey door gave access to some steps leading down to the canal. This time he looked at the surroundings more carefully and noticed a small garage across the road. It must also front onto the canal, he thought, but on the opposite bank to Pattenson's warehouse, the existence of which came as a surprise to him.

At the bottom of the steps he looked around carefully. The towpath widened as it emerged from under the bridge. In front of the warehouse it broadened to form a small wharf. Big doors fronted onto the wharf, but looked as if they had not been used for a long time. Near the far corner of the building there was a smaller door, and beside it, a very dirty window: probably that of an office. He knocked but there was no response. The door was unfastened and he pushed it open. Inside it was very dark but he could see that he was in a small lobby. There was an inner door ahead of him and another to his right. He knocked on the latter, supposing it to lead to the office. "Come in," said a rather brusque voice. He opened the inner door and stepped into a modest sized room. It was lit by a small unshaded bulb and the daylight filtering through the grimy window. As his eyes became accustomed to the gloom, he saw that there was a large desk below the window. There were two men in the room, one seated at either side of the desk. They had been deep in discussion and looked up impatiently. "What do you want," said the smaller man sharply. Before the newcomer had time to reply the other man, looked at him intently and asked in a very different tone, "are you Max?"

There was a moment's pause before he replied, "I am." At once both men rose to their feet. The bigger of the two was well-built and smartly dressed: a man in his late forties: a professional man almost certainly. He held out his hand. "You are more than welcome. We have been expecting you and are eager to learn about "Operation Chainbreak". By the way I am George Pattenson and this," indicating his companion, "is Walter Riddle. I practise as a solicitor and Riddle is my managing clerk as well as my assistant here. He served in U-boats in the last war and is an expert on codes and radio. We have only one other man working with us in the intelligence unit in Birmingham and you will probably meet him tomorrow. He runs the barge which carries our radio transmitter." "Tell me the extent of your network," said Max. "The Kriegsmarine were not very informative and in any case I had a very short time to prepare for my mission and much of that was taken up with the technical aspects of the operation." Pattenson smiled ruefully. "Network is a rather flattering description," he said. "Berlin did not anticipate the need for extensive intelligence cover in Britain. After the Munich pact, it was not really expected that the British would go to war at all. Intelligence resources were concentrated on Poland and the Low Countries. Apart from the three of us here, we have one man in Cardiff, a small unit London and a very good agent in Glasgow. An IRA unit in Liverpool gives us information about shipping movements in the Mersey area."

The newcomer eyed the other two. Then he addressed Pattenson. "There are twenty or so targets which must all be attacked simultaneously using special packs brought in by submarine." Pattenson and Riddle seemed completely taken aback. "We can't possibly find twenty agents," said Pattenson, "let alone twenty teams!" Max drew himself up, looked hard at each of them in turn, then said sternly, "the Fuehrer's orders are explicit. I have them here." He tapped his case. "This operation will be carried out regardless of risk. It is so important that the usual precautions will be over-ridden. Berlin has authorised the recruitment of elements not normally regarded as sufficiently reliable for work with the German intelligence services." The other two looked aghast and Riddle would have protested, but before he could utter a word Max continued, "My information is that there is to be a large gathering of peace protesters here in Birmingham this weekend. Is that correct?" Pattenson nodded. "That is certainly so, and our Glasgow agent, who has established a reputation as a Communist trade union agitator by way of cover, is using the meeting as an excuse to come to Birmingham and up-date us with information from the port of Glasgow." Max nodded. "That is well, but you will instruct ALL your existing agents to attend this meeting. They are to bring anyone known to them who might be prepared to strike a blow in favour of an early peace settlement, regardless of sympathies or background. We may be able to use militant pacifists, any British Fascists who haven't been interned, IRA sympathisers, and Communists and perhaps other disaffected persons. Provided that they remain unaware of each other's sympathies and motives, and of the fact that they will actually be working for Germany, members of any such group may be useful to us. At the meeting we shall identify and recruit the most promising individuals. As far as they are concerned they will be striking a blow to discredit the warmonger Churchill and so allow moderate politicians to take over and negotiate peace with Germany! We shall explain that this has been the Fuehrer's wish since the onset of hostilities; that it was never his intention to go to war with Britain or the British Empire. Our recruits will be told that his plans have always been directed to the unification of Europe under German influence and that the ambitions of the German people have now been fulfilled!"

"Riddle," said Pattenson, "kindly contact our men immediately and relay the instructions." He turned to Max. "What arrangements do you wish to be made for your accommodation and for communications with Berlin?" Max allowed himself a dry smile. "My personal requirements are simple. I shall remain here at your centre of operations and will use your existing communications system as necessary. However, as Chainbreak is already planned in very great detail only the minimum of contact with Germany will be necessary. It is safer so. The most urgent work will be here in Birmingham, although I have several lesser assignments from the Reichsluftfahrtministerium which will necessitate my absence for short periods. I shall require your fullest co-operation and your existing agents will be needed to help in the recruitment and training of the sabotage teams. This must be our first priority. All I shall require for my own use is a mattress on the floor of the office here and some bedding. I shall take my meals at local restaurants. In the unlikely event of any enquiry being made about me, you will say that I am an engineer sent to Birmingham to investigate improvements in machine tool design. Now kindly explain to me why you are working from this warehouse. I expected to find you at your solicitor's office.

For an instant Max thought Pattenson looked very slightly uneasy, and he noticed Riddle look up rather sharply. It was all over in a flash and Pattenson spoke perfectly normally when he replied. He explained that the warehouse accommodated a business which was a better cover for their intelligence work than the legal practice which had always been a small one and which had been very quiet since the war started. "In the new business I buy up surplus civilian cars. They are very cheap owing to the shortage of petrol and the strict rationing. We collect up the cars here at the warehouse and then, using subcontractors, convert them for use as ambulances, fire pump towing vehicles, light rescue tenders and so on. They are then sold to local authorities for Civil Defence use. Before conversion each car is checked mechanically by a garage over the road. Any found to be unreliable are sold as scrap. Because we are careful to ensure our vehicles are sound and the conversions carried out to a high standard we have established a good reputation and the business is actually quite profitable!" Once again Max had a fleeting impression that Riddle was uneasy, or perhaps disapproving. Pattenson continued, "The third member of our group here in Birmingham is Alfred Barnes. He has no connection with the car business or the legal practice but is a bargee. As the warehouse is beside the canal Riddle and I can easily meet with him, as if by chance, and pass on and receive information. Our radio equipment is concealed on the barge. As it is never in one place for very long there is little risk of our brief transmissions being picked up by British counter-intelligence. Unlike Riddle and I, who are both German, though we both pass as English and have lived here for many years, Barnes is a Britisher." Max looked up sharply. "How, then, can you be sure of his loyalty to the German cause?" he asked. "Barnes was a British soldier," replied Pattenson. "He joined up in 1914 and served in the trenches all through the war. In 1917 his younger brother was called up. He was a bit simple and while serving at the front he misunderstood an order and panicked. He was court- martialled and executed. When Barnes learned about it after the war he swore revenge. He contacted our embassy in London secretly and they recruited him for intelligence work. He has been in the service longer than any of the rest of us and is totally loyal to Germany."

The organisers of the Great Birmingham Peace Meeting of November 1940 proclaimed it as a triumphant success. There had certainly been quite a number of people present in the City Hall and most of the speakers departed well satisfied. They had put forward a logical case for ending the war in a civilised fashion. Surely, it had been explained, the air raids were proof enough of the overwhelming might of the German military. It should, they said, be possible to live at peace now that Hitler had so amply satisfied the need of the German people for "lebensraum" and for a wider sphere of influence! Secretly some of the organisers might have wished for rather more publicity and press coverage. They would have preferred an appearance by Lloyd George, rather than a polite note from his secretary explaining how frail the old man had become. They recalled the enormous impact of the riotous meeting, held in the same hall in 1901, when he had spoken so vehemently against the continuation of the Boer war. It was a pity that this meeting, forty years on, could not have attracted the same sort of attention!

Others, however, were very satisfied with the outcome. As anticipated by German intelligence, the event had drawn together a motley collection of individuals and groups. Some were willing to do a lot more than speak against the continuation of the war! For example the Communist party had sent delegates and while all of these wished Britain to follow the example of the Soviet Union and sign an accord with Hitler, some amongst them were extremists. Such men and women regarded Churchill's government with deep hatred. They were willing to take considerable risks to overthrow it. Most of the numerous pacifists present abhorred all forms of violence. A few, however, believed that any means of ending the war and stopping the bloodshed was justified. Then there were IRA agents who were more than willing to further their own cause by damaging Britain. They were only too happy to seize any chance that might present itself. Most of the British Nazi party had been interned at the start of the war but there were still a few sympathisers at large. Several of these attended and decided that a peace settlement would greatly benefit their interests. Amongst the various conference delegates members of the small band of German intelligence agents moved unobtrusively. Wherever there seemed to be an enthusiasm for militant action, rather for than mere words, a quiet verbal invitation to attend a small private meeting after the main event was given.

The private meeting was chaired by George Pattenson, a large man of dignified appearance. He had greying hair and a round reliable looking face. His expression was serious, befitting the gravity of the situation under discussion. He was a figure calculated to reassure the sceptical and the suspicious. He allowed the meeting to develop a momentum of its own, encouraging speakers to come onto the platform and put forward their ideas. With his minimal but discreet guidance the meeting evolved a proposal to form a movement to be known as "People for Peace". This movement was to have the secret objective of forcing the British government to sue for peace. At this stage Walter Riddle raised his arm.

He was called forward by the chairman. Neither gave any indication of knowing the other. Riddle seemed at first an unlikely person to take a major part in such a gathering. Of moderate height and slightly built, with a long narrow face and balding hair, he appeared diffident and, at first, almost apologetic. Then as he spoke he seemed to gain in confidence and, imperceptibly, the confidence developed into firm authority. "I believe," he said, "that if a great blow was struck against the air defences at a number of different places simultaneously the nerve of our arrogant and obstinate government, which is at present leading the country to disaster, would crack! Saner politicians would take over and, recognising the true situation of the country, would seek negotiations for peace." Somebody asked how the defences could be disrupted badly enough for this to happen. "I, and one or two of my associates have direct links with the Soviet Union," he said. "We know that the Soviets have a great desire for world peace. They could, and would supply the means that we need." This announcement was greeted with enthusiasm by many of those present, but it was clear that one or two waverers were reluctant to become involved in action of this sort, now that the means might actually be available.

At this point the chairman announced that refreshments were available in the next room and that those present would have an opportunity to talk amongst themselves.

This allowed the weaker-willed and the waverers a chance to slip away, just as the organisers had anticipated. During the interval the German agents once again moved unobtrusively about the room listening to the conversations going on and picking out the genuine militants from the rest. When the meeting was re-convened Pattenson asked for views from the floor. These were forthcoming. Some were expressed at length. This gave a further opportunity for assessment of both the speakers and the listeners. By the time the meeting closed, in the small hours of the morning, the names and details of about thirty men and women were in the hands of the Germans. Each of those chosen was asked to attend an "action meeting" the next evening. This arrangement allowed just sufficient time for a few discreet enquiries to be made. Any of those invited who seemed to have a background which might be "suspicious" was skilfully side-tracked and excluded from the campaign. Anybody who failed to respond to the invitation was obviously too lukewarm to be of much use. Only the most ruthless, determined and fanatical were going to be tough enough to carry out the daring and dangerous operation that German Intelligence had planned!

During the next few weeks the little group at Birmingham, reinforced by several carefully vetted helpers, worked desperately to organise the twenty or so teams considered essential to the success of the scheme of sabotage envisaged. Vital radio-location sites, carefully selected by Heimgarten and his opposite number at the Reichsluftfahrtministerium, were to be targeted. Visits were made to various parts of the country to assess the men and women who had been chosen. Some of them had attended the Peace Rally themselves while others had been recommended by friends who had been present. A few of the easier assessments were carried out by Pattenson and Riddle, but most of this work was done by Max. He stated that, as the officer in charge, he must personally size up any "doubtfuls".

Once the personnel for the operation had been selected there was the task of planning which team would be most suited to attack which site. At this stage documents from the case brought by Max when he arrived were studied intensively. Captain Heimgarten had provided detailed information about some locations. There were deficiencies, though, where a site had been identified by the Luftwaffe but where little more was known beyond the fact of its existence. Cautious local exploration and enquiry had to be made, but Pattenson, Riddle and Max all agreed that anything more than fairly superficial inspections at this early stage would be dangerous and might arouse the suspicions of the authorities. It was decided that each team should make an individual plan of attack and should be responsible for its own reconnaissance. Every team would be visited by one of the three men from the Birmingham headquarters. He would vet their plan and instruct the team in the use of the specially designed explosive pack which would be used in the attack. For this the demonstration explosive pack and instructions included in the contents of Heimgarten's case would be used.

They discussed the problem of transferring the explosives from the Scottish coast, where a German submarine would land them, to the various places where they would be used to destroy the big masts of the RAF radio-location units. Distribution, they thought, would be a very difficult problem, involving considerable risks of detection. At first no-one could think of a solution. Then, late one afternoon, when Pattenson and Riddle were working on a complicated legal contract to supply ARP vehicles to a large local authority, Pattenson suddenly pushed aside the documents and said, "I think I've got the answer to the explosives problem!" The other two were immediately alert.

"We have an organisation which can do the job for us!" said Pattenson. "We can get "People for Peace" to arrange a special meeting, with a dinner party for the executive committee. Representatives can be invited from various parts of the country and we can include one person from each of our teams. The meeting can be held in London a night or two before "Chainbreak" is due.

What could be more natural at such a prestigious event than to have some really good fresh fish sent directly from Scotland! We can invite plenty of well-known people with pacifist sympathies to act as cover for the real purpose of the gathering. There are several distinguished academics and one or two sympathetic politicians who could be included. We might even try for Lloyd George again! The explosive packs can be concealed in the boxes of fish. If we stress the importance of the occasion and the status of the guests, it won't seem too odd if we make a fuss about the "fish" and insist on it being collected personally. Later in the evening those in the know can collect their explosive packs quietly and take them home in cases that they will bring with them. Nominally the cases will be for Peace leaflets to take away and distribute!"

Max and Riddle were impressed with the suggestion and neither could think of any major snag, nor could anybody think of a better alternative. The arrangements for the London meeting were therefore put in hand. Max then asked for ideas as to how a submarine could be met at some remote spot on the Scottish coast, the explosives transferred and then packed into boxes of high quality fish. The boxes would then have to be taken to the railway and dispatched to London. "That," said Pattenson firmly, "must be a job for Hector Sedler, our Glasgow agent. You met him briefly at our private meeting after the peace rally. That's not his real name, of course. He is of German parentage but was brought up in England till he was about ten. His father was a chemical engineer who came over from Germany to work with the British chemical industry. After the war they realised how much more advanced we were in that field! Anyway when the lad returned to Germany with his parents he joined the Hitler Youth. It was quickly realised that he was intelligent and tough and totally dedicated to the Nazi cause. He and his troop were involved in one or two fairly bloody clashes with the young Communists. Then someone realised he was wasted on that sort of thing. He was recruited into our intelligence service and it was then decided he would be of most use in Glasgow. Once there he lost no time in picking up the dialect and chose membership of the Communist party as a cover. He got work in the shipyards and being hard-working and intelligent he became a useful craftsman. He was exempted from military service due to being in an "essential occupation" and, having got deeply involved with the local Communists, he eventually became a shop-steward. He finds out most of what goes on locally through his contacts and gives us very reliable information about ship movements." Max looked thoughtful. "Landing and forwarding the explosives is a vital part of Chainbreak. I will travel to Glasgow and discuss it personally with Sedler."

The heavily laden train toiled up the incline towards Shap. Clouds of black smoke billowing back from the locomotive blotted out the view of the fells with their dry-stone walls running up the steep hillsides and their little, fast-flowing becks gushing down into the valley. Max, who had been enjoying the scenery, turned to the book on his lap. The quality of coal was poor now and locomotive maintenance was not up to the pre-war standards. Max had been very lucky. He had secured a corner seat in that crowded train. The journey had been more interesting than he had expected. The train was packed with servicemen laden with packs and accoutrements. He noticed that the soldiers carried their rifles at all times. He supposed this was necessary in case of invasion or an attack by parachutists. At first the train had rumbled through the flat plains of Cheshire: mostly small fields with cattle and sheep grazing. Here and there Max had noticed a farm hand at work hedging or ditching: the usual winter chores in that sort of country. Most of the men were old and weather-beaten. Once he had spotted a two-wheeled cart driven by a lad who could not be more than twelve lumbering out with a load of manure to tip on an empty pasture. The placid Clydesdale pulling the cart looked as if it could do the job just as well without the boy!

Then the flat fields had given way to rolling country. The surrounding land had started to lift away from the railway. Little lanes led off into the distance. Farmhouses grew fewer. There were clumps of woodland here and there. The bare trees stood out black against the winter sky, looking so dead that one could hardly believe that they would burst into life again within a few brief months! It crossed Max's mind that this was a wonderful and a beautiful country. A country that men and women might risk much to protect and preserve.

He roused himself from a state of torpor induced by tiredness, and the strain of the last few weeks, as well as by the length of the journey. There was a hollow rumbling sound. The long train was grinding its way slowly across a big bridge. They were crossing the Clyde. Over to the right he could see a road bridge. On it there were green and orange tramcars. Lorries were crossing in either direction and he saw a dark red bus. He guessed it was taking city workers home to the country area to the south of Glasgow. There seemed to be a general greyness about everything - grey buildings - grey streets - a thin grey mist; and now a grey dusk gathering.

Outside the Central station the streets were crowded with people. There were plenty of trams. He remembered to be as inconspicuous as possible. A tram pulled up at the stop. On the front the destination board read "via Charing Cross". Max climbed on board, paid his penny fare and settled to watch the busy scene. A few minutes later the conductress shouted "Charing Cross". Max was pleased not to have had to ask anyone where to get off! He looked about the confused jumble of busy streets. He realised that now he would have to ask his way. "Can you tell me how to get to the Bath Hotel, please." The middle aged woman seemed happy to help. "Certainly, hen!" Once she had shown him where to go she seemed inclined to prolong the conversation. Later Max realised that the citizens of Glasgow never missed the chance for a chat, but at that stage he was worried about giving anything away to anyone, however seemingly innocent. He pretended an urgent appointment and hurried away. The woman returned, rather reluctantly, to the tram stop where she had been waiting. He must be a commercial traveller with an appointment to meet a prospective customer.

The Bath hotel had been a private town house in more prosperous days. It was shabby but very, very respectable. He was shown to a ground floor room towards the rear of the building. The window overlooked a passage leading to the back premises. Hector had sent strict instructions about what Max must wear. He must blend as much as possible. By the time Max had unpacked his small case and changed there was a knock at the door. The fourteen year old maid announced there was "a gentleman asking for Mr Smith".

Hector was a muscular, dark-haired man in his twenties. He had an air of restlessness about him and somehow gave the impression that he was always anxious to be somewhere else: that he had never quite caught up with his own intentions. They would go, he said, to a tearoom at Charing Cross for high tea. While they ate they would only be able to talk in general terms. After that Hector would take him to a meeting at the University where he, Hector, amongst others, had been asked to speak to the Socialist club. The walk along Woodlands Road to the University Union gave Max a chance to discuss the matter of meeting the submarine and dealing with the transfer of the explosive packs to London. Hector was distinctly discouraging. He pointed out that the only sort of area where a submarine could land a cargo secretly would be in the prohibited zone in the North-west of Scotland where access by the general public was severely restricted. Max, as his superior, felt it necessary to speak to him sternly at this point reminding him that the enterprise on which they were embarking was being carried out under the direct orders of the Fuehrer. Hector, Max felt, was probably very efficient, as Pattenson had said, but he appeared to be a strong willed young man who would need firm handling!

The meeting at the University was not particularly well attended. The speakers were of very varied ability. Several expressed doubts about the war. The burdens and losses were mainly borne by the working classes, they said. The rich were making big profits from the manufacture of war materials. Some felt that a move to make peace with Germany would be in the best interests of the workers. Hector made a fiery speech in which he pointed out that if the Soviet Union was able to live at peace with Hitler's Third Reich, Britain should be able to do the same. Britain undoubtedly would do so, he said, if the capitalist warmongers of the present government were thrown out and replaced by a Communist popular government like that of Soviet Russia. His speech was greeted with the loudest applause of the evening. After this an interval for coffee was announced. Twenty minutes would be allowed, then the speakers would re-assemble on the platform to answer questions.

Max kept very much in the background, but during the interval he listened carefully to conversations around him. Nearby were two earnest-looking female students. One of these was red-headed with a rather square face and determined jaw. She was obviously the leader of the two. Her accent was soft and quite unlike the voices of the Glaswegians he had talked to so far. After the girls had discussed the speakers - and both thought that Hector was by far the best - the other girl, slightly built and dark-haired, asked the red-head, "How was your journey back from Ardmurnach at the start of term. Did you have any trouble getting your pass renewed?" This was interesting. Max moved as if to get some more coffee and then, apparently as an afterthought, turned to the two girls and asked if he could get either of them a refill. The dark- haired girl smiled and accepted his offer. When he returned he asked casually if they had come far to attend the meeting. "No," they said. It appeared that both stayed in a students' hostel quite nearby. The dark girl explained, "We both come from far away so we can't live at home like most Glasgow students. I'm from Galloway and my friend here is from a very remote place on the west coast called Ardmurnach. You'll not have heard of it?" she added. Max shook his head. "I couldn't help overhearing you mention Hector Sedler," he said, as if changing the subject. "He's a grand speaker isn't he? I had the good luck to have a talk with him earlier on. Would you like to meet him?" The dark girl's brown eyes lit up and she nodded enthusiastically. The red haired girl made no objection.

Max crossed the room and Hector broke away from the small group he had been talking with. "I want you to latch onto that redhead over there," said Max in a low urgent voice. "She comes from up the West Coast somewhere and if you can make friends with her it could be very useful." They went back across the room to where the girls were standing and Hector was introduced to Mary Dunbar from Galloway and Morag McClean from Ochshiel in Ardmurnach. Mary was obviously impressed by Hector. Morag gave away nothing of her thoughts or feelings. There was only time for a brief conversation before Hector had to return to the platform, but Max noticed that Morag's green eyes seldom left Hector's face during the second half of the meeting. At the end Hector rejoined the girls and asked if they would be interested in attending a meeting of the Communist party at Pollockshaws the evening after next. Mary looked disappointed. "It's Friday," she said, "and I've promised to catch the bus home after my last lecture and stay with my mother for the weekend. Dad's away in the army." Morag looked at Hector and spoke directly to him for the first time. "I'd be very interested," she said. "I'm getting a bit impatient with these Socialists. They seem to do nothing but talk. I want to meet people who are actually prepared to do things. Your lot sound a bit more hopeful!"

Hector walked back to the hotel with Max. "I think you're right" he said. “That girl may be quite useful to us. I might be able to get up to the West Coast with her help." "It's essential to our plan," emphasised Max. "The only way we can get the explosives we need is to have them delivered by sea. You must stick to that girl like a limpet! Get engaged to her, marry her, seduce her or do whatever else is necessary! I watched her carefully and I think she is quite interested in you." In the privacy of the hotel bedroom Max handed over the plans of the radiolocation site which Hector would be responsible for destroying. Hector, Max had decided, was entirely ruthless and very capable. He would work out his own method of attack. It would be a waste of time for Max to spend any longer in Glasgow. The young man would make his own preparations and then go personally to the Birmingham headquarters in about six weeks to report progress.

The meeting of the Communist party at Pollockshaws was a long drawn out affair and many girls would have soon become bored. Morag was not bored. She listened to what was said and planned. There was talk of strikes and of working to rule, of stoppages and of industrial sabotage. Direct action was favoured by many present. Morag was fascinated. The meeting went on into the small hours of the morning. When it finally ended trams and buses had long since stopped running. "Are you up to the walk back to Gilmorehill?" asked Hector. Morag looked indignant. "Of course I can walk," she said. "Where I come from we've to walk further than that to get anywhere. I had to walk seven miles to school when I was little!" "I'll walk with you," said Hector. "How do you find Glasgow after living in such a remote place?" "Och, I miss the sea and the hills right enough but I want to do things and I know that's impossible in Ardmurnach." "Have you always been a Socialist?" "As long as I can remember," replied Morag. "I was brought up by my mother and my granny and we had to survive on a tiny pension. I never knew my father. He joined the navy in 1914 and came all through the war: then, when my mother was expecting him home any day, word came that his ship had been sent to fight against the Bolsheviks up near Archangel. He would never have wanted to do that of his own accord. They sent him ashore with a landing party and he was killed. My mother never got over the shock and she's never been quite right in the head since. Granny came to look after me and mother and run our wee croft. She's dead now and my mother just struggles on as best she can. I've never forgiven the navy and the government for what they did to my mother and father!" "Aye," replied Hector, "I'm not surprised you feel bitter. And now a similar sort of government is dragging us through the same sort of thing all over again! You said the other night you were interested in action rather than talk. Some of my friends are planning something pretty drastic to try and bring the country to its senses. We want to force the government to come to terms with Germany, just as the Soviet Union has done. Would you to join us? It's likely to be a risky business though. Are you up for it."

They had left the main road now and were walking through a passageway with tenements on one side and the high wall of a warehouse yard on the other. Round a corner and into the passage from the other end came three men who had obviously been drinking heavily. As the men got closer one of them lurched over towards Morag and made a grab at her. "Give us a kiss, hen," he mumbled, and tried to embrace her. Morag gave him a sharp shove. He toppled and fell flat on the pavement. "What call had you for to do that?" said the big man who had been walking next to him, with the righteous indignation of the moderately drunk. He gave Morag a hard push and she staggered back against the wall. "That's right, Jock," said the third man who was carrying the bottle of spirits from which they had all been drinking. "We'll teach the besom, “and he advanced on her lifting the bottle over his head. Hector did not wait to see if he would hit her. He caught the man's arm and, using the drunk's own impetus, hurled him aside. The man went sprawling onto the ground and the bottle smashed leaving him clutching the remains by its neck. At that the bigger man turned on Hector and swung a massive fist at his head. Hector sidestepped and hit the other as hard as he could in the pit of the stomach. The man doubled up and Hector hit him again and caught him on the side of the head. He fell senseless to the pavement. "Look out behind you," Morag yelled. Hector turned abruptly and saw that the man with the broken bottle was on his feet again and about to attack him with the jagged glass. He backed away. As the man advanced in triumph his foot caught on an uneven paving stone and he stumbled. Quick as a flash Hector kicked out and caught him hard on the front of the knee. The man yelled in pain and dropped his deadly weapon. Hector chopped at his attacker's neck with the side of his hand. The man went down for the second time and lay still.

The sound of breaking glass had woken somebody in the tenement. A window above them shot up and a powerful female voice shouted, "Polis, Polis. Murder, murder!" There were sounds of other occupants of the tenement rousing too. From the main road that Hector and Morag had recently left there came the sound of a police whistle. Hector pointed towards the road at the far end of the passage. Police enquiries and appearances in Court were the last things that any German agent wanted! It was too late! An answering whistle came from the road onto which he had hoped they might escape. He hesitated. but Morag grabbed his arm. "Come into the close," she whispered. "If anyone asks, we're just saying goodnight!" By the time they had got inside the mouth of the close leading to the stairs and the front doors of the occupants of the tenement, the first policeman had arrived, rather breathless, and was examining the three men on the ground. One was trying to get up, another was swearing incoherently while the third lay very still. "Did anyone see what happened?" he called in the general direction of the tenement. Quick as a flash Morag called back, "Me and my fellow saw it. They were well away wi' liquor and started to quarrel.

Then they set on each other." A middle aged woman in curlers appeared in the close behind them. "Aye, the lassie's right," she said. "Drunken wretches, disturbing our sleep and giving Burnside Passage a bad name!" The second policeman had arrived by now. He spoke with a Highland accent, similar to Morag's. "And what would you young folks be doing in that close at this hour?" he asked. "Och, me and my fellow was just saying goodnight. He's away to the army the morn's morn and we've just got engaged!" The policemen were at once sympathetic. "You two just let on nothing's happened then. We'll soon have these shifted." He turned to the older woman. "If there's a witness needed we may have to ask you to come to Court, so I'll just take your name and address."

Morag put her arm round Hector's waist and, taking his cue from her, he kissed her and put an arm across her shoulders. They nodded to the two policemen and walked on up the passage and, reaching the road at the far end, turned right in the direction of the University. Hector was impressed despite himself. In his restless toil on behalf of the Nazi party he had never allowed himself to become involved with or even interested in girls and he had a fairly low opinion of females in general. This girl had got them out of a very difficult situation with apparent ease. She would almost certainly be a resourceful ally. Until ten minutes ago he had had no particular fancy to get involved with her except in the line of duty. Now, with her warm body close to him and her very generous kiss still fresh on his lips, he began to feel that seduction or something very like it might be enjoyable as well as being useful in terms of Operation Chainbreak! Nothing was said for a while and they walked in companionable silence. As they neared Gilmorehill, Hector said, "it was generous of you to pretend we were engaged. I would very much like us to get better acquainted. Do you think that one day you might really be willing to consider me as your fiance!" Morag said nothing but stopped walking and, turning, kissed him firmly on the mouth. Hector felt a strange and wholly unfamiliar stirring within his body.

Chapter 8

Christine Turner said good-night to Miss Griggs, manageress of the Birmingham Fiveways branch of Turners Tearooms, and left to walk back to her bed-sitting room while the older woman locked up. Christine had been fortunate in finding accommodation in a modest house in Wheelers Lane, only ten minutes walk from the tearoom. Her landlady was a shy woman in her seventies who had lived in the house all her life and had only taken to letting out the room because her inherited investments were now bringing her very little income. The stock markets had fallen. Fifteen months of war had left Britain in virtual isolation, apart from the loyal support of the distant countries of the Empire. Old Miss Tubbs was grateful to have a quiet tenant, who paid her rent punctually every week. To Christine's relief she was left to come and go freely. Fortunately Miss Tubbs appeared to have no interest in Christine's movements.

Once back in her room, Christine changed into Red Cross uniform before making herself a cup of tea and preparing a poached egg on toast. Her parents had been very distressed when she had returned home on indefinite sick-leave in November. Gradually, however, they had accepted that she needed a change from her stressful job in London. After a little while they had come to appreciate her more frequent week-end visits home to see them. They had been pleased, too, when she told them that she had decided to join the Red Cross. They felt it would give her an outside interest which might help her recovery from her "nervous breakdown". Her father, going round his businesses, had got into the habit of having lunch at his Fiveways branch once a week, and was mildly amused at being waited on by his daughter. When the meal and the service were to his satisfaction he left a three penny bit under the plate!

The Commandant of Christine's Red Cross detachment had soon recognised her as a capable young woman and advised her to take her nursing certificate. This involved attending a hospital for practical experience. Christine asked to go to the Accident Hospital, which was near her lodgings, and this was arranged. She had spent her first evening on a very busy ward where everything had seemed to her to be quite chaotic! She had felt that she was more of a nuisance than a help to the hard worked nurses. However, when she went to get her book signed by the ward sister, at the end of her three hours "duty" she was greeted with a smile and thanked for her help! After a few weeks the nurses seemed to look forward to her visits. Unlike some of the volunteers, she was willing to take on any job she was asked to do, pleasant or otherwise, and had never allowed herself to show feelings of disgust or horror at what she saw. When she had completed the twelve sessions required for her exam, the ward sister asked Christine if she would be willing to continue helping out. She had agreed readily and after that was quite often asked to do extra sessions when the ward was short staffed. While she was working at the hospital one Sunday afternoon she happened to look out of a window which overlooked the canal running alongside the hospital. On the other side of the canal there was a large, rather shabby, warehouse. She had never seen it before because up until then her time on the ward had always been spent during the evenings when the hospital windows were blacked out. She now realised, with a tingle of excitement, that this warehouse must be the place where her "contact" spent much of his time. She was careful not to show any outward sign of interest but was, nevertheless, quite intrigued.

She only saw the "contact" infrequently but had begun to take a sort of proprietorial interest in this uncommunicative but determined-looking man. He must be in his late thirties or early forties, she thought. He looked physically fit but rather strained and she thought he seemed more tense and preoccupied each time she saw him. He came to the tearoom for lunch three or four times a month, but at irregular intervals. Sometimes he would sit at a table served by one of the other waitresses. When he did that, she knew that there was no message for her. She guessed that he deliberately varied the table he used in case he was being watched. Only three times so far had she had to take a message. This was passed to her with the bill when he paid for his meal. He always asked for a receipt. So far none of the messages had been urgent and in these circumstances her orders were to keep the information received until the weekend. The message was always in a code, which Christine did not understand. The message was clearly intended to sound like a simple conversation when repeated over the phone. At the weekend, she would telephone a certain London number, either from a call box or from her parent's house, being careful to vary the procedure on each occasion. She had very different instructions as to what to do in the event of an urgent message. She had also been given a completely different number, which she had to learn by heart. This was for use in an emergency if there was any sign that she or her contact was in danger.

The 400 bomber raids on Coventry and Birmingham had taken place in November of 1940, when Christine was still in London, but as the winter continued Birmingham suffered a number of lesser attacks by the Luftwaffe. One night Christine and her landlady, old Miss Tubbs, decided to retreat to the cellar during a raid which seemed to be concentrated unpleasantly close by. As they sat on deckchairs, with rugs tucked around them, drinking cocoa from a thermos flask they heard the ominous drone of an unusually low-flying aircraft grow louder and louder. Then there came the whistle of falling bombs. The first crumping explosion sounded close enough. The second was even nearer! The third explosion seemed to be right on top of them. The whole house shook violently. Bits of mortar showered down from the cellar roof. They could hear the rumble of falling debris. The sound of the aircraft rapidly faded away and Christine said, "I think I'll go upstairs and investigate. It sounded as if the house may have been hit!" Miss Tubbs protested feebly but Christine told her she would be quite safe in the cellar for the time being. With the aid of a torch Christine made her way up the cellar steps and opened the door into the hall. As she had expected the blackout curtains covering the windows had been ripped down by the blast. She knew she must not put on the lights - even if they were still working!

A brief inspection with aid of the torch showed that the place was strewn with broken glass and plaster from the ceiling, but apart from this the house seemed to still be in one piece. Christine cautiously opened the front door. Once her eyes had adapted to the darkness she noticed something wrong with the shape of the house next door. There was also an unpleasant smell. Gas! Using her torch she scrambled over the remains of the fence that had separated the two houses. Now she could see that most of the front of the next door house had been blown away by the bomb, leaving the basement exposed. The gas meter was usually down there! She lowered herself gingerly into the basement and then, using the torch, searched for the meter. There was a sound of running feet and a rough voice shouted, "put out that light!" Christine ignored the demand and continued to work her way systematically round the wall of the front basement room. There it was. Thank God! The meter seemed to be undamaged and, more important, the valve beside it was intact. "What's that smell" shouted the voice?" Christine did not bother to answer. She knew the dangers of coal-gas poisoning only too well and was trying to hold her breath. She reached the valve and closed it. Now she must get out of the gas-filled basement! At last the man who had shouted at her seemed to realize what she had been doing. "Grab my hand," he called, "and I'll pull you out." He was as good as his word and must have been very strong. She felt herself becoming a little faint, but the hand gripping her right wrist propelled her firmly upwards, assisted only to a small extent by her own efforts. Once she was clear of the cellar her rescuer lifted her bodily in his arms and carried her well away from the damaged house - and the gas!

By now others were beginning to arrive on the scene and she recognised the voice of the local air raid warden. The rough- voiced man called to him, "There's been a big gas escape, mate! Keep everyone well back till it clears, and for Gawd's sake don't let anyone strike a match or come near with a cigarette!" "Has anyone turned off the gas?" asked the warden anxiously." "This young lady's done it all by herself!" said the man. "She jumped down into that basement and found the valve right away: ought to get a medal! She might have been asphyxiated if I hadn't come along." He turned anxiously to Christine, now propped rather limply against her landlady's garden gate. "Sorry I shouted at you, dearie. I was a bit shook up with those three bombs coming so close." Christine smiled feebly: "It doesn't matter. I think you saved my life!" Her head was throbbing as if it would burst and she felt very weak. A light rescue tender pulled up, and then an ambulance. Summoned by the warden, the woman ambulance driver took Christine by the elbow and helped her into the saloon of her vehicle. She settled Christine on one of the bunks. "Shall I take this one to the hospital right away?" she called. "If she's not too bad you'd better wait. There may be some more casualties for you when we check the house," the air raid warden shouted back.

The rescue men took ladders from the roof of their tender and made an improvised bridge to get into the ground floor of the damaged house. "There's normally an elderly lady and her very old mother lives there," the warden told them. He walked over to the back of the ambulance and spoke to Christine. "Do you know if Miss Dyson and old Mrs Dyson were at home when the bomb fell?" he asked. Christine nodded. "As far as I know they never go away. I haven't seen anyone else at the house, so I think they're on their own." "Thanks," said the warden. "How are you feeling yourself?" "A bit better now, thank you, but I'd like to rest here for a bit longer, if that's all right," she said, turning to the ambulance driver. There was a good deal of shouting going on and Christine recognised the voice of a very agitated Miss Dyson, whom she had sometimes met in the road or at one of the local shops. Miss Dyson was very stout and evidently unwilling to trust her weight to the ladders bridging the gap where the front door steps should have been! Eventually she was coaxed across and brought to sit in the ambulance with Christine. "Thank goodness that's over," she said. "That was much worse than the bomb! It will be all right getting mother over. She's much lighter and anyway she can't see too well, so she won't know what a terrible drop there is where our front door used to be!"

Now she was over the gap Miss Dyson seemed quite relaxed. "Are you and your mother injured at all?" asked Christine. "Not a bit," said Miss Dyson, "dirty and dishevelled but not a scratch. We'll go to my married brother in Edgbaston and have a good bath! He and his wife will put us up till the house is mended." At this stage a problem arose. The old lady adamantly refused to get into the ambulance! "I'm not getting in one of those things!" she said. "I'm not injured and anyway what would my son think to have that pull up at his front door. He'd probably think we'd been killed and they were bringing the bodies! His wife wouldn't be pleased, either, with the neighbours all gossiping. You better get us a taxi!" After a little delay an ambulance car was summoned and the old lady, thinking it was a private car, which indeed it had been until a year previously, graciously consented to get in. She and her daughter were driven away. Now that the Dyson problem was settled the warden and ambulance driver turned their attention to Christine. "How are you feeling, miss?" enquired the warden. "Quite a lot better, thank you, but I'm a bit worried about Miss Tubbs. I left her in the cellar and she will be wondering what is happening." At that moment the long wailing "All Clear" started up. Everyone relaxed to some extent. "If you think you are all right and don't need to go to the hospital I'll come with you and we'll see Miss Tubbs and try to get things a little straightened up for you," said the kind-hearted warden. Christine was truly grateful. She did not feel up to much clearing work, even to the extent of just getting their two bedrooms habitable! They got down from the ambulance and the driver closed the rear doors and set off for her depot. The rescue men were still at work checking the next-door house and making sure that things were as safe as possible until building repairs could be done. When Christine and the warden reached the cellar, Miss Tubbs was dozing uneasily in her deck-chair. She was relieved to hear that nobody had been injured but was very interested to hear about her neighbours' adventures!

Next morning Christine reported for work at the tea-room as usual but when Miss Griggs saw how wan she looked and heard about the bomb on the house next door, she sent Christine home to "rest". In the event, when she got back to Wheelers Lane the place was a hive of activity and rest was obviously quite out of the question. Builders were at work next door, noisily demolishing an unstable wall. Miss Tubbs was sweeping up broken glass and plaster with considerable gusto, creating clouds of dust in the process! "Oh, I am so glad to see you, Miss Turner," she said. "A policeman has just called round to say that if we go up to the end of the road there is a distribution of roofing felt so that we can cover the broken windows and make the house weatherproof. I was wondering how I could manage to carry one of those heavy rolls of felt by myself, but if you will take an end we can easily do it between us." They brought back two rolls of felt and were given a supply of broad-headed tacks. They spent much of the morning doing first-aid repairs to their broken windows. It made the house pretty dark but this would be preferable to having the wind and rain driving in! As the morning wore on Christine felt better. The fresh air helped her headache and although she was rather tired the work had probably done her more good than harm. At twelve she told Miss Tubbs she must get back to the restaurant. She knew Miss Griggs wasn't really expecting her back, but it was essential for her to be there over lunchtime in case there was a message.

It was just as well she had gone. At a quarter to one her contact came in and headed straight for one of her tables. Their eyes met momentarily and she knew instinctively that something important was afoot. Without appearing to hurry she was soon at his side. They exchanged casual and conventional waitress/customer greetings, then he said, "You don't look at all yourself today, are you all right?" "We had a bomb on the house next door last night and I didn't get a lot of sleep, but I'm fine otherwise, thank you sir," Christine answered with a slight smile. She hoped the short conversation sounded natural and in keeping with their supposedly minor degree of acquaintance. She had the impression that this man from Air Intelligence, with whom she worked, was relieved to be, for a short time, with the one person he could trust, in his present hazardous situation. Her tiredness was forgotten in the excitement of the moment and she felt curiously aware of her role as his protector, as well as his messenger. This time the message was urgent. After lunches had been served and the tables cleared she asked Miss Griggs if she might go home for an hour to see how her landlady was getting on. This gave her a chance, on her walk back to Wheelers Lane, to slip into a phone booth in the corner of a busy post-office. Here she could be fairly certain that no-one was watching her or eavesdropping. Her brief message was passed on in less than a minute and she was back at Wheelers Lane with the minimum of delay and in possession of a book of stamps which she did not really need.

At first light the following morning an RAF Sunderland flying boat took off from the Coastal Command base at Milford Haven and headed out over the Atlantic. As far as the crew were aware they were on a routine patrol. Only the captain knew of something unusual. He had received highly secret verbal orders to search in a certain area for a U-boat pack known to be lying in wait for a large convoy. Should he find an enemy submarine he was to attack it. If he failed to locate one, he was to make a dummy attack at the location given. His crew would believe that he had momentarily glimpsed a likely target. After that he was to find the convoy and make contact with the escorting warships by Aldis lamp. His message to the senior naval officer of the escort would be that enemy U-boats had been located in the stated area. By giving the impression that the German submarines had been found purely by chance by a patrolling aircraft, Air Intelligence hoped that excessive losses of shipping in the convoy might be avoided, while still preserving the secret of their penetration of the German spy network!

Chapter 9

When he arrived back from Glasgow Max returned immediately to the warehouse which was both his temporary home and his headquarters. On entering the little office he was surprised to learn from Walter Riddle that George Pattenson was away in London. Pattenson had left Riddle to cope single-handed with the work of receiving information from various sources around the country, collating it and then forwarding it to Berlin by one of the several routes available. Anything urgent was transmitted by radio from the barge. This sometimes meant that one of them had to cycle to wherever Alfred Barnes and his barge happened to be at the time. Such messages were not particularly common but, with both Pattenson and Max himself away, Riddle was left in the position of having to close up the warehouse, leaving nobody available to take any new messages, and then to set off on a lengthy bicycle ride to locate the barge. With some relish Riddle recounted how he had had to do just that the previous day. His implied criticism of Pattenson was unmistakable.

Max frowned. "Show me the copy of the message you transmitted, if you please," he said. The message had been from Liverpool. It was about a particularly important convoy which had been assembling there and was expected to sail imminently. There were details of the cargo and of the IRA agent's speculation, from conversations he had overheard, as to its likely destination. "Tell me, Riddle, where has Mr Pattenson gone, and when do you expect him back?" Max enquired. "Mr Pattenson told me he was going to London to make further arrangements in connection with the "People for Peace" dinner. I was a little surprised. I believed that, apart from minor details, the arrangements were almost complete. He said he would be away for a few days." Max found this puzzling but he sensed that Riddle wanted to say more, and looked at him expectantly. After a short pause Riddle went on. "Actually, sir, I am glad to have a chance to talk to you privately about Mr Pattenson. As you know I have worked with him for some years but lately I have been worried about his loyalty to Germany!" "That's a very serious charge," Max replied. "You must tell me exactly what you mean. What grounds have you for saying such a thing!" Of the two men Max rather preferred Pattenson, who seemed to have the more normal personality of the two. Riddle had an intensity and a fanaticism about him which could be rather disconcerting. With Pattenson, on the other hand, Max could enjoy an occasional joke or a quiet half-hour smoking a pipe. Riddle seemed to be entirely devoid of a sense of humour. He appeared to have no interest in anything other than work.

Max now recalled several occasions when there had appeared to be some sort of tension between the two men. He remembered that he had first noticed this on the very day he had arrived and had asked for an explanation about the move from the solicitor's office to the warehouse. It had surfaced again, though barely perceptibly, when he had questioned Pattenson about the new business centred in the warehouse. He wondered what the background to this underlying discord between them might be. Perhaps Riddle was about to enlighten him!

"As you know," said Riddle, "our unit is funded by the Kriegsmarine and both Mr Pattenson and I are paid for our intelligence work by the German navy. Mr Pattenson is graded as Oberleutnant and I am graded as Chief Petty Officer. We have, of course some income from the legal practice as well, but not very much. From the start the purpose of the practice has been as a front for our intelligence work. Anyway, a few months after the war began I read in the paper that the price of second-hand cars had fallen sharply because of the petrol rationing. I mentioned this casually to Mr Pattenson. A week or two later I read that Wolverhampton Corporation had bought a number of large cars and was having them converted to ambulances for use with the ARP services. I mentioned this also, and suggested to Mr Pattenson that it might be a good business opportunity for somebody. To my surprise he came in the next day and said he had talked to a golfing friend of his who owned a small coach building firm. This man had been complaining about lack of work, as very few people had been ordering luxury cars or specialist vans since the start of the war. He said that when the orders he had in hand were completed there would be nothing left for his workers to do. Mr Pattenson had asked him about building other types of vehicle body, and the man said his firm could easily convert to that sort of work. I then remembered the small garage across the road from here. I occasionally meet the proprietor at lunchtimes and we sometimes chat about our work. He too had been complaining of lack of work. He thought he might soon have to close up his garage. Mr Pattenson became very interested and went to see him. Soon he had arranged for the man to start buying up large cars in good condition and to overhaul them mechanically with a view to conversion if sound. Mr Pattenson then arranged to rent this warehouse to store the cars awaiting conversion."

"Very well," said Max, "I can see how the business started up, but that does not explain your charge against Mr Pattenson." Riddle continued, "I have been his clerk for some years and I know a good deal about both Mr Pattenson's business and his private affairs." Max decided that this was probably correct. He had noticed that Riddle took an unusually close interest in the private affairs of almost anybody they had dealings with. Riddle continued, "I am virtually certain he had nothing like enough funds of his own to pay for all the cars he bought at that early stage. I am sure no bank would have lent him that sort of money! I worried about it for a long time, then I discovered that he had sent a message to Berlin around that time asking for extra funds on the grounds that he had hopes of recruiting some new agents. I am almost certain that he used those funds to set up this business for his own private gain! The business has done very well but the only one to benefit has been Mr Pattenson himself! I think, sir, that you should look into the whole business with a view to disciplining him and recovering all the profits for use in our intelligence work - or for setting up Nazi organisations in this country when we have won the war against England."

Max folded his hands and rested his chin against his fingers, deep in thought. He could well understand Riddle's discontent. The man appeared to have been at least partly responsible for a very profitable idea, but had not benefited personally in any way. He also seemed to be a genuine and dedicated Nazi, though perhaps with somewhat idealistic concepts about the party and its activities. It was not surprising that he regarded Pattenson as something of a traitor. Max lifted his head, sat up very straight and addressed Riddle. "I am glad that you saw fit to speak to me about this. From now on it will be your duty to collect any evidence there may be about misuse of official intelligence service funds. You must keep copies of any documents and other information that may be relevant; but keep them at your own house, and in a very secure place! However at this stage in our work it is essential that nothing occurs to interfere with Operation Chainbreak. Remember that we are under direct orders from the Fuehrer himself and that the success of Chainbreak takes priority over all other considerations! We shall both have to be on our guard. We must not give Mr Pattenson any cause for suspicion. Even the whiff of an idea that he was under a cloud of some sort could affect his concentration on the work in hand! Once our task is successfully completed it is probable that most of England will be under German control within weeks." Riddle broke into one of his rare smiles. "Do you believe that things will move as fast as that?" he asked. "Most certainly," replied Max. "Then," commented Riddle reflectively, "will come the time to deal with traitors and criminals!"

Max had spoken sternly, as he did deliberately from time to time when dealing with members of the German intelligence. It was essential to maintain discipline and to exercise firm control over the little band of agents. Nevertheless he was relieved to see that Riddle gave at least the appearance of being satisfied with his response to the complaint against Pattenson. Max had, in any event, decided to take up the matter of Pattenson's unexpected absence as soon as the latter returned. On the face of it the man had acted irresponsibly and out of character. Riddle left the warehouse soon after their discussion and Max went over in his mind all that had been said. He would have to tread warily. They must continue to function as a team. Personal conflicts must not interfere with his assignment. He looked again at the urgent message Riddle had transmitted to Berlin the previous evening. It certainly appeared to be of considerable importance. The U-boat packs out in the Atlantic were trying desperately to break the flow of goods and materials both into and out of Britain. Precise information about potential targets for their torpedoes would undoubtedly help them.

Max had already been weary when he arrived back after the long journey from Glasgow. He had been less fortunate on the return trip than on the journey north. The train had been so full that he had had to spend the entire journey propped in the corridor. Every time someone wanted to pass along the train he had had to get up from a suitcase on which he had been sitting. Added to that, the train had been running hours late by the time it reached Birmingham! He decided to retire early and get some much needed sleep. Even in this he was frustrated. The air raid sirens started up as he was preparing to settle on his makeshift bed on the office floor. The raid turned out to be a noisy one! During the next hour or two the warehouse was shaken several times by explosions. Max was certain that some of the bombs had fallen quite near. Eventually the "all clear" sounded. At last he was able to settle into a deep sleep on his improvised bed.

The chance to cross-examine Pattenson occurred a couple of days later. Max had sent Riddle to look for the barge once again, in order to pass on a further urgent message to Berlin. He was settling down to study details on a revised list of "reliable" individuals in the "People for Peace" movement, when Pattenson breezed into the office. He was obviously taken aback to find Max there. "Oh," he said, "Max! I thought you would still be in Glasgow with Hector Sedler." "Evidently!" said Max austerely, "And might I enquire why you thought fit to leave Riddle here on his own!" Pattenson, who had been in sole charge of operations until Max's arrival, was clearly none too pleased to be questioned! With a rather casual air he replied, "Riddle's a competent enough fellow in his way. I've learned to rely on him a good deal over the years." This gave Max the chance to tell his second in command about Riddle's having had to leave the headquarters unmanned for some time while he searched for the barge. Max then gave Pattenson a quite severe dressing down on that score.

Once he had exhausted that topic, Max went on to take up the matter of Pattenson's activities in London. "Now," he said, "perhaps you can tell me what you, yourself, have been doing. Riddle told me you were dealing with arrangements for the formal dinner for the hierarchy of the People for Peace movement which we have planned for May. I must confess I was surprised. I understood the arrangements were virtually complete!" Pattenson blustered a little, then said he was very concerned that everything should go without a hitch in view of the importance of the event with regard their plans. He also appeared very concerned that a good impression should be given to the distinguished men and women who would be guests. He said that giving a favourable impression of the organisation was of great importance. At first Max was surprised at this concept. The purpose of inviting such people was merely to disguise the real reason for the dinner which was, of course, to distribute explosive packs to the saboteurs, who would also be present. The venue was convenient and central. The event was timed to take place shortly before the night on which it was expected the order would come from Germany to attack the radio-location units. Max then recalled what he himself had recently said to Riddle about England coming under German control within a short time of a successful Operation Chainbreak! This was the answer! Pattenson must have seen the potential for him to become a powerful figure in a German-occupied Britain! In alliance with senior political figures with pacifist sympathies and with clandestine Nazi supporters amongst the well-to-do he could achieve much. He hoped to become an important man in the post-war era which he imminently expected. His ambition would, no doubt, be easier to achieve if he had previously ingratiated himself with various influential individuals!

Max remained silent for a minute or two. It would do no harm the keep Pattenson in suspense for a little while as he thought things over. If Max's theory was correct, it would be in Pattenson's best interests to ensure that the operation went according to plan. Operation Chainbreak was much the best prospect for the early German victory, which would give Pattenson the chance to acquire the position of power that he hankered after. Max had shown his authority. That would suffice for the present. Now he would take the opportunity of finding out what Pattenson's view of Riddle might be! "Very well," he said, as if dismissing the matter of the trip to London from his mind. "While the two of us are here together, I may as well take the opportunity of obtaining your confidential assessment of your assistant. It is likely that, before long, I shall have to make personnel reports to the higher authorities. The time for us to launch our attack on the British radio-location sites is drawing close. Once that happens, events will move very rapidly indeed. Soon we may have the task of assisting the occupying forces in the running of this country. Riddle, like yourself, has lived in England for many years and speaks the language like a native. He could be exceedingly useful. Is he totally reliable? Would he be able to work without direct supervision?"

Max noticed a curious, almost wistful, look flit across Pattenson's face, but he immediately resumed the rather bland expression of the dependable family solicitor that he normally wore, like his business suit, most of the time. "Riddle," he said, "is in many ways well fitted to his assumed name. He is a curious mixture of a man. He worked for me for several years before I really found out very much about him. Then, one day, he did not come in for work. I was concerned - he is a very precise and predictable person. I went round to his lodgings and found him looking very ill. The woman who owned the place had done nothing whatsoever to look after him. I called a doctor at once. He diagnosed pneumonia and asked me to stay with Riddle till he could arrange for him to be taken to hospital. While I waited Riddle became delirious. He talked a great deal about his childhood, which had evidently been a rather unhappy one. He was brought up in a poor district of Bremen. While I waited for the doctor to return Riddle lapsed into German. This worried me as we had both been accepted by everyone locally as bonafide Englishmen. When the doctor eventually reappeared I persuaded him to get the ambulance to take Riddle to my house. This was readily agreed. The doctor was actually quite relieved. Hospital beds were very short that winter. My late wife nursed Riddle and afterwards he became devoted to her in his odd, rather distant, way. We learned that his father had died when he was very small and his mother had brought him up as best she could by working as a washerwoman. The one bright spot in his childhood had been the wife of one of their neighbours. She had more free time than Riddle's mother and had no children of her own. She had often looked after him while his mother was working. She was an Englishwoman, who had been nursery-maid with a rich German family before she married. From her Riddle had picked up English at a very early age. As a result he has always spoken English with an authentic, slightly Cockney, accent.

When the war started in 1914 Riddle was just old enough to join the Imperial German Navy as a boy-seaman. He was transferred to submarines in 1916 and became a radio operator. After the war he could not find work in Germany so came to England, where he got a job with the Standard Telephone and Cable Company. He was obviously well placed to obtain information from many parts of the British Empire and was eventually recruited by German naval intelligence. A few years later he was put under my control to act as my assistant and to develop our communications system here in England. We got on reasonably well, but after my wife died in 1934, our relationship became less personal. Then, to my surprise, he asked for leave to attend the 1936 Olympic Games in Berlin. I was puzzled as he had never shown much interest in sport previously. When he returned from Berlin I noticed a change in him. He seemed to have become more secretive and I noticed a hardness in his attitude that I had never encountered before. I now believe that he was asked to Berlin by the Gestapo and was recruited into their own intelligence network, probably through the influence of somebody who had known him during his time in the Imperial Navy. Our relations have gradually become more formal since then, although we have continued to work together efficiently enough, both in the business and in the intelligence field."

Max was extremely interested in what he had heard. Pattenson had been surprisingly frank. Most Germans were rather guarded in what they said about the Gestapo and its agents! Who could know whether an acquaintance might turn out to be a Gestapo agent, and might report one for suspected disloyalty to the Party or to the Third Reich and its Fuehrer? Max had now learned quite a lot about both men. Pattenson was clearly one of the old-style officer class. He must have been away from Germany for so long that he was out of touch and must know little of the fear and distrust which now controlled everybody's actions and words at all times and in all strata of society. Pattenson obviously assumed that Max came from a similar background to himself and so took it for granted that they could speak to each other freely and without restraint. This was useful to Max, but would certainly not have happened had they been in Germany! That Riddle was a Gestapo agent and detailed to watch over the activities of Naval Intelligence did not surprise him unduly. The Gestapo had infiltrated everywhere in Germany, so why should Germans working in other countries be exempt? The man was naturally inquisitive and as he was in overall charge of communications he was ideally placed to pass on any information he thought significant. There would undoubtedly be agents of the Gestapo planted in the Kriegsmarine headquarters intelligence section to whom Riddle could report. In his mind Max wryly congratulated whoever had recruited Riddle on a very astute bit of work! He felt that since his visit to Glasgow he had learned a good deal about his subordinates. This might be very helpful in the future!

The final plans for the overall control and execution of Operation Chainbreak were perfected over the next few weeks, and, as winter gave way to spring, the men and women involved in this most ambitious of all Hitler's "fifth column" operations felt that their efforts were starting to blossom. Each team had by now been allotted a radiolocation site, or RDF unit as the British called them, to destroy. Each had secretly reconnoitred the allotted site and had evolved detailed plans for their attack. The teams had been arranged in groups - four or five teams to a group, for the purposes of co-ordination and command. The lead team of each group was headed by a German agent but, of course, the other team members were quite unaware of their leader's allegiance to Nazi Germany! It was assumed that all were peace activists, though from a variety of backgrounds. Only the German agents knew what the signal for the attack was to be. It had therefore been arranged that once all personnel were in position and ready to strike, a member of each team would phone the group leader every evening at a pre-arranged time. When the leader gave the message "it is time to unchain the door" the team would go into action. They would proceed to blow up one of the radio masts at their particular site at precisely 3am the next morning! By this means the operation would be initiated from Germany but without anyone, other than the few German agents involved, being aware of the fact! With the saboteurs in place the Luftwaffe commanders would pick the optimum conditions for the attack!

Reidel, or Riddle as he would still have to be called until the invasion was successfully completed, was placed in charge of a group covering sites on the important sector north of the Thames estuary. His team was to attack the unit at Bawdsey, which had been the first RDF station to become operational, back in 1938. The other teams in his group would attack the stations further up the east coast, north of Bawdsey. Pattenson, as the most senior agent, had responsibility for a group attacking the particularly vital units in and near Kent. These were the units which covered the coastline on which the Wehrmacht's landings were to be made. Pattenson's own team had the especially difficult task of dealing with the RDF unit near Dover. Here there was always a great deal of military and naval activity. They hoped to resolve the problem of access to the area by arranging for Pattenson himself to pose as a senior naval officer. He looked the part and it was hoped that he and his "naval rating" driver, together with a younger man posing as a junior RAF staff officer, would be able to bluff their way onto the site, pretending that an immediate spot inspection of all defence installations had been ordered by the naval officer in command of the port of Dover! With a bit of luck the Flight Sergeant in charge, having had to tumble out of his bed at about 2.45am on the arrival of the inspecting officers, would be sleepy and perhaps overawed by the sudden appearance of a very senior officer from another service and would make no difficulty about the little group entering the site! Once inside the site they would rely on speed and, if necessary, their automatic pistols!

The area to the west of the Kentish coast was considered important because of the many RAF fighter airfields and sector stations guarding the southern and western approaches to London. After some debate it was decided that Hector Sedler should head the group responsible for dealing with the sites in this part of the country. Pattenson had expressed doubts, but Max overruled him saying that, although Sedler was young and relatively inexperienced, his ruthlessness and determination would make him a strong leader. When informed of his role Sedler had decided that he and Morag Maclean could tackle their own target without other assistance. There was a shortage of dependable saboteurs! The third member of their team was to be an elderly pacifist who was keen and reliable but unfit for any active role. His job would be to watch the RDF site from a mile or two away. When he heard the explosion, and, if possible, had seen that one of the masts had actually fallen, he would phone from a public call box and give a pre-arranged message to the Birmingham headquarters. This arrangement struck the others as an excellent one. From it there evolved the idea that every target site should be watched in this way by somebody who was independent of the actual attack team. The attackers would be relieved of the responsibility of reporting the outcome of their operation to headquarters and information would be received at the Birmingham HQ more far quickly and reliably than if one of the attack team had to find and use a phone in the confusion that was likely to follow their operation. The saboteurs could concentrate on escaping from the moment the charge had exploded!

Max informed the others that he personally would man the warehouse office headquarters in Birmingham and that Alfred Barnes would moor his barge at the wharf outside and maintain the radio link with Berlin throughout the operation. Max sensed that neither Pattenson nor Riddle was entirely happy with this arrangement, though neither of them commented. He was not surprised. Both had been allotted particularly dangerous jobs for the night of Operation Chainbreak and, while both were accustomed to the risks of working as a secret agent in a hostile land, it must appear to them that Max was taking the safest job for himself. More importantly Max would be the one who was in touch with Berlin! Nobody counted Barnes. He was content to do what was asked of him. He had no ambitions for the future! Pattenson on the other hand would undoubtedly have liked to have his name prominently linked with the operation which would enable Hitler to conquer the last remaining obstacle to the achievement of his ambitions. Direct contact with senior German commanders at such a moment would almost certainly help to establish his position as a big man in the post-war German-occupied Britain he expected would follow shortly after their night of action. Riddle also would have liked to have direct contact with Berlin, but for different reasons. He would almost certainly have sought to make contact with some senior Gestapo officer. Then, once the main operation was over and the invasion successfully completed, he would hope to be in a position to help direct or, better still have charge of, a radical purge of anti-Nazi elements in Britain. The idea of such a purge was gradually becoming an obsession with him! Max was well aware of the ambitions and discontentment of his subordinates but was careful to conceal his insight from them.

The time to mount the operation was getting close. Alfred Barnes was away from Birmingham with the barge and Max decided it was time to talk to him. They must ensure that the barge would be at the warehouse wharf at the right time. Barge traffic is necessarily slow and for their communication equipment to be at a distance from the headquarters at the crucial time would be disastrous. It was Riddle's responsibility to keep a note of where Barnes was travelling at any particular time. Max consulted him. "Barnes should be returning from Worcester by now," said Riddle. "He had a load of coal to deliver there and was hoping to pick up a return cargo." Both Riddle and Pattenson were in the office at the time and Max told them he would take the old bicycle they kept at the warehouse for the purpose and contact Barnes. He set off along the towpath. It was a sunny morning and the canal towpath was pleasantly sheltered. Max found himself relaxing in the unfamiliarly peaceful surroundings. He enjoyed the warmth of the sun and the blossoming of wild flowers along the canal banks. The clean fresh green grass was speckled with sparkling white daisies. So many were there that he was reminded of the stars of the milky way. The hedgerows beside the towpath were green and lush. Birds were busy everywhere and were surprisingly noisy along the deserted canal bank. Max, anticipating a longish ride, stopped at a small pub at Lifford. Here he had a half-pint of beer and bought a ham-sandwich to take with him for his lunch. At the junction with the Stratford and Avon canal an old man was fishing. Max stopped and passed the time of day with him. He was a retired bargee and knew Alfred Barnes well. "'Recon you'll have a long ride," he said. "Alf told me he was expecting he might have to wait a day or two at Worcester to pick up a return cargo." This was rather annoying! Max did not want to be away from his headquarters for too long - for several reasons. He cycled on for three miles or so then, rounding a bend, caught the sound of an engine. A quarter of a mile further on he sighted a barge. It looked familiar. Then he saw Barnes waving to him. Something unusual in his manner attracted Max's attention. The usually placid Barnes seemed excited! As Max approached, Barnes throttled back his engine and, with practised skill, brought the barge neatly to a standstill alongside the bank. He threw Max first a bow rope and then a stern one. Max made them fast to a fence post and tree root handy nearby. Barnes ran out a small plank and Max, spared the risk of slipping on the muddy bank, boarded the barge in style!

"I'm right glad to see you, sir," was Barnes's greeting. Despite strict orders that, for security reasons, all agents should use the official code name "Max", Barnes always addressed Max as "sir"! "I left Worcester without waiting for another cargo and I've been pushing on as fast as I could. Just outside Worcester I got an urgent radio message from the Kriegsmarine! I could hardly wait for the wharfmen to get the coal unloaded and let me turn the barge around! I dared not phone. The message is coded as highly confidential and is for you personally. I don't fully understand the code, Riddle does all the coding and decoding, but over the years I've picked up a smattering, almost without noticing, and I've a fair idea of what this is about. Max studied the paper Barnes handed him. "You were right to return as fast as possible," said Max, "but won't your leaving so suddenly without a return cargo arouse suspicion?" "I said that I had to hurry back to see a cousin who was ill in hospital in Birmingham," said Barnes. "I told them I could easily pick up a cargo there after I had seen my cousin." "Well done," said Max. "I'll have to go back directly to make some arrangements, but before I go we'll have something to eat. I need to talk to you!"

Barnes made tea and produced bread and cheese. Max contributed his ham sandwiches. They settled in the low roofed cabin near the stern of the barge and, as the canal was deserted, Max decided that it was safe for them to talk freely. "I anticipate," said Max, "that we will be called on to set our operation going very soon now. I shall be at the warehouse controlling the teams and receiving information from them. It will be essential to pass news of our achievements on to Berlin without the slightest delay! This means that I will need your barge moored beside the warehouse, all ready, with your radio equipment set up for immediate use. Can we arrange this without people starting to ask awkward questions?" Barnes pondered for a while. Of all the

German agents Barnes was, thought Max, the least complicated. He accepted instructions and got on with his work. His only motive appeared to be to serve the country to which he had pledged his allegiance. At length Barnes replied. "By the time I reach Birmingham my imaginary cousin will be too ill for me to leave the wharf from where I can visit him easily, so I won't want to take on even local jobs for the time being. That story should go down all right with the other bargees and the folk who work along the canal. They're a nosey lot but they don't really know that much about me and the story of the sick cousin should satisfy them!"

Max was happy with this arrangement. They wasted little time on the remainder of the meal and as soon as it was completed Max remounted his cycle and set off back to his headquarters. He did, however, make a brief phone call from a little used public call box at Lifford, which he had noticed on his way south a couple of hours previously. The whole trip had taken him much less time than he and Riddle had expected. As he cycled Max's brain was working like a dynamo! He would have a great deal to attend to within a very short space of time. An immediate visit to Hector Sedler in Glasgow was essential! That determined and fanatical young man was going to have his abilities tested to the full in the near future!

Max was still thinking about his plans and the information he had just received via Barnes when he reached the warehouse. He leaned the bike against a wall and, deep in thought, headed for the office. Nobody appeared to be about. The outer door was open and he walked through but when he glanced through the inner doorway into the office he saw that Riddle was at the far side of the room. He was clearly on his own and obviously quite unaware that Max had returned. He seemed to be examining Max's mattress, which was in its usual corner on the floor. He saw Riddle feel carefully along each side of it and then slide a hand under it and feel it from below. Max watched, quite puzzled. Riddle must suspect that Max had something concealed in the room! When Riddle had finished with the mattress he took out a knife and, very expertly, picked the lock of the corner cupboard where Max kept his few personal possessions. Max stifled his initial impulse to march in and demand to know what the devil the man thought he was doing! Much better that Riddle should remain unaware that Max now knew that he, Max, was under the suspicion of this agent of the Gestapo! Just as well that Riddle should not know that Max had rumbled him!

Max tiptoed back out onto the wharf and over to the cycle. He moved it a few feet forward and then parked it against the wall of the office as clumsily and noisily as possible. Its bell sounded as it knocked against the wall.

Then Max walked back towards the office with heavy footsteps. This time when he entered Riddle was working at the desk. "Hello, Riddle," said Max cheerfully. "I found Barnes was already on his way here so my cycle ride was a lot shorter than we had expected. He's had an urgent message from Berlin which we shall have to discuss together. By the way, where is Mr Pattenson?" "Mr Pattenson has gone over to Selly Oak to look at a large car which is for sale there. He thinks it may be suitable for conversion as a towing vehicle for one of the fire brigade's heavy trailer pumps. We have an order for such a vehicle from the Auxiliary Fire Service in Burton on Trent," Riddle replied, perhaps a little more suavely than was usual. Other than this slight change from his normal rather abrupt manner there was nothing to suggest that he had not been working at his desk all afternoon.

Max continued, "I shall have to leave here tomorrow and may be away for a day or two. Will you make sure Mr Pattenson knows that I want both of you to stay at the warehouse throughout the day while I am away, and I also want one of you to be here at nights until I return. I will telephone at frequent intervals in case of any further messages for me come through from Berlin. Barnes will probably arrive here within an hour or two. I have arranged with him that his barge will stay at the wharf from now on." Riddle asked no questions, but Max could sense his excitement as he resumed work on the contract he had laid out on the desk. He left the office as usual at five o'clock. In the meantime Max got together some things ready for his journey the next day.

Chapter 10

The mid-day train from Birmingham to Chester stood at platform 4, wisps of steam drifted back from the waiting locomotive. There were smuts, and faint smells of hot oil and wet coal. The carriages were almost empty but in a first class compartment near the front of the train a big man in a pin-striped suit sat looking intently down the grimy, largely deserted, platform. The copy of the Financial Times on his knee, his neatly rolled umbrella and the bowler hat stowed on the rack above his head proclaimed him to be a business man. At this time of the day passengers were few. He could see the guard and the ticket inspector chatting at the barrier. He saw the guard look at his watch and start to unfurl his green flag in a leisurely fashion. At this moment a well-dressed man of early middle age presented his ticket and then marched purposefully up the platform towards the first-class carriages. As the guard blew his whistle the man wrenched open the door of Group Captain Avon's compartment and stepped in. The train started to move. Avon, his eyes still on the barrier, saw the ticket collector halt a slim figure in a dark raincoat who was attempting to get onto the platform. "1 think you've been followed, Max," said the Group Captain. "Your Gestapo friend is obviously suspicious and wanted to see what you were up to!" "Blast," said Maxwell, "I'm afraid he really does think I'm up to something, but I doubt if he realises whose side I'm on! He's got such a devious mind himself he probably thinks I'm a Soviet agent or someone from the CIA getting mixed up in European affairs!"

Avon allowed himself one of his rare smiles. "If I didn't know you better," he said, "I might be wondering that myself!" Max laughed, then he looked serious. "You forget that I've seen a little of what's been going on in Germany these last few years. Some of it's pretty unpleasant, I can assure you. Anyway," he continued, "it's not so important now if he does have his suspicions. We are almost certain to get the signal to proceed within the next couple of weeks. The explosives are to be landed from a U-boat next Friday around 2am. at Ardmurnach. Can you make sure the Navy and Coastal Command keep well clear? As I told you when I phoned from Lifford I'm off to Glasgow to give the German agent there his orders about meeting the sub. and forwarding the cargo. By the way, what a bit of luck you happened to be in your office when I phoned, and that we were could arrange this meeting! It's our first chance to talk directly since the whole business started." "That's not been your only bit of luck, Max," replied Avon. Max looked up surprised. "Have you forgotten that night when you went to investigate the crashed Junkers 88?" said the Group Captain. "I doubt if you would be alive now if that gamekeeper hadn't been suspicious and stalked that parachutist. Then he saw him produce a pistol and creep up on you, with obvious evil intent. Rescuing you and capturing him - all in the space of a few seconds - was a pretty handy bit of work! Luckily, like most gamekeepers, he's discreet. He's followed our request to stay silent to the letter and, wisely, he asked no questions!" "Heavens yes," said Max. "When all this is over I must go and see him and thank him properly. By the way, what have you done with the prisoner?" "We're still holding him. He won't admit to anything except to say he thought there must be something valuable in the case and he wanted it for himself! There's no direct evidence to prove he's a German spy, except that envelope, and of course we can't use that! Not at present anyway. Even the pistol he had was British made! He was obviously well prepared for his assignment."

Avon changed the subject. "Do you know yet what the starting signal for Operation Chainbreak is going to be?" he asked. "The signal will come in one of Haw-Haw's regular "Germany Calling" broadcasts", replied Max. We don't know precisely what he will say but it will be something or other about breaking chains." "That's useful," said Avon. "All the sites will be covered by our counter-espionage agents who will shadow the saboteurs, but just in case any of our men fail to grab their quarry in time I'd better warn the sites to be on the alert once we hear Haw-Haw's message." Max was a bit dubious. "Better make your warning pretty non-specific," he said. The last thing we want to do at this stage is to frighten our quarry and let any of them escape the bag!" "Yes," said Avon thoughtfully. "Perhaps just a formal signal ordering the sites to double their guards for 24 hours from midnight, with no reasons given. Where will you yourself be when the operation takes off?" Max smiled grimly. "I am expected to be at headquarters throughout but, once the others depart, the only other person around will be Barnes, and he will be on the barge, manning the radio. I intend to slip away from Birmingham once the coast is clear. There's one particularly nasty bit of work I want to deal with myself! He's the agent from Glasgow that I'm on the way to visit now. I wouldn't trust him to anyone who didn't know him! He's the most fanatical and ruthless of the lot!" Avon was not entirely happy with this plan. He would have preferred a regular counter-espionage agent to do the job. Still, he reflected, Maxwell had done remarkably well to take on the role of head of German secret operations in Britain and to keep up the deception for so many months, undoubtedly at a great risk to himself. Avon supposed it was only fair that Maxwell should be in at the "kill" if he wanted to! "Right," he said, "tell me which site this friend of yours is planning to sabotage and I'll withdraw my man and leave the field to you."

When Max had given the details, Avon asked him, "and how exactly do you plan to slip away from your headquarters, without Barnes spotting you, and how will you get to Hampshire in time for zero hour?" "Ah," replied Max. "I will need a bit of help. There is an old fire escape at the back of the warehouse, on the side away from the canal. It leads onto the roof of another building. From there I can get into a back lane which leads to Islington Row. That part is quite easy. However I won't leave till I have heard Haw-Haw give the signal and have confirmed it with Barnes. After that, time will be critical. Once I'm out on the road I can be at New Street station in seven minutes. Meanwhile, Christine, who knows what the signal is going to be, will go to the station immediately she hears it. She will wait in the Refreshment Room and watch for to me arrive. She will note which train I catch and will then phone Air Intelligence. At that stage I'll need your help! Can you arrange for someone to be on hand to take the call and to dispatch a fast car and a couple of armed plain-clothes men to meet the train and then go with me to the RDF site at Hamden Down?" Avon nodded. "That should be no problem, and even if there is a hitch, Hamden Down will have had the general warning to be on the alert, so the site should be pretty safe. I must say you and Christine seem to have got it worked out pretty well between the two of you. By the way, the messages she has passed on have saved several convoys from being badly mauled! Now," he continued, "Have you discovered what the enemy plan to do if they succeed in knocking out a good number of our RDF sites?" "No," said Max. "The Nazis work on the principle that their people are told exactly what they need to know to carry out their particular role but no more. We have only a vague idea of what is to happen after Chainbreak, but it's pretty certain they plan to follow up almost immediately with major air attacks followed by an invasion!" Avon stroked his chin reflectively. "It's a pity you haven't been able to get hold of details about likely targets. I would have liked to have given Fighter Command some ideas about where the attacks may come. In the circumstances all we can do is to issue a general alert about the time the saboteurs are due to strike." "Yes," said Max, "but remember if you do that any earlier, a sudden increase in airfield activity might give the game away and foil our plans!"

Avon left the train at Stafford and set off for an RAF airfield not far away. He was to attend a conference of intelligence officers there, this having been the official reason for his absence from London. Max continued on his journey as far as Crewe. Here he boarded an express on route from London to Glasgow. Once he arrived in Glasgow he would seek out Hector Sedler and give him orders which were much too confidential for transmission by any other means than direct face to face contact! Sedler would be given the exact time at which the German submarine bringing the explosive packs for Operation Chainbreak would make its landfall! The site chosen for the landing would be confirmed. Sedler would then have to find some way of reaching the spot. This was in an area where access by the general public was restricted! After that he would have the task of moving the explosives to a certain hotel in London, by means which they had discussed previously. Such an assignment might have been too much for a less resourceful and determined man but Max had little doubt that Sedler would succeed.

Morag Maclean waited impatiently at the roadside. She was in a state of high excitement. This was very unusual for her. Morag normally kept herself and her emotions under firm control, but today she would see Hector again and he could not fail to be pleased with the way she had arranged everything. Of course it should really have been wonderful to introduce him to her mother as the man she was going to marry, but she had now come to accept what she had really known all along. Her mother's mental state was such that she had almost no comprehension of anything beyond the most basic everyday crofting routine: feeding the hens and milking the cow she could cope with. She was able to make the porridge that was her sole diet much of the time; yhe could cook a herring if some kindly fisherman called in with a present of one; but any more abstract idea was quite beyond her understanding. Morag had told her that a friend was coming on a short visit, hoping that for once she would show at least a flicker of interest, but there had been no reaction at all. So Morag's excitement was focused on the thrill of being with Hector again and on the prospect of the dangerous but thrilling adventure ahead of them. For a start it would be wonderful to see a Russian submarine. Perhaps one of the crew would speak English, or possibly French, which was included in her syllabus at University! To converse with someone from the USSR, the fountainhead of International Communism would be an unforgettable experience!

Acting on urgent instructions that Hector had given her she had left Glasgow a couple of days ahead of him. She had made arrangements for supply of the fish which were to disguise the explosive packs brought by the submarine. She had obtained plenty of empty fish boxes. She and Hector would use these to re-pack the fish - with the explosives underneath! This job could be done in a little stone building near the shore, where her father had kept his nets in the days before he went off to the navy in 1914. Then she had arranged for a boatman to take Hector and her and the fish boxes the 15 miles or so to where the railway touched the sea at Hemel. Here there was a tiny, little-frequented, harbour. Before leaving Glasgow she had managed to get a permit so that Hector, as her fiance, could visit her mother at Ochshiel. Hector could not fail to be pleased with all her efforts, and Hector's approval was like a warm sun shining on her! She had waited at the roadside for nearly half an hour, standing in the soft misty rain, before she caught sight of the red and green bus rounding a bend in the road half a mile away. She had come early, fearing that Hector might miss the stop. The bus was late as usual. The driver and several of the passengers waved to her and then the sliding door at the front opened and there was Hector! He looked tired and travel stained after the long slow journey but his embrace was as warm and as firm as ever and the kiss that accompanied it made the wait in the rain worthwhile a hundred times over.

Events do not always live up to expectations. It came as quite a blow when Hector explained that Morag would not be able to meet any of the crew of the submarine. In fact she would not even see the submarine itself! Hector was, he said, most anxious that there should be no risk to the Soviet vessel or its crew. Any incident would not only be acutely embarrassing for the Soviet government, but could also jeopardise the whole scheme. It could so easily undo all the careful work done by the militant branch of the "People for Peace" movement during the past six months. A reliable person must watch the only road that passed near that lonely stretch of coastline so as to be able to give warning in case intruders of any sort should appear. That person must be Morag. There was nobody else available and nobody else was as trustworthy as Morag! Hector was very sorry she was so disappointed but said he knew she would understand that in the cause for which they were both working there must be boring jobs as well as exciting and dangerous ones. Sometimes, said Hector, the boring jobs were the most important ones.

Hector had given a lot of thought to keeping Morag out of the way when the German U-boat arrived. His specially warm embrace when he got off the bus was part of the programme. Secretly he was very relieved when she accepted the role he had outlined for her! Hector knew that Morag had a strong personality and very firm ideas of her own. Once the German conquest of Britain was over, he reflected, it would be necessary to dispose of her. For an important member of the Nazi party to be discovered to have had a previous romantic association with a dedicated Communist would be most embarrassing! Later it would be desirable for him to acquire a wife of unimpeachable Aryan origins. Hector intended to rise rapidly within the Nazi hierarchy and nothing whatsoever must compromise his progress.

They were up early next morning and went down to the beach as soon as they were dressed. Old Donald Maclain, who was to ferry them and their boxes of fish to the little port of Hemel, arrived with four big blocks of ice he had brought from the depot there. He helped Morag and Hector unload the blocks from his boat. They staggered up the beach to the old stone net store with the heavy blocks, one after the other. "I'll be along with some fish for you this evening," he said, "and I hear Hamish is to catch some for you as well. That must be quite a party your London friends are planning!" They laughed. "There's a good few folks coming," said Morag. "It's not just Hector and me going to make pigs of ourselves with sea-trout!" "Ah yes," said the old man. "Thon's your intended, of course. "He turned to Hector. "You're a fortunate young fellow. Morag's the brightest lassie hereabouts. Aye, and she's one o' the boniest too!" He pushed his boat off the beach where it was grounded and climbed back in.

Morag and Hector knew the night would bring them no rest. They went back to the croft where Morag cooked a substantial breakfast for them both. Her mother, who had been up and about since daybreak, took little notice of them. After they had eaten, Morag took Hector up through a little field above the croft-house and out onto the heather, to the highest point on the rocky ridge that ran the length of the Ardmurnach peninsula like a backbone. Hector could trace the course the U-boat would follow when it slipped in from the Atlantic at dead of night. It should have a clear passage, he thought. On the other side of the ridge the ground sloped quite gently away to the south and at a distance of a mile or more he could see the glint of the sea on the other side of the peninsula. A few hundred yards away there was a massive boulder. They walked over to it. Hector could see that to the east the peninsula narrowed as it approached the mainland. He could see the path they had walked along in the rain and mist the previous evening. He noted that the path disappeared over another, higher, ridge well before it reached the place on the road where the bus had dropped him. Anyone waiting close to the road would be invisible both from the ridge on which they were standing and from the shore. He would post Morag close to the road on the pretext of having her watch for any police or military vehicle which might appear. It was most unlikely there would be any other sort of traffic. From the road she would be able to see absolutely nothing of the submarine or of the landing of its cargo! He knew her well enough to be quite confident that once she had undertaken a task on behalf of the cause she was dedicated to she would see it through, come what may. Her commitment to the Communist party and everything it stood for was absolute! She would not leave her post until he came to tell her that the Soviet submarine had departed safely and that they could now be confident that the USSR would be in no way compromised as a result of the generous help given to the cause of peace.

The young heather was green beneath their feet. Amongst it grew tussocks of rough bent and patches of spiky green rushes. The gentle sunshine was warm on their backs. Hector took off his jacket and they sat down on it, sheltered by the giant boulder. The ground was soft and yielding beneath the jacket. They kissed. Both were passionate and impulsive by nature. Almost immediately their instincts took possession of them and swept them away into temporary oblivion. For a while nothing mattered in the world except their two selves.

Morag was the first to wake from the sleep which had come on them suddenly and unawares. It was colder. The sun was now behind a filter of hazy cloud and it had moved on quite alarmingly since they had first climbed the ridge! Soon the fishermen would be arriving with their catches. She and Hector must be there to pay them and then pack the fish in the ice, which they had still to break up ready! Later, of course, once the explosives arrived, everything would have to be repacked. There was no time for a meal! It was just as well she had insisted on their having a really good breakfast. "Wake up," she said urgently. "We must get straight back down to the shore. Do you have the money to pay for the fish on you or will we have to go back to the croft?" Hector grunted. He felt in the recesses of his jacket. There was a sort of poacher's pocket from the depths of which he produced a package. "Here it is," he said, his customary assurance and self-confidence returning rapidly as he threw off the last vestiges of sleep. He rose, stretched, put on his jacket and was soon striding down towards the beach with Morag following hard on his heels.

At a quarter to eight next morning an anxious Morag, who had spent much of a cold night huddled by a deserted roadside, and the rest of it packing explosives into fish boxes, was knocking on old Donald's door. She had walked a mile and a half along the shore to reach his house, the nearest-croft house to her mother's. It had been arranged that Donald would come at 7am to collect Hector and Morag and their very special cargo. This would have left ample time to load it and to sail along the coast to Hemel, and so to the railway. Donald was a reliable old man and Morag was astonished when he did not appear. Hector was very obviously annoyed that her arrangements had led to their carefully prepared plan faltering at this stage. He had not taken any pains to conceal his anger!

The door was opened by the old man's wife who was clearly in some distress. "Donald has been taken ill in the night, Morag," she said. "He hasn't the use the use of his left arm, you see, and he's got an awful bad head. I've sent word for the doctor to call." Morag wondered what on earth they would do. The timing of the delivery of the fish and explosives to coincide with the "People for Peace" dinner in London was critical. She was very careful to conceal her terrible impatience. She said sympathetically, "that's awful bad news Mrs Maclain. You must be very worried about Donald." "Indeed I am, Morag, but come you away in and see him for yourself. Maybe you can cheer him up a bit." Morag went through to the little bedroom. The old man was flushed and looked anxious. His left arm lay spread limp and lifeless on the counterpane. "Och Morag," he said in distress, "I'm so sorry to let you down, but I could never take the boat over to Hemel the way I am today." Despite her worry and the urgency of the situation Morag answered quite calmly. "Never mind that, Donald, how are you feeling?" "I've a very sair heid and no life at all in my left arm. I just feel useless!" "Well," said Morag, "you just stay quiet till the doctor comes and do not worry yourself or Mrs Mclain over a thing." Poor Donald groaned. "I can't rest quiet with the thought of all that grand fish going to waste!" Morag seized the chance. "Donald," she said, "Hector and I will take the boat over to Hemel ourselves. It's a fine morning and the weather's settled. I've been out with you often enough and know how to handle your boat and Hector is a good hand with engines and is used enough to boats himself." The old man looked doubtful but his wife jumped at the idea. It would relieve Donald of his anxiety over the fish and his distress at letting Morag down. "That's a grand idea," she said, "and when you get to Hemel you can leave the boat with Fraser, Donald's cousin, and he will look after it till Donald is fit again."

Twenty minutes later Hector, pacing the shore impatiently, heard the noise of an engine and, looking round, saw Donald's boat heading towards the beach beside the little stone net store. He was surprised, and impressed despite himself, to find Morag alone and in full control of the situation. They wasted no time. Working together, they swiftly loaded the fish boxes that they had packed with such care in the early dawn, after the U-boat had left and Hector had recalled Morag from her weary watch on the empty road. They had already said farewell to Morag's mother who, as usual, barely seemed to notice them. They flung their rucksacks into the boat and pushed off. There was a gentle wind blowing from aft to speed their voyage. The sky was clear. The sea was calm. On their right they could view of the whole north coast of the Ardmurnach peninsula. Far ahead they could just discern the outline of the little stone pier at Hemel. The beat of the engine was steady and reassuring. Hector checked the fuel tank. It was almost full. They would be at Hemel in not much more than a couple of hours. There would be ample time to transfer their fish boxes to the station and catch the train. Suddenly they both relaxed. Morag edged close to Hector, who had taken over the tiller. He put his arm round her. Together they watched the little coves and beaches of Ardmurnach slip past. Above the shore the hillside was dotted with sheep, peacefully grazing. Some had lambs beside them. Sometimes the lambs collected together in little groups and frolicked, chasing each other and jumping off and on the rocks that dotted the rugged heathery slopes. Occasionally there was a croft-house, white and low, with peat-smoke curling up from the chimney and then billowing away on the light westerly breeze. For a brief interlude they almost forgot their deadly cargo and the tremendous mission ahead of them.

At Hemel everything changed. By the time they had tied up the light breeze had freshened. There were several old men at the pier. One of them had a hand-cart. Yes, he would take their boxes up to the station for a shilling. Certainly, he would tell Fraser Maclain to take charge of Donald's boat when Fraser came back from the fishing. The old fellow was infuriatingly slow and would not be hurried despite their pleas. At the station there was more frustration! At first it seemed totally deserted. Eventually they succeeded in locating the man on duty. He was in a little office eating his sandwiches and drinking tea which looked almost black. He said there would probably be no train to the south at all that day! Morag sensed that Hector could hardly contain his anger. This sort of intolerable inefficiency would be ruthlessly stamped out when a Fascist government took over after the invasion! So he reflected. Morag, however, knew her fellow highlanders better than to lose her temper. She laid a gentle restraining hand on Hector's arm. Although she was just as frustrated as he at this unexpected problem, which could so easily upset all the carefully laid plans made by their fellow-Communists and various allies in the militant peace movement, she remained outwardly calm. "What is the problem today then?" she asked the porter. "We have a load of fresh fish that is urgently needed in London. Can you help us at all?" "Well," the man replied, "we've had word that the locomotive of the train from Kyle to Glasgow has broken down." Morag frowned. "Will they not have a spare engine at Kyle, then?" "Och, they'll maybe borrow one of the shunters that's kept there but its certain the train will be very late, anyway, and very slow. One of those wee tank engines will be hard put to it on a long haul with a heavy train, and there's plenty of steep gradients to climb between here and Glasgow!" Hector and Moray decided that all they could do was to wait and see what would happen.

By now a chill mist was drifting in off the sea. The cold was miserable after the pleasant sun of the early part of the day. The grate in the small bleak waiting room was empty. Morag and Hector huddled together, hungry and depressed. Two and a half hours later a different railwayman arrived to take charge of the little station. He was a more cheerful fellow than his colleague of the early shift: also he knew Morag slightly. At her request he telephoned Kyle and reported that there would definitely be a train in the late afternoon. "Get you down to Mrs McCrachen's wee shop, Morag," he said. "Tell her I sent you and that you're stuck at the station because the train has broken down. She'll surely find you something to eat to keep you going. I know food is pretty short but she's a good soul and will find something for you and your young man. You've plenty of time, for the train won't have left Kyle yet."

When, at last, the train pulled in they stowed the fish crates in a van which already contained fish loaded at Kyle. The van was marked for direct transfer to Euston. They found out from the friendly railway-man to which of the London trains the van would be attached when they reached Glasgow. After that they bought their own tickets through to London at the little booking office. They were determined to keep as close as possible to their hazardous freight until it reached its destination. After further delay and much discussion amongst the railway staff, the little engine's whistle blew and the train started off on its long journey on to Glasgow.

Morag and Hector were very weary, and were hungry again by the time they reached the city which was so familiar to both of them. They had several hours to put off before the night train for the south left. They hung about the dreary, blacked-out station, trying to follow the progress of the luggage van from Kyle as it was shunted. Eventually, to their great relief, they saw it coupled onto their own train. Then they were able to find a couple of seats, fortunately together, where they resigned themselves to another eight or ten hours of unpredictable wartime travel.

They reached Euston late the next morning. As the train ground to a halt Hector seemed to take on a new lease of life. Morag was too exhausted to think, but Hector was out of the compartment and onto the platform almost before the train had stopped. He managed to get hold of one of the few elderly porters still left to man the terminus and, with the porter trundling his barrow after him, he hurried up the train to the van at the rear. He located their boxes and noted with satisfaction that they appeared completely undisturbed since he and Morag had packed them, what seemed a lifetime ago, in the little stone building by the shore of Ardmurnach sound. They were soon loaded onto the porter's barrow and Morag, who by now had roused herself sufficiently to heave their rucksacks out onto the platform, joined Hector. The porter added the rucksacks to the load on his barrow and helped them find a taxi. This was by no means easy at this stage of the war. Many former taxi drivers were in uniform and away serving with the forces. Numerous taxis had been converted for use by the Auxiliary Fire Service. Eventually they were successful and, within an hour of arriving in the capital they were at the “Wolds” Hotel, a little west of central London.

The proprietor of the “Wolds” was, unbeknown even to his wife, an IRA "sleeper" who had established himself in England years before in preparation for just such an opportunity as that afforded by Operation Chainbreak. He had been recommended to Pattenson by one of the latter's IRA contacts and his hotel had been chosen as the ideal venue for the "People for Peace" dinner. As soon as Hector had introduced himself the man took them under his wing and, watched closely by Hector, supervised the unloading of the fish boxes and their transfer to a small secure back pantry. The hotelier's wife, a Londoner, who had appeared soon after her husband, saw the utter weariness in Morag's eyes and, with the quiet, undemonstrative kindness of her sort, led an unprotesting Morag upstairs to a little attic bedroom. Here Morag found just enough strength to wash and undress before falling into bed and dropping almost at once into a long deep sleep. No need for Morag to be involved in the grand dinner party scheduled for that evening, nor in the distribution of the explosives - at a considerably later hour. She had played her part for the time being and had more than earned her rest!

Chapter 11

Maximillian von Straussen sat, cramped and uncomfortable, in the canvas- covered rear of the little military Austin pick-up truck. Although the flaps at the back had been rolled up to allow the occupants some fresh air his view was very limited. This was due to the presence of two military policemen who sat at the back, one on either side, facing each other. The day was mild and he could see glimpses of blue sky and could tell that the sun was shining, but von Straussen's mood was far from cheerful. He had been told nothing, but had a pretty shrewd idea that his removal from solitary confinement in the military prison where he had spent the past five months was a preliminary to his being brought before some sort of tribunal. This would certainly result in his being shot as a spy! Various interrogators had asked him why he had threatened a plain-clothes police inspector with a gun, why he was at the wreck of a crashed enemy aircraft and why his British identity card had the same number as that of an elderly lady living in Stepney. He had said nothing. He did not know whether operation Chainbreak had continued without him, but he would not risk giving away any vital information to the British. Once he answered any one of their questions, who knew what might follow! They had got the brief-case, of course, but Heimgarten had assured him that there was nothing in it which could harm existing German agents working here in Britain.

Von Straussen did not know about the envelope! This was a used one, empty but quite genuine. It had been sent through the British post to Pattenson & Co, Solicitors, and bore a Birmingham postmark. The envelope had been the idea of the young Kriegsmarine intelligence officer who had been responsible for obtaining the clothing and other effects - all of genuine British origin - needed for von Straussen's mission. The officer had thought the envelope might be useful as an aid-memoire if, after the hazards of a night-flight over enemy territory and the excitement of a parachute landing in the dark, von Straussen had difficulty in recalling the precise address of his ultimate destination. The young man had fully intended to tell both Heimgarten and von Straussen about the envelope. However he had been sent on an urgent mission to Danzig at short notice.

In the haste of his departure, he had forgotten all about the envelope and its purpose! When the British had captured and searched von Straussen shortly after his parachute landing it had been found and removed without his ever having known of its existence. The envelope had led von Straussen's British replacement straight to the headquarters of the German intelligence service in England!

Despite his limited view Von Straussen could see that the road behind was straight for a mile or more. He could tell that the truck was travelling quite fast now. The military policemen were holding onto the metal frame which supported the canvas canopy at the back of the vehicle. Von Straussen himself was bouncing uncomfortably on the box they had provided for him to sit on. The young officer in charge of the party, travelling in rather pleasanter conditions in the cab, was probably not particularly concerned about the increasing speed, but in the rear conditions were even more unpleasant than they had been during the earlier part of that very unpleasant journey. Suddenly von Straussen heard the screech of tortured rubber and felt the vehicle start to judder and then begin to tilt over to the right. The driver was struggling to negotiate a bend in the road which was a great deal tighter than he had expected! He lost control. The truck skidded violently, rolled onto its offside then dipped nose down and came to an abrupt halt. The larger of the two military policemen, a sergeant, was thrown on top of his companion. Von Straussen was thrown against the back of the cab but was cushioned to some extent by the smaller policeman who was crushed against one of the metal supports. Von Straussen was momentarily dazed but then found that, by wriggling, he could free himself from the jumble of bodies. To his surprise he was uninjured! He instinctively struggled towards the back of the truck and the open air. "No you don't!" shouted the sergeant and von Straussen saw his hand move towards the revolver at his side! Quick as lightening von Straussen's right hand, fingers extended, rigid as a board, shot out and struck deep into the side of the man's neck. The sergeant collapsed without a sound and slumped on top of his colleague. Von Straussen pulled himself through the opening at the rear and hauled himself up the side of the deep ditch into which the truck had plunged.

He looked about him cautiously. The road was deserted. Tall overgrown hedges, dazzling white with a profusion of blackthorn blossom, screened the countryside beyond. The roadside verges were thick with tall grass and with cowparsley, some already bursting into flower. There was no sign of any other living thing. Von Straussen looked down into the ditch. There was no movement. He could see that the truck's cab was partly buried in soft mud. He brushed down his threadbare suit - the one provided for him before he left Berlin. It was the only outfit he had possessed since his capture. He set off down the road. The chance of life and freedom was a small one but he would seize that chance with both hands! The road ahead, in contrast to the straight stretch they had just covered, twisted in a series of bends. After von Straussen had covered about half a mile he noticed a plume of black smoke ahead. Shortly afterwards, rounding yet another twist in the road, he came upon a steam-roller and three road-men at work. They appeared to be repairing a large pot-hole. He broke into a run and shouted to the men. A plan was forming. "What's up, mate," called one of the men. "Bad accident," von Straussen called back breathlessly. As he came up with them he added, "An army truck has gone in a very deep ditch and the soldiers in it are trapped. It might be possible to get them out if you can pull the truck back onto the road with that steam-roller!" One of the men took charge of the situation. "Bill," he called, "You get the roller going. Alf, you chuck that rope on and go with him. I'll have to get my bike and go for the ambulance."

"If you'll lend me your bike" said von Straussen, " I'll go to the phone. Those two will need all the help they can get to pull that truck out," he continued, nodding towards the two men now setting off up the road as fast as the steam-roller would go. The foreman seemed relieved.

"You'll find my bike in the next gateway on the right, propped behind the hedge. The phone's in the middle of Sladewick village, outside the post-office." Von Straussen set off at a run. Once on the cycle and out of sight of the road-men he had a chance to think things out. If he just disappeared the road-men would soon become anxious and one of them would go for help. Then they would tell what they knew and the hunt would soon be on. If he actually phoned and the ambulance came, everyone would be taken up in dealing with the injured. In fact the sergeant was almost certainly dead. That special "chop" he had used, learned on a crash course with the SS before he left Germany, was usually fatal. The other members of the escort were probably quite badly injured: in fact they might all be dead! In any event none of them was likely to remember the prisoner for a while! By the time the authorities at the military prison they had come from were notified he should, with any luck, be some distance away!

He cycled on as fast as he could go, but when he reached the sleepy village he slowed down and went quite casually to the red telephone kiosk. He did not want to draw any attention to himself! He lifted the receiver. An impersonal voice asked, "Number please?" "Ambulance," he replied and a moment later he was giving the name of the village and details of the accident. Once this was done he left the kiosk and cycled quietly on through the village. When he was well clear of it he put on speed again. After he had covered a couple of miles or so he heard the urgent clangour of a powerful electric gong. A moment later a large cream and blue ambulance swung round a corner ahead of him and raced past and on towards the village of Sladewick. He noticed that the driver and attendant were staring intently at the road ahead. They did not seem to notice the solitary cyclist going in the opposite direction. Von Straussen then recalled that when an ambulance is summoned to a road accident the police are usually notified too. He was particularly anxious to avoid their interest! When he got to the next gateway, therefore, he dismounted and wheeled the cycle into a field of growing corn. He closed the gate and then waited behind the thick hedge, invisible from the road. Within a couple of minutes he heard another vehicle. Peering cautiously through a small opening in the hedge he caught a glimpse of a black Wolseley car speeding by in the direction of Sladewick. It contained three policemen.

When the car had disappeared von Straussen wheeled the cycle back onto the road again, carefully closing the gate behind him. He then resumed his rapid progress away from Sladewick and the injured military police in their wrecked truck. Half a mile further along the road he found a side turning leading off to the right. He took it without hesitation. The road was a single track one, little more than a lane. It led from the relatively flat area around Sladewick, over a low crest and on, into a more undulating country. By now the sun was high and it was becoming really warm. The air was still with no breath of wind apart from that due to his own progress. Von Straussen had had little exercise while he was in prison. He began to tire. Once he was over the brow of the hill and into the next valley he thought it would be safe to take a short rest. The countryside was deserted and seemed to be sleeping! As he freewheeled down into the valley ahead he saw that there was a stone bridge at the bottom of the hill. The road crossed a little stream before starting to climb again. He stopped and dismounted beside the bridge and, after carefully concealing the cycle among the long grass at the roadside, he scrambled down the bank to the water's edge. There was a faint but delightfully fresh smell of marjoram and wild mint. The stream looked crystal clear. The fast-flowing water sparkled in the sun, and gurgled comfortably over the stones that formed the stream's bed. A little downstream from the bridge he could see a small pool. As he watched there was a splash. A trout, which had been lurking under the shadow of an alder close to the bank had risen to take a fly. So still was the air that, although the trout was many yards away, von Straussen heard the plop as it dropped back into the water quite distinctly. He hesitated no longer. He was thirsty and hot. The water looked pure, and trout do not flourish in contaminated streams. He cupped his hands and drank his fill.

Once he had quenched his thirst he rested in the shadow of the bridge for a full ten minutes. Then, with an effort, he roused himself to continue his journey - to wherever the lane and fate would lead him. He retrieved the bicycle and set off up the next hill. It soon became so steep that he had to dismount and push the bike. When he finally reached the top he could see a wider valley ahead of him. Here there were fields of lush grass on either side of the road. In the distance, over to the right, a herd of placid cattle lay chewing the cud under the shade of a group of tall elms. Beside the road, where he had paused to recover after the stiff climb, young ash trees grew among the hedge. He noticed that these laggards were still in bud while all the other trees he had passed were dressed in the richly varied greens of early summer. The ash buds were black and bulging. The twigs supporting them curved gracefully upwards in a way which suddenly reminded him of the handsome candelabra he had seen when, as a boy, he had peeped into his mother's dining room in that gracious Edwardian era, when his father had been a diplomat serving in the London Embassy of Imperial Germany. In those days his parents had entertained lavishly and often. He felt curiously reassured. He suddenly knew that his life was not going to end in front of a firing squad, being executed as a spy. He was quite certain of this even though he had not yet worked out any definite plan of escape. The valley he was now crossing was flatter than the previous one. He felt his confidence rising and, pedalling hard, he began to travel quite fast. Beyond the field of cows the road ran into a little wood and then started to climb again, though not as steeply as before. Then there a was a steep descent followed by a sudden sharp bend to the right which almost proved to be his undoing. He just managed to scrape round it without coming off. Almost immediately there was another turn, to the left this time. He found himself at the top of a long downward slope. The lane continued through dense woods, until, quite unexpectedly, it debouched onto a wide dusty main road.

Von Straussen stopped and leant against the cycle, having no idea of where he was or which direction he ought to take. There had been no traffic visible when he emerged from the lane but then, as he hesitated, unsure of his next move, a steadily increasing rumble heralded the appearance of a large lorry. It was grinding along at about twenty miles an hour but when the driver saw von Straussen he slowed down and pulled up beside him. Looking down from his cab he signalled the latter to open the passenger door. "Want a lift, mate," he shouted above the racket of the engine. "It's too hot for cycling!

Shove the bike on the back. I'm going to Brum if that's any use to you." Von Straussen could hardly believe his luck. Within a couple of minutes he was in the cab and they were off, with the tell-tale cycle well out of sight, concealed in the rear of the vehicle. Even if his escape was discovered quite quickly the police would be looking for a cyclist, not a heavy lorry. In any case the lorry, although heavy and slow-moving, would soon be well clear of the Sladewick area!

The driver obviously liked company and was well pleased at having someone to talk to. Fortunately for von Straussen the driver did most of the talking himself! Without bothering to ask any awkward questions he launched into a long dissertation on the progress of the war, the London "blitz" of the past winter, his son's adventures in the navy and the difficulty of getting any decent grub on the road these days! By sympathetic grunts and an occasional agreement von Straussen managed to keep the flow going without much mental effort on his part. He soon realised that he was picking up some very useful background information which would help him in any conversations with such other people as he might encounter. In prison there had been no contact with the outside world and he was profoundly ignorant of the events of the past five months. "Did you know you was in the company of a very rich man?" said the driver suddenly, turning to von Straussen with a wink.

"Yes," he continued, "The wife's always on at me about it but last night she was over at her sister's and I slipped off to the dog-racing. My luck was in!" He patted his jacket, hanging between them from a hook at the back of the cab.

By now they were running into a built-up area and von Straussen wondered if this was "Brum". His companion pointed to some wrecked houses down a side road. "The bastards really blasted the heart out of this place," he said. "This is nothing to what it's like in the centre." "Do we pass through there then?" asked von Straussen. "Yes, and if you haven't been in Coventry since the raids you're in for a shock." Sure enough the road led on through an area with fewer and fewer surviving buildings. There were gaping acres of rubble with odd gables and the corners of walls sticking up here and there like the wrecked superstructure of some battered warship. Amongst the ruins purple willow herb was blossoming. It stood tall above the other wild plants beginning to colonise an area which, less than a year previously, had been a hub of human activity. The driver was obviously depressed by the sight. He fell silent for a while. As they left the devastated city behind he said, "I came through here the day after one of the big raids: nearly broke my heart. Kids with pale dirty faces dressed in rags and wandering about aimlessly; an old couple trying to salvage a few bits and pieces from what was left of their little house; next door, rescue men in filthy overalls struggling to get at the old folk's neighbours trapped under the stairs; dust and debris everywhere. That dust! It seemed to get in your eyes, up your nose, down onto your chest, everywhere. 'Took days before I got rid of the smell of it. Seemed to be the same story in every road I passed." "'Must have been hell," said von Straussen tersely and for a time there was silence between them. Von Straussen had never seen a badly bombed city before. His companion had seen several and, with his wife, had lived through quite a number of air raids.

When he next spoke, the driver was his old cheery self again. "Got to stop in the next village and see a man about a dog!" he said. Shortly afterwards he pulled up in the yard at the front of a small pub, climbed down from the cab and disappeared behind the building. Von Straussen's mind had been at work. He realised he must have money to survive; not much perhaps, but some. A man without money can't last very long, especially in enemy territory. He leaned across and gently patted the jacket hanging at the back of the cab. He felt the bulge of a wallet. He extracted it gently. Inside were several dozen pound notes. Most were well worn. If he took one it would probably not be missed, at least not for a while. The theft was completed in seconds. By the time the driver returned von Straussen was quietly reading a newspaper he had found beside his seat. "That feels better," said the driver, "now for Brum." Although outwardly calm and at ease, von Straussen was, rather to his own surprise, troubled by guilt. Had he, a German officer and son of a Prussian diplomat of good family really been reduced to stealing from this decent working man? He tried to console himself - reasoning that the driver was not in danger of being summarily shot, whereas he himself most certainly was! Perhaps in the circumstances what he had done was excusable.

Half an hour later they were heading in towards Birmingham city centre. Von Straussen recalled his briefing of the previous November. "Do you go anywhere near Fiveways," he asked the driver. "No, mate," was the reply, "but I'll drop you within a couple of miles and you'll soon make it on that bike of yours." Five minutes later von Straussen was standing at the roadside with the stolen bicycle. He was about to mount when he noticed a small cycle shop a little further down the road. If he could get a few pounds for the bike, he would be disposing of a piece of potentially incriminating evidence and would, at the same time, increase his rather limited funds! He wheeled the machine to the shop. The shabbiness of his suit decided him on his approach to the shopkeeper. "Excuse me," he said rather diffidently, "but do you buy bicycles?" The man nodded. "Sometimes," he said. "This is my son's," continued von Straussen, "but he's away in the navy and has written to say we can try to sell it. Times are hard with his Mum and me just at the present." The shopkeeper, a tall, balding, rather lugubrious man in an oily brown overall looked the machine over with a critical eye. "Pretty dirty, and its seen a lot of hard use," he said. "Still, it's been a good enough bike in its day. I could give you three pounds for it." Von Straussen looked disappointed. "We'd been hoping for a fiver," he said sadly. The other man was by now squatting by the cycle, looking at the brake blocks and tyres which were good. "Tell you what," he said, "I'll give you three pounds fifteen shillings, but that's my last offer." Von Straussen hesitated, not wanting to seem too eager. Then he said, rather reluctantly, "I think I'd better take it if that's really all I'm likely to get."

He had escaped from the crash in a shabby blue suit and riding a bicycle. Now he was rid of the latter and it was time to part with the suit! At least he had a little money in his pocket now. He would, no doubt, get access to more funds once he contacted George Pattenson, the principal German secret agent in Birmingham, but he already had enough money for a change of outfit. The matter of his appearance was urgent. He walked on down the road and turning a corner found himself in a quiet little side-street. Here were small terraced houses with shabby, green-painted, front doors opening directly onto the pavement. There were several little shops. Some sold groceries, ironmongery or newspapers and confectionery, but eventually he saw what he was looking for. He walked in boldly. There was a faint aroma of musty damp and of stale sweat. The elderly lady behind the counter seemed short-sighted. She wore thick glasses and peered at him as he entered. This pleased von Straussen. In the event of enquiries she was unlikely to give the police much of a description of her customer! He smiled at her and said confidentially, "I am going to visit my brother in Wales and hope to go fishing while I am there. I have nothing at all suitable to wear. Do you have a jacket and a pair of trousers that are not too expensive? I can't afford anything fancy." Second hand clothes seemed almost to fill the shop but this was not all that she had available! She led him through to a room at the back which was also stuffed with clothes of all descriptions. "All my cheaper stuff is in here," she said. "The gent's items are over on that side. Have a good look and see if you can find what you want. You can try it on if you like. I'll be through in the front when you want me." After some poking about he found an inconspicuous tweed jacket and a pair of old but quite sound grey flannel trousers. Both items had originally been of good quality. There was still some wear in them. These were certainly more serviceable than the shabby blue suit that had been to Berlin and back during its earlier days and which he had had to wear every day of his five months in detention! He went back into the shop wearing the jacket and flannels. "You probably know more about clothes than I do," he said, "do you think these are a reasonable fit?" She looked him over casually through her thick glasses. "Those fit all right and that looks a good outfit for the country," she said. "You can have the jacket for five bob and the trousers for three and sixpence." "Right, I'll take them," he replied. The woman produced some used brown paper and string. Von Straussen said he would keep the new outfit on so as to get used to it and she obligingly parcelled up the old suit for him

Five minutes later he was in a tram heading for Fiveways and the rendezvous he had expected to make many months previously! Von Straussen had an excellent memory. From his briefings in Berlin he could recall the layout of the streets around Fiveways quite clearly. He quickly identified Islington Row and was glad not to have had to risk drawing attention to himself by asking for directions. Within a short time of getting off the tram he was ascending the stairs to the first floor offices of Pattenson & Co, Solicitors. From behind the glass door at the top of the stairs he could hear the sound of typing. When he followed the neatly typed instruction to "knock and enter" on a notice pinned beside the door he found himself confronted by a rather severe-looking middle-aged lady wearing glasses. Von Straussen put on his best formally polite voice using the Oxford accent which, like many variants of English, he could adopt at will. and said "Good afternoon madam. I'm looking for Mr George Pattenson who was recommended to me by a mutual acquaintance." The typist looked up at him sharply. "What is the name, sir?" she enquired. "Mr Pattenson would know me from conversation with our mutual acquaintance as Max," he replied. She looked at him with some surprise, but merely said, "I am afraid that Mr Pattenson is away for a few days, can I help?" Von Straussen was shaken. He had been so sure of finding a safe refuge as soon as he had contacted Pattenson. For once in his life he let his feelings show. "It is a very personal matter upon which I want to see him," he replied. The dragon weakened. She sensed that for some reason this man was exhausted and near the end of his tether. She knew that Mr Pattenson had some rather odd friends in connection with his car conversion business. She decided to direct him to the warehouse. Perhaps it was a matter he could not discuss with a woman! One of the men who worked down there might conceivably help.

After thanking the woman in the same rather formal manner he had used throughout, von Straussen descended the stairs. Emerging from the main door onto the street he turned to head for the canal where he had been told the warehouse was situated. Suddenly he caught sight of two policemen walking up Islington Row towards him. As they approached he got the impression that they were looking at him suspiciously. He felt the sweat break out on his back and trickle down towards his waist. The cool resolve which he had maintained throughout that eventful day suddenly deserted him. He desperately wanted to hide: to escape back up the stairs to the sanctuary of the dragon's office! With a terrible effort he forced himself to walk on towards the officers. As they passed him one of them nodded and said, "Good evening, it's been a grand day!" Almost overwhelmed with relief he managed to give a little smile and nod back. He found the gate leading from the roadway to the canal towpath quite easily. He pushed it open. The steps leading down from the gate were in shadow. Beyond he could see a warehouse beside the canal but it seemed to be deserted. There were big double doors opening onto a small wharf but weeds grew in front of them and they had obviously not been used for a long time. There was a rather curious smell pervading the whole area. He remembered from his briefing of the previous November that there was a brewery nearby. He noticed, but barely registered, the presence of a long, narrow, rather battered barge tied up to the wharf. Blackish smoke curled up from the little chimney on top of the cabin at its stern. The whole set-up seemed depressing and desolate. He could not face struggling down to the wharf to investigate further. He felt utterly depressed and was suddenly aware of his extreme weariness. He must get some food and drink inside him and take a rest while he worked out his next move. He pulled the gate shut and turned back towards Fiveways, where he now recalled having seen a nice, respectable looking tearoom.

An hour and a half later a much more relaxed Maximillian von Straussen sat back in his chair and toyed with a Danish pastry. He glanced through a newspaper, conveniently left behind by the previous occupant of the table. It was the first newspaper of any sort he had seen for six months. At his side was a cup of coffee. He had struggled with himself before taking the risk of ordering the coffee for which he had craved. He knew that tea was a much more usual drink in England but the longing, prompted by the smell of freshly roasted coffee beans which had hit him immediately he entered the place, had been too much of a temptation! He had not tasted coffee for months. To his relief the waitress had shown no surprise whatsoever when he ordered it. He had not been aware that this particular establishment prided itself on serving both tea and coffee of the best quality. So far they had managed to obtain reasonable supplies, despite the wartime shortages which, by now, were beginning to be felt almost everywhere. The steak - pie they had produced for him had also been pretty good: a vast improvement on prison fare! "Have you got everything you require, sir?" The waitress was at his side. He nodded and thanked her. A few minutes later he saw the same rather attractive brunette walk through the restaurant in her outdoor coat and heard her say to the woman at the cash desk near the door, "good-night Miss Griggs. I'll see you in the morning."

He watched her set off down the road and reflected that it was very pleasant to have the opportunity of admiring a pretty girl once again after so many months of solitary confinement! She disappeared in the direction of Islington Row and von Straussen's thoughts drifted back to the bitter disappointment he had felt at Pattenson's unexpected absence. Then he recalled the desolate appearance of the warehouse to which he had been directed. He pictured it again in his mind. Now he was rested, relaxed and well-fed. His brain was working much better than it had been when he had arrived at the top of those steps leading down to the canal. At the time his nerves had been strained to the limit by the sudden shock of encountering the police just as he had emerged from Pattenson's office, bitterly disappointed at being told that the man was away when von Straussen so urgently needed to contact him! His body had been utterly exhausted by all that he had done since his escape early that morning. Now his mind was much clearer. He recalled the barge and the smoking chimney of its little cabin. Vile barge! Of course! That must be why

Pattenson had been using the warehouse. Now it all came back to him. Heimgarten had explained the secret communications system linking the German agents in Birmingham with Berlin. It depended on a barge! He reasoned that there must be someone on board that barge he had seen moored beside the warehouse, otherwise there would be no fire in the stove and no smoke from the chimney. That someone was most probably the renegade Britisher that Heimgarten had told him about. What was his name? Barnes, if he recalled correctly.

Was there some special reason for Pattenson's absence and for the presence of the barge, tied up outside his headquarters? Could they actually be mounting "Operation Chainbreak" at this very moment? It was an exhilarating thought. He knew that the operation was scheduled to take place in May. That month was now well advanced! It would be a tremendous thing for Germany if the plan could be pulled off despite his capture. If it succeeded the gain would be tremendous. For the RAF to be deprived of its invaluable early warning system, even for 24 hours, would give the Luftwaffe the chance it so badly needed. They could destroy the British fighter defences at long last! Once that was done the invasion plan, carried out with the Wehrmacht's usual efficiency, might well end the war within a month or two, resulting in yet another resounding triumph for his country. What if he could help in some way even at this eleventh hour? It would be a boost for his own morale and might make up in a small way for the ignominy of his having been captured within half an hour of landing on English soil. Such an adventure would help to blow away the tedium of those long months in that awful prison!

Von Straussen decided he must act cautiously and deliberately. He must not in any way jeopardise the operation, whether it had actually begun or not. It would be best to think things over for an hour or so. He could see that the staff of the restaurant were beginning to clear up. The establishment would soon be closing. He could not linger here while he marshalled his thoughts and worked out a plan. He must find some quiet spot where he would not attract any unwelcome attention. He rose leisurely from the table, paid his bill and strolled out with as casual an air as a spy and escaped prisoner could muster in the heart of enemy territory! A little way down the road he saw a projecting canopy on which he read "Panorama News Cinema. Continuous programme of news, short films and cartoons." That would suit him well. He might catch up further with current affairs and learn rather more detail than he had been able to glean from the newspaper he had just been reading. It would be a good thing to be able to talk to anyone he met in a reasonably well-informed manner.

In prison he had had no access to news of any sort and the information he had gleaned from the friendly lorry driver had been rather patchy. The cinema would be dark. Nobody would notice him and during the parts of the programme that were of no importance he could think out his next move.

The newsreel was fascinating. In spite of the patriotic overlay thickly applied by British propaganda von Straussen learned that Greece had already been conquered by German forces and that a desperate battle was going on in Crete between the British and their allies and German parachute troops. Clearly Germany had made amazing progress since he had left Berlin in November of 1940 and subsequently lost touch with world events. If his country could achieve such triumphs in the Balkans and Greece, the sort of attack envisaged by the planners of Operation Chainbreak must be feasible. By now he had convinced himself that the operation was either under way or just about to be launched! He sat through cartoons and "Food Fact" films, quite oblivious of his surroundings. He cogitated about his next move. It would probably be best to wait until near dusk, when he would still be able to see reasonably well but would not be too noticeable himself. He would then go boldly to the barge and ask casually after Mr Barnes. If it was the wrong barge, little harm would have been be done and he would in any case get the chance of a closer look at that warehouse. If he managed to contact Barnes he should be able to convince him that, he, von Straussen, was a member of the German intelligence service. He could relate some of the details of Operation Chainbreak which no outsider could possibly know! Also, von Straussen now recalled he himself knew something of Barnes' own background and this too would help to establish, his, von Straussen's bona fides in Barnes' mind. Pattenson, von Straussen speculated, might well be away supervising the active part of the operation. He had probably left Barnes to deal with the communications. Barnes would presumably have an assistant, but it would be best to try and contact Barnes himself. After that he would have to rely on Barnes to allocate him to some useful duty on the spot or alternatively tell him where he could find, and link up with, Pattenson.

Chapter 12

Morag Maclean knocked at the back door of the old Hampshire farmhouse and waited, a little anxiously. After a minute or so she heard the sound of footsteps on the stone floor. Eventually the heavy door jerked open with a creak and a graunch and there stood Mrs Grey blinking in the bright sunlight. Her kindly weather-beaten face lit up when she recognised her visitor. "Come in my dear," she said. The pleasure in her voice was unmistakable. "Are you on your own or is your friend Mary with you? I'm sorry I was so slow in coming but I was in the dairy putting some milk through the separator. We've an order for cream." Morag genuinely liked this gentle middle-aged woman. If only her own poor mother was a bit more like this! Mr and Mrs Grey had no family but, when Morag and Mary Dunbar had called at Easter and asked for permission to camp, the couple had made them very welcome. By the end of the holiday they were treating the girls almost like daughters! Morag had let Mary Dunbar think that the Easter camping holiday was entirely Mary's idea. Actually it was Morag who had subtly instigated the plan with the objective of reconnoitring RAF Hamden Down and the surrounding area.

Some weeks before the Easter break, using an Ordnance Survey map from the University library to supplement the sketch-map that Hector had given her, she had discovered that the radiolocation site at Hamden Down was only a couple miles or so across country from Ferny Farm. Quite early on in their visit the girls had been to a dance in the nearby village and had met some of the aircraftsmen from the site. Mary had fallen for one of the young airmen and during the rest of the week's holiday the couple had met whenever Jack Stanley was off duty. As a result Morag had been fairly free to explore on her own. She had wasted no time in finding out as much as she could about the site. She had discovered that a good way of approaching the perimeter fence without being seen was to follow a small, rather overgrown stream whose course ran up through some fields and a wood towards the RAF site. The lower reaches of the stream passed close to Ferny Farm. Before the holiday was over and the girls returned to Glasgow for the University summer term, Jack Stanley had arranged for them to have a very unofficial visit to the site. This took place one evening, when the senior NCO's were out and when one of Jack's friends was on guard duty at the gate. The visit had given Morag an excellent opportunity to study the layout of the place. She had never anticipated such a stroke of luck when she had begun her investigations!

Now Morag had to prepare the ground carefully for what was to come next. She and Hector had decided that if they were to convince Mr and Mrs Grey of their respectability and obtain permission to camp at the right spot for their attack on the RAF site they would have to be "a married couple". They had decided that Hector was to be a young soldier on embarkation leave before being posted abroad. They thought it best to say that they had known each other for a long time but had married on the spur of the moment before they were separated, perhaps for the duration of the war! Morag was a good actress. By now her feelings for Hector were very strong and this helped to make the fiction seem real - and desirable too! It required very little mental effort to become a newly-wed wife, deeply in love with the young man of her choice! By the time she had finished telling Mrs Grey all about it she had half convinced herself of the story! The older woman was thrilled by this exciting development. "But where is your Hector?" she said. "I would not let him come up here till I had talked to you and Mr Grey," Morag replied. "He's waiting at the station with our bicycles and tents. He said that if you did not approve we would find somewhere else to camp. He did not want to cause any embarrassment."

Mrs Grey was horrified. "Just get down to the station this minute and fetch him up here - yes, and all your things too. Of course you're most welcome to camp, but wouldn't you rather stay in the house here? It would be a great pleasure to Mr Grey and me to have a young soldier and his wife here, and indeed an honour too." This, of course, would never do! Morag knew that she and Hector must have complete freedom of action for the dangerous work that lay ahead. If they were guests in the house they might be trapped by their kind hosts at some vital moment! They would certainly find it very difficult to slip out in the middle of the night with explosives and wire cutters! "You're so kind Mrs Grey," she said, "but I'm sure you'll understand that with so little time before he goes abroad Hector and I want to be together, just the two of us, as much as possible." "Of course, dear, I should have thought of that," said Mrs Grey, but Morag could see that she was disappointed.

When, half an hour later, Morag returned, accompanied by Hector and the cycles and baggage, there was a great introducing of the "young soldier on embarkation leave." Mr and Mrs Grey shook him by the hand and Mr Grey clapped him on the back and told him he was a lucky chap to have found such a lovely young wife. "I can see you're responsible young folk and won't leave gates open or start fires or anything of that sort," he said. "You can put your tent where-ever you choose, but there's several good spots up towards Durton Wood, beside the little stream. There's one especially nice spot. The stream takes a bend there and there's a lovely flat area with very short grass where the sheep have cropped it over the years. More like a tennis court than a field it is! Don't go beyond the wood though. You see those two big masts sticking up on the high ground above the wood?" They nodded. "They belong to an RAF wireless station. There's supposed to be some sort of secret equipment up there and they don't like folks going too near!" "Thank you for warning us," said Hector. "We'll keep well clear. All we want for these few days is to enjoy each other's company and the peace and quietness of the country. With a girl like Morag and weather as good as this, who could ask for more!"

They wheeled their laden bikes up a track through the fields and after passing through several gates, they found a grassy area shaped like a half-moon. On one side there was a thick hawthorn hedge and on the other the clear, gently-flowing, stream, quite open in its lower reaches. The grass was as short and as fine as might be found on a bowling green! The ground was fairly soft but quite dry. This must be the spot that Mr Grey had spoken of. They pitched the tent near the hedge, for shelter. Having set up the camp to their satisfaction, they carefully concealed some equipment of a sort not normally carried by campers or honeymoon couples! Neither had much experience of camping but Morag, always thorough, had read several books on the subject before she and Mary Dunbar had set off at Easter. She had put her theoretical knowledge into practice and learned enough on that trip to ensure that she and Hector would be comfortable, and that their camp would be easy to run. In the early evening Mr Grey and his dog passed by and they exchanged "Good evenings". He complemented them on their arrangements. There was no hint of the armaments and explosives that the little camp concealed!

In the sunshine of that warm May evening Hector and Morag stretched out in front of their tent and finalised their plans. Hector had one essential duty of which Morag knew nothing. Each evening he must listen to the propaganda broadcast from Berlin! As soon as the "news" item by William Joyce - "Lord Haw-Haw" - was over Hector had to make four brief telephone calls. He had told Morag that he must keep contact with the other four teams in the sector. So as to allay any suspicion she had mentioned to Mrs Grey, casually, that Hector's mother was a widow lady and rather nervous and that he liked to phone her each evening. They thought this would be a plausible explanation if he was seen by any of the locals, who might be curious about his regular evening trips to the call box. Hector had to telephone each of the four sabotage teams under his control to ensure that they were ready and to tell them when to strike. None of these teams was staffed by German agents and therefore none knew that the signal to attack would emanate from Berlin. Morag knew that Hector had supervision of the other teams but she, too, was, of course, quite unaware that the whole operation was ultimately controlled from Germany! She imagined that Hector got his instructions by phoning the headquarters of the militant peace movement in London and that he then passed the orders on to his four teams. He had persuaded her to arrange to visit the Greys at their farm at the critical time each evening on the pretext that, by chatting to them, she might glean valuable local information. She could also listen to the BBC nine o'clock news on their wireless set. Hector said that it was essential that they should not lose touch with the general situation on the eve of the peace movement's great coup to end the war. Morag's absence from the camp when she went down to the farm each evening gave him just enough time to listen to the "Germany Calling" broadcast on his own compact, and highly secret, portable radio set before setting out for the village on his cycle to contact the other groups under his control by telephone.

On the evening of their third day in camp Morag returned from the farm to find Hector flushed and excited. He was just back from making his phone calls. "We go tonight," he said. Teams all over the south and east of England are ready. We strike at 3am tomorrow!" Only the German agents amongst the saboteurs knew just how critical the timing really was. At 3am all the radio-location units covering the south and east coasts of England were to be immobilised simultaneously by destruction of one of the two huge masts which made every site such an unmistakable landmark. By 3.30am the "observers" would all have telephoned headquarters at the warehouse in Birmingham to report the result of their own team's attack. A precise call time had been allotted to each observer so that the telephone at the warehouse would not get jammed. Each call would last for less than 30 seconds. The message would be simply "Peacestrike complete" followed by a code name for the site successfully attacked. In the event of failure no message was to be sent. This would avoid confusion: also the organisers considered that the idea of failure was not to be encouraged amongst their followers! At 3.30am the collated results of all the phone messages would be passed to Berlin by Alfred Barnes, using the transmitter on his barge. As soon as it was known that a huge hole had been blasted in the chain of radiolocation stations along the English coast, the waiting Luftwaffe fleets would head for their various targets. They would attack shortly after 4am. The rising sun would be behind them and would blind any British fighter pilots who might succeed in taking off despite the absence of any early warning of the attack. By 5am the RAF fighter defences should be devastated and out of action for good!

Naturally Morag, and all the others amongst the saboteurs who were not German agents, were quite unaware of the Luftwaffe's key role in the plan! As far as they were concerned the reason for making the attacks simultaneously was to take the guards at the radiolocation sites by surprise and to impress upon the government the power and efficiency of the peace movement. It had seemed likely, too, that attacks made shortly before daybreak, when sentries were less than fully alert, would have the best chance of success.

Morag felt a tingle of excitement, not without an element of almost pleasurable fear, run down her spine. This was what they had worked for so long and so hard. All the exhaustion of that journey to deliver the explosives, all those weary hours beside that empty highland roadside, all the disappointment of not seeing the Russians and their submarine were as nothing. This was the moment they had been anticipating for months and months! By tomorrow evening the war-monger Churchill and his hateful gang of reactionary politicians would be on the ropes! Soon there would be a new government. Soon there would be world peace. Best of all she and Hector would have striven, and triumphed, together in the glorious cause of international socialism. In working for that cause they had fallen in love. Soon they would really be married, not just pretending! The brave new world that would come once there was peace would be their world. Power would soon be in the hands of the workers, as was their rightful due. She and Hector would have earned a place of honour in a new and just Britain, freed at last from capitalist oppression.

Morag's thoughts were interrupted. "Tell me," Hector asked her, "When you did your reconnaissance at Easter did you find any specially difficult places that could hold us up when we follow the stream up to the perimeter fence tonight?" During their few days in camp Hector and Morag had been most careful to avoid going anywhere near the RAF site. They had not wanted to arouse the slightest suspicion and had deliberately shown no interest whatsoever in the radiolocation unit. They had decided in advance that they would rely entirely on Morag's previous explorations. If anyone had spotted her near it at that time and had been curious as to what she was doing they would almost certainly have forgotten all about it by now. "Look over towards the wood," said Morag. "You can see patches of elderblossom all along the edge of it, but where the stream goes into the wood there is a single very big elder tree absolutely covered in blossom." Following her gaze, Hector saw the distant splodges of creamy elderblossom here and there along the margin of the wood, but sure enough at one point there was a much bigger and more prominent light patch standing out against the dark green of the trees. "That will be fairly easy to pick out in the dark and will be quite a good guide for us when we start out," she continued. "There is an easy fence to cross at that point. At the far side of the wood the hedge is very thick but we can get through by walking in the bed of the stream itself. It took me and hour and a quarter from where we are now to the perimeter fence but that was in daylight and with no equipment." Hector nodded. "We'd better allow ninety minutes to get to the perimeter and a quarter of an hour to cut through the fence. We might have to wait a little while the guards pass on their rounds." "The nearest mast is only a couple of minutes away from the fence," said Morag. "Right," said Hector. "We should be able to place the explosives in under ten minutes. We'll leave here at 1am." "What about the equipment," asked Morag. "You take the wire cutters and I'll take the pack of explosives. We can't risk failure. One of those masts must go down at 3am precisely or we'll be failing the movement. By the way old Grimes, our "observer", is around. I met him on my way back from the phone box. I've told him tonight is the night! He'll phone Birmingham at his allotted time - 3.12am - to confirm that one of the Hamden Down masts has gone down."

Hector decided that it was time to check the equipment. After a careful scout around the whole area to be sure that there was nobody else about they settled down to this vital job. Their earlier preparations had been thorough so it did not take them very long. Soon they were satisfied that everything was in perfect order. They dropped the flap of the tent to conceal its contents and, as the sun was still quite strong, they sat down on a groundsheet outside then stretched out to rest. After a couple of minutes Morag turned to Hector and kissed him lightly on the lips. He responded with a much firmer kiss. They kissed again - and again - more and more passionately. With each kiss their need of each other grew and with each kiss that need became more urgent. Very soon they were they were inside the tent, the flap closed, oblivious to the world and its problems! After all there was nothing more than they could do to play their part in the great peace endeavour until 1am came!

Not very far away, on the low summit of Hamden Down, Flight Sergeant Sutton sat in his little office reflecting on life - over a stiff whisky. He was depressed. His thoughts were bitter. His wife was dead - killed six months ago in the London blitz. They had no family. All that was left to him was his job on the lonely radiolocation site that he commanded. Until last month he had had the support and companionship of Sergeant Baker, who had been his second in command and sheet anchor. Now Baker was gone; promoted and posted to command a site of his own. Sutton was left with young Corporal Strange. He did not like Strange. Strange was at least as good a radio technician as Sutton himself, and Sutton had been in radio since the early days of wireless-equipped aircraft back in 1916! Sutton resented Strange's expertise, although he would not have admitted this, even to himself. Corporal Strange, too, was a poor disciplinarian and Sutton could sense the rapid slide into slackness that had occurred in the short time since Sergeant Baker had departed. Sutton himself just could not seem to make the effort to rise above the lassitude, which had now become a habit, and step in himself. Baker had taken care of all the daily routine on the site. Sutton knew now that he had come to rely on him far too much. He missed Baker's down to earth common sense and also the company of a man of his own age. He rose, marched out, made a cursory round of the unit and checked the cathode room and the duty operator. All seemed quiet. He made his way to the NCOs' hut and slowly prepared for bed.

It was 1am when the Flight Sergeant was woken from a heavy sleep by his second in command. "Sorry to disturb you "Flight"," said Corporal Strange, "But we've just had a signal from the Air Ministry. It's an "operational immediate" so I thought I better speak to you." Sutton tried, half-heartedly, to focus his mind on what this tiresome young man was saying. Subconsciously all he wanted to do was to get back to sleep again as soon as possible; to get rid of this nuisance; to slip back into the oblivion which he found preferable to his waking hours these days. "It says we've to double all the guards immediately," continued Strange. "Just some staff officer panicking, Corporal," growled the Flight Sergeant. "When you've been in the service as long as I have you'll learn to take these things with a grain of salt. Put it on my desk. I'll deal with it in the morning." He turned over and was in a deep sleep before his second in command could protest. Strange knew that he was unpopular with Sutton. Strange was a radio-technician. His general service experience was very limited - and he could smell that the older man had been at the whisky again! He shrugged his shoulders and left the room. Probably the Flight Sergeant was right. Strange was certainly not going to stick his neck out and double the guards on his own responsibility. The airmen would hate it and he would have to explain himself to a resentful Sutton in the morning. To salve his conscience he walked the perimeter fence himself and spoke to the three men on guard duty before retiring to bed, still a little uneasy in his mind.

At 3am precisely a series of three explosions in quick succession shook the whole of Hamden Down. Seconds after the last explosion there was a long drawn out grinding rending noise followed by a tremendous crash as one of the site's two huge masts hit the ground. It fell on the cathode tube room, destroying it completely. The masthead struck the NCOs' hut. Flight Sergeant Sutton was killed instantly but Corporal Strange crawled out of the wreckage shaken but, to his surprise, unhurt. He pulled himself together with commendable speed for a man who had never seen action before. "One man stay on the gate," he shouted as he struggled to his feet, "the other two guards come with me." As he hurried towards the base of the wrecked mast, off-duty airmen started to appear from the barrack huts over towards the guard-room. Rubbing the sleep from their eyes, the men tried to make out, amid the darkness and confusion, what on earth was going on. Some followed the sound of the running footsteps of the two guards as they responded to corporal Strange's shouts.

The moment the charges were set Morag had started to move towards the perimeter fence, followed by Hector. When she heard the detonations she turned instinctively and watched, fascinated. The mast, clearly visible against the night sky, started to tilt and then fell with a rending crash, splintering and crushing the two wooden huts nearest to it. She was momentarily dazed, partly by the shock of the explosions and partly by the dramatic success of their operation! The explosive pack had worked perfectly - it had performed exactly as they had been told to expect. The delayed timing had allowed them to get quite close to the small opening they had made in the perimeter fence. She marvelled at the superb technology of the Soviet Union whose scientists, so Hector had told her, were responsible for the design and manufacture of the packs. She turned towards Hector. One of the wrecked huts had started to burn and by the light of the flames she could see him standing, gazing at the place where the mast had stood moments before. There was a look of wild exultation on his face. As she watched he sprang to attention and, to her astonishment, his right arm shot up. "Seig Heil," he shouted at the top of his voice, "Heil Hitler. Deutchsland uber alles." For a moment Morag did not understand, then an unquenchable rage flared within her. She had trusted this man as a Comrade: she had taken him as her lover: and he was a traitor! A traitor to the cause of International Socialism. A traitor in the struggle for peace. He was a Nazi! And she had been duped by him - and used by him!

Then she saw the glint of a steel helmet, reflecting the flames from the burning wreckage of the cathode ray hut. An RAF guard was kneeling on one knee, partly concealed by some debris from the fallen mast. His rifle was at his shoulder and he was aiming carefully. As she watched Hector dropped to the ground, rolled over, raised a pistol and fired. Corporal Strange, who was running towards them stumbled, staggered forward a few steps and then collapsed not far from Morag. Hector aimed again and a second RAF man coming up behind the corporal fell to the ground. The kneeling guard fired two shots in quick succession. Hector seemed to lift from the ground. He shuddered convulsively and then lay still. In the darkness and confusion nobody appeared to notice Morag, standing in the shadows.

There was a shout from further along the perimeter fence. Somebody had found the gap. The guard with the rifle jumped to his feet and ran off in the direction of the shout. He was followed by a straggle of airmen in various stages of undress, roused from their sleep by the explosions, the crash of the falling mast and then, by the ominous sound of small arms fire. With the vague idea of finding some blankets to cover the injured men Morag made her way to one of the, now deserted, barrack huts. She shivered and suddenly felt cold. Hanging on a peg near the door of the of the hut was an RAF man's tunic. She slipped it on, then pulled a few blankets from some of the beds in the hut, and made her way back to the injured.

Down at Ferny Farm Mr Grey had woken with a start. He was a light sleeper and years of rising through the night to calve a cow had accustomed him to respond to any unusual sound. Surely that was an explosion he had heard! Then, in quick succession, there were two more.

His wife was awake by now and both of them heard the distant crash of the falling mast. As they puzzled over the cause of the disturbance there came another sound. The noise of gunfire. This was quite familiar. There were plenty of pheasants around Ferny Farm. Before he had gone off to France with his regiment, early on in the war, Major Johns, their landlord, had often organised shooting parties. Frequently they shot over Mr Grey's fields after the harvest had been taken in. Sometimes, following a shoot, the Major had called in to leave the Greys a brace of birds. The shooting they heard now sounded different, though, and anyway most people don't shoot pheasants out of season and in the small hours of the morning! Mr Grey slipped out of bed and drew back the curtains. Almost at once, looking out towards Hamden Down against the skyline, he could see that something was very wrong. One of the two big masts, which had dominated the little hill for the past three years, had disappeared! "Alice," he shouted, "one of them great big masts is away!" Mrs Grey was out of bed and at his side in a moment. "Best phone the police, Jack. Something pretty bad must have happened!" Mr Grey stumbled downstairs to the little room he used as an office. He grabbed the telephone receiver from its hook at the side of the mahogany box fixed to the wall. He cranked furiously at the handle on the other side of the box. Eventually, a sleepy voice answered and he shouted into the mouthpiece, "Get me the police, its urgent!" Soon he heard the reassuring voice of the village constable. "Police station here." "George, this is Jack Grey at Ferny Farm. One of those big masts on Hamden Down has been blown up. We heard the explosions and looked out and sure enough one of them has gone." "Leave it to me, Jack," said the constable. "I'll get onto the army right away. This sounds like a job for the military. That Canadian camp is only a few miles from Hamden Down. I'll contact them, then I'll call the fire brigade from Frimbridge. After that I'll cycle over myself and sort things out. Just leave it to me." Constable George Roberts was a confident man. He had a calm assurance of his own ability to deal with any problem from a lost cat to a major disaster.

When PC George Roberts called him on the phone, Captain MacKay, duty officer at the Canadian army camp, wasted no time and asked no unnecessary questions. Within five minutes a 15 hundredweight truck with half a dozen soldiers of the camp guard was on its way to Hamden Down, closely followed by a military ambulance. A three ton lorry, with a full platoon of Canadian soldiers, and a second ambulance would follow shortly. At the gate of the radiolocation site the sole remaining RAF guard received the reinforcements with relief. He had very little idea of what was going on and was thankful to be relieved of all responsibility by this efficient Canadian officer! The latter detailed a couple of his men to take over the gate and then, with the RAF man as guide, set off swiftly with four more soldiers to investigate the perimeter fence.

The ambulance proceeded straight to the huts which had been shattered by the fallen mast. Morag signalled urgently to the two men in the cab. The medical orderly jumped down and ran over to her while the driver turned the vehicle. "These two are pretty bad," Morag greeted the Canadian orderly. She indicated Hector and Corporal Strange, lying not far apart. "1 think we ought to get them off to hospital right away, but there may be others trapped under the buildings." By now the driver had opened the rear doors of the ambulance and was bringing over a stretcher. "I'll tell you what, miss," said the orderly in his rich Canadian accent, not too far removed from Morag's highland one, "if you can go to the hospital with these two, I'll look after any others. There's a second ambulance on the way." Then he noticed the second of Hector's victims. He examined the fallen airman briefly. "This poor chap's as dead as mutton," he said. "We can leave him for now." Morag nodded but said nothing! She had suddenly realised that, because of the jacket she had taken to keep herself warm, the soldiers had assumed she was a WAAF - perhaps a "medic".

The ambulance soon moved off. Morag began to look at her two "patients" aided by the lights inside the vehicle.

The corporal's jacket was heavily blood stained. She unbuttoned it and felt inside. There was a horrible squelching sensation. When she withdrew her hand it was covered in blood stained froth! On the partition of the ambulance, behind the driver, there was a cupboard. Morag opened it. She found a khaki pack labelled "field dressing - large". She ripped open the pack and, as quickly as she could, unfastened Corporal Strange's jacket and shirt and fastened the dressing firmly on the wound that was revealed. Then she buttoned the jacket over the dressing. After that she turned her attention to Hector. She would never know that by sealing his open chest wound with the dressing she had saved Corporal Strange's life!

Morag tried to feel Hector's pulse but could not. His face was deadly pale and, despite the blankets tucked round him with practised skill by the Canadian medical orderly, he felt very cold. Her emotions were numbed. In her fury at his betrayal of herself and of the Cause she had wanted to kill him. Now she was relieved that it was the RAF Guard who had done the job. What was she to do now? Their mission had succeeded but now it was obvious that what they had done had not been for the cause of peace at all but to further some hideous Nazi plan! Now she must think of herself.

She could do little for Hector, even if she had wanted to. The ambulance, which had been moving at a steady pace for some time was slowing down. Shortly it came to a halt. She could hear that some sort of shouted conversation was going on between the driver, his voice easily recognisable by his distinctive Canadian accent, and some other men. Morag switched off the interior light and, leaning across the stretcher on which Hector was lying, she slid open the shutter covering a little window high up on the side of the vehicle. It was daylight by now. She could see that the ambulance had halted at a railway level crossing. The gates were shut. Beyond them she could see a dark green electric train standing at a station platform. On the destination board at the front she could just make out the name "Waterloo". She guessed that the ambulance driver was trying to get the men to open the crossing gates so that he could get the casualties to hospital as quickly as possible. She saw one of the men run towards the signal box at the far end of the station. The other two men walked over to the ambulance and started talking to the driver. Morag slipped off the RAF jacket she had been wearing on top of her own clothes and laid it over Hector's blankets. She opened one of the rear doors very quietly. Corporal Strange opened his eyes. Hector did not stir. Morag stepped down and closed the door gently. Nobody seemed to have seen her. The men were still at the front of the ambulance talking to the driver. She walked over to the railway station, feeling in the pocket of her slacks for the return half of the ticket from London she had put there a lifetime ago when she and Hector had arrived with their cycles and camping equipment.

The crossing gates started to open. The ambulance driver waved to the railwaymen and the vehicle moved on across the tracks and accelerated away. Morag got into an empty third class compartment of the train. It was the first train of the day and there were very few passengers. It would pick up more and more as it got nearer London. Someone had left last night's evening paper on one of the seats. Morag picked it up and started to read. She took in absolutely nothing but it was best to look like a regular traveller on this, the first stage of her journey back to Glasgow, the University and her work for the Communist party. She did not then know that very soon Hitler's forces would attack the USSR, nor that, before the year was out she herself would have joined the WAAF - an eager volunteer in the united struggle against a common enemy!

Chapter 13

Christine Turner sat alone at a small round marble-topped table in the empty refreshment room at New Street station, Birmingham. She was trying to make her second cup of coffee last as long as possible. As she sipped it she forgot, for a moment, her preoccupation with immediate worries. She had barely noticed the first cup. The excitement of her errand and the prospect of seeing her "contact" again had fully occupied her mind. The coffee had just been part of the job! Now the horrid taste of the second cup, with its hint of bitterness, distracted her, temporarily, from a growing impatience and anxiety. It was quite irrelevant, but the thought suddenly struck her - how different this dismal refreshment room would be if her father had the running of it! Lately she had become quite proud of the high standards he had achieved with his chain of "Turner's

Tearooms". Until she had started to work in one of them she had taken only a superficial interest in his business activities, though she had always been vaguely aware that the high standard of living the family enjoyed was not due to chance or to inherited wealth, but was solely the result her father's hard work and business skill. When, last November, she had been suddenly uprooted from her job as a WAAF driver in London and sent by Air Intelligence to work in one of his tearooms in Birmingham the contrast between the two occupations had been quite a shock! At the time she had felt very resentful at having to leave the job she loved and her friends in London. She had been upset, too, at having to deceive her mother and father into thinking that she had had a nervous breakdown due to the stress of working in the blitz. Slowly, as she had come to terms with the situation, she had started to quite enjoy working as a waitress. Miss Griggs, who was in charge of the Fiveways tearoom, was not one to make anything special of Christine being the boss's daughter! She had treated Christine exactly the same as the other waitresses. They had to be punctual, meticulously clean and tidy and invariably polite, however difficult the customers or the circumstances might be!

On arrival each morning every waitress had to lay up her tables exactly to Miss Griggs liking. Thereafter they had to be maintained in pristine condition throughout the day. Woe betide anyone found to have dirty crockery or an unemptied ashtray on one of her tables when Miss Griggs made one of her frequent inspections! After the early weeks of inward rebellion Christine had come to accept the ordered routine of her new life. She had begun to get to know her regular customers. Some were charming like old Mr Prendergast from the gentlemen's outfitters down the road. He came in for lunch at exactly the same time every day and always enquired courteously as to Miss Griggs' and Christine's health. He usually gave his copy of the Times to Christine when he went back to work. This was appreciated. She took it back to her bed-sit after work and read it over supper before passing it on to her landlady, who was too hard up to buy a paper for herself. Certain other customers took some coping with! There had been one young man who, she thought, should have been in the forces. He had sometimes made unpleasantly suggestive remarks to her. When, after a month or so he asked if she would like to spend a weekend with him at Blackpool, all expenses paid and nothing barred, she had put him down with Icy politeness! He had not returned.

The refreshment room coffee cup was made of thick white china: ugly to look at and awkward to hold. Mr Turner, by contrast, always insisted on attractive china and cutlery being provided for his customers. "Decent things last just as well or better," he had told Christine once, when the subject cropped up. "People instinctively take care of a thing that looks and feels nice, even if it belongs to somebody else. Anyway," he had added, "Why should my customers put up with things I would not like my family to use." Her father, thought Christine, would probably have had the refreshment room decorated in relaxing colours to tempt his customers to linger (and to spend more!) and would have had some attractive pictures on the wall. He would most certainly have insisted on decent quality tea and coffee being served and would never have allowed slightly stale biscuits, like the ones provided with her disagreeable coffee, to tarnish the reputation of one of his establishments!

Christine suddenly jerked back to her present situation. She glanced at her watch and checked it against the huge clock above the station concourse. Max should surely have reached the station by now! She had expected that he would arrive quite soon after her, presuming that he would follow the plan he had outlined when he briefed her on her own disappointingly minor role in tonight's major operation by Air Intelligence. Christine was seriously worried. She assumed her worry was about the success of the operation on which she and Max and many others were engaged. She knew it was so critical that Britain's very survival might depend on its success.

Had she been more objective she might have admitted to herself that a good deal of her anxiety was really about Max himself. She knew that the job he had been doing for the RAF was a very dangerous one. She had been his sole contact with the British Intelligence Services during the past six months. During that time she had felt herself getting close to him as a person. Of necessity their contacts had been brief and irregular, but she had come to look forward a good deal to his appearances at the tearoom. Recently she had started to feel restless when a week or two went by without her seeing him. From the start of their curious relationship she had admired the way in which he had tackled the job of posing as the senior Nazi agent of the group of genuine German spies which he had infiltrated. She suspected that, using her as a messenger, he had passed on a good deal of valuable information about German submarine activities. She again suspected that this information might have saved quite a few sailors' lives. Lately she had noticed that he was getting thinner and seemed very tense. She guessed that the strain of the role he was playing must be telling on him. Now she was desperately worried that he had been unmasked by the real German agents. She hardly dared to think of the consequences.

Christine had listened to the radio in her bed-sit earlier that evening and had heard the broadcast from Germany by "Lord Haw-Haw" as she had done regularly for some days now, in accordance with her instructions. This particular broadcast had, she was certain, been the one about which she had been briefed and which was the signal for the start of the great German sabotage plan which would precede the invasion of the British Isles. That signal meant that tonight Nazi agents would attack the numerous British radio-location stations which, ever since the start of the war, had been giving accurate advanced warning of every enemy air attack. The wording in Haw-Haw's broadcast had been quite clear. "Under the inspired leadership of their Fuehrer the German people have CAST OFF THEIR CHAINS!" It could not have been plainer to anyone who had been told about the message. Probably very few of King George VI's subjects had been listening to the Nazi propaganda that evening. Haw-haw was recognised as a purveyor of some very exaggerated claims. For example, according to Haw-Haw, HMS Ark Royal had been sunk several times over! Some people listened for amusement, of course, to see what he would claim next and to laugh at the curious nasal accent of the broadcaster. A small minority with Fascist sympathies followed him more seriously. For those few in the know, however, tonight's item was of vital importance!

Christine decided to abandon the remains of her unappetising coffee. She got up, walked out of the refreshment room, and over to the ticket collector standing at the barrier. "Can you tell me when the next London train leaves, please?" she asked. "Yes, miss," the man replied. "The 11.40 leaves from platform 6 and gets in to London at 1.56 am. It's really a mail-train: never many passengers." "Thank you," said Christine, pleased to have learned all she wanted to know without having to ask too many questions. She realised now that Max had not the slightest hope of reaching the radio-location site in southern England that he was supposed to be guarding before the zero hour of 3am. She decided that she must act on her own initiative. There were several telephone booths on the concourse and she entered one of them, inserted some coins into the box, and dialled a number. When she heard a voice answer at the other end of the line she pressed button A and repeated a code word. Seconds later she was speaking to Group Captain Avon. "Max has not arrived at New Street station, so his site won't be covered," she said. "I'm going to find out what has happened to him." She hung up immediately. Avon might have tried to dissuade her or might have given her some order she would not have been prepared to obey. Better to cut him off before he had the chance!

Outside the station there was a solitary taxi. She roused the sleepy driver and asked him to take her to the Accident Hospital as quickly as possible. The man, she supposed, would imagine her to be an anxious relative called to the bedside of some unfortunate casualty and so would not be particularly curious as to why a young woman was out alone, late at night, in the blackout. He dropped her at the front entrance of the hospital and, having collected his fare and a sixpenny tip, drove away.

Christine paused for a moment. Everything seemed quiet. There was nobody else about. She slipped down a little alley leading to a small yard at the side of the hospital. From here she could see across the canal to the warehouse on the opposite bank. As her eyes became accustomed to the gloom she could make out the shape of a barge, moored at the little wharf just in front of the warehouse. She knew that Max spent much of his time at that warehouse. Could the barge have some connection with the German agents? There was something odd about it! Surely it should not have had a tall thin mast rising from the little cabin at its stern? Canal barges never carried sails. Was this a radio mast? It was certainly rather suspicious. Christine wondered if she should get in touch with the local police. They would probably be willing enough to investigate but might want to confer with the intelligence services first. That would mean a delay. It was also quite likely that their arrival would cause a disturbance and this might alert any German agents in the warehouse or on the barge. If Max was being held prisoner the sudden arrival of the police could put his life at risk!

The thought of Max, perhaps helpless, and in the power of the Nazis decided her. She retraced her steps up the alley and out onto the main road. Here she turned in the direction of Fiveways junction. The blackout deterred most people from venturing out at nights and she saw nobody else. Christine knew that there was a door which led from the road down onto the canal towpath. When she reached it she found it was unfastened. She pushed it open gently and cautiously descended the worn steps which led down to the canal, moving as silently as she could and looking about her all the time. It was very quiet and very dark. When she reached the front wall of the warehouse she felt her way along the brickwork until she felt the edge of a doorway. She pushed but the door felt solid. Working her way forward she felt for the fastening. It was a large padlock. She could tell by it's gritty feel that it was rusty. As she became accustomed to the deep gloom she realised that this was the main entrance to the warehouse. Probing the lower edge of the door with her foot she felt the uneven roughness of overgrown grass and weeds. This door had not been used for a very long time. There must be some other way of getting into the building!

Standing in front of the disused main door, Christine paused to take stock of the situation. She looked at the barge. Now that she was quite close to it and she could see the outline of the mast more clearly; slim and even darker than the night sky. It was certainly not a normal feature of a canal barge. The more she looked the more certain she became that it was some sort of illicit radio mast, probably specially rigged up for tonight's sinister operation. She was now convinced that this must have already begun! To her right she could see the faint oily glitter of the canal and could just make out the square outline of the bridge which carried the main road over the waterway. To the left the canal ran straight for a few hundred yards, then it seemed to curve gently and disappear from view. In this direction she could see a faint red glimmer from a partially blacked out railway signal reflected on the surface of the water. She could hear the distant hiss of steam and guessed that there was a railway junction or shunting yard further along the canal. Immediately opposite was the dark outline of the Accident Hospital on the other side of the canal. It was very effectively blacked out and its bulk shut out the sky to the south.

Christine had to locate Max without being spotted herself. He might either be on the barge or in the warehouse, if indeed he was here at all. The warehouse was near at hand. Best to try and find a way in and investigate that first. By now her eyes were fully adjusted to the darkness and, looking along the front of the warehouse towards its far end, she thought she could just make out the faintest yellowy glow. She moved very carefully towards it, feeling the front of the building as she went. Eventually she came to another door. This was quite a small one, but the handle felt smooth, as though it was in frequent use. It turned easily. She opened the door very, very slowly and, summoning up her courage, stepped cautiously and silently through the doorway. Once inside she closed the door again. It had obviously been well lubricated and closed smoothly and almost noiselessly. Christine felt around her with the tips of her fingers starting at the edge of the doorway. She was in a small square lobby. She could feel a further door ahead of her and another to her right. At the bottom of the latter door a faint light was just discernible. This inner door must have been fairly efficiently sealed against the escape of light, she decided, but at the lower edge the seal was not quite perfect.

She paused for a full two minutes, her heart beating much faster than she would have liked. No sound was to be heard. She felt for the handle of the right hand door and turned it. As she opened the door light seemed to flood out, although once she entered the room, she saw that it was illuminated only by a single, small, rather grubby, unshaded electric light bulb. The room seemed to be a sort of office. It contained a big desk, littered with papers and folders. There were a few chairs and also a large cupboard. In a corner she saw a gas ring. Beside this was an empty saucepan, a mug and a half-empty bottle of milk. Thankfully the room was unoccupied. Christine gave an involuntary sigh of relief! She closed the door carefully and started to examine the room and its contents. She found that the mug contained an inch or so of rather strong smelling coffee. The mug felt quite cold and so did the saucepan. On the floor to one side of the desk she saw a sleeping bag. To her surprise this seemed to have been badly damaged. It had been cut into time and again and reduced to a series of strips of dusky red material. All that held these together was the zip fastener. Had someone been looking to see if anything important was concealed in the bag, she wondered? On the desk there was a telephone. Beside this she saw a pencil and a writing pad. She looked at the pad and saw what appeared to be a sort of mathematical table. The first column was made up of a series of number and letter combinations. In the next column, beside each number and letter combination, a time was written. The times started with 0305 and continued at one minute intervals. The third column was blank. There were twenty entries altogether in each of the first and second columns.

In what Christine took to be the front of the room there was a small window. It was very heavily blacked out but Christine guessed it was from here that the very faint suggestion of light which had first drawn her to this end of the building had come. The cupboard was on the far side of the window, beyond the desk. It was lying open and appeared to have been ransacked. The contents were in complete disarray. On the floor in front of it was scattered a jumble of men's clothes. There was also a strongly made attaché case. This was open - and empty. She saw that on the lowest shelf of the cupboard there was a partly used loaf of bread and some crockery. At one side of the shelf there was a cardboard box containing a few bits of cutlery, a packet of salt, a bag of sugar and a jar of jam. There was also a bottle of coffee essence. This was a quarter full. On impulse Christine undid the screw top and smelt the contents. There was a strong coffee smell but also a faint hint of something that was neither coffee nor chicory. She replaced the cap. There seemed to be nothing further to be learned from the contents of the cupboard and she looked around the room once more. On the wall facing the window there was a wash basin. Above it was a shelf and on this she saw a razor and shaving brush, a glass, a toothbrush and toothpaste. It looked as if somebody had been living in the room as well as using it as an office.

Christine now noticed a man's raincoat hanging on a hook on the back of the door. It looked somehow familiar. She examined it carefully and saw that, like an army trench coat, it had epaulettes at the shoulder. The button securing the epaulette on the left side was loose - held only by two or three strands of thread. Now she was certain that it was her contact who had been living in this room! She had noticed that loose button some weeks before when he had come into the tearoom at lunchtime one very wet day. She must be on the right track but if he was not here and had never turned up at the station, where on earth was he? Could he have been overpowered and imprisoned somewhere else in this big old warehouse or was he perhaps on the barge? She was now certain that he was being held against his will. She hoped with all her heart that he was still alive! Christine decided to search the warehouse first. Getting onto the barge without being seen might be difficult and dangerous. Anyway she was here and, as far as she could tell, there was nobody about to prevent her exploring the place. She noticed a small electric torch beside the remains of the sleeping bag and, deciding it might be useful, she slipped it into her pocket.

As Christine could see nothing more of interest in the office she went back into the lobby and closed the door, shutting out the light. She stood, silent, in the darkness, listening. After the lightness of the room her eyes took a while to adapt again. There was no sound of any sort. She felt around cautiously and located the second door. The handle turned easily and silently. She noticed a slight oiliness as she touched it and she wondered if somebody had lubricated it recently for some special reason. When she opened the door and stepped through she sensed that she was in somewhere very spacious. There was a slight smell of petrol. This part of the warehouse was not blacked out. In the gloom she could just make out that there was a row of windows along one wall. These windows lessened the darkness just enough to reveal numbers of large objects standing about on the warehouse floor. She went close to one of them and realised that it was a car. The place was full of cars! She felt her way past the one nearest to her and found that a passage had been left between some of the vehicles. Moving with great care she made her way along this alleyway, trying to avoid knocking her shins on car bumpers. It would have been much easier and quicker had she dared to use the torch!

When she reached the far wall of the warehouse she found herself at the foot of an iron staircase. She tested it and it felt perfectly secure. It would be very easy to make a noise going up those stairs! Christine slipped off her shoes and jammed them into her handbag. The knobbly surface of the metal steps was unpleasant to walk on in stocking feet but at least she was able to climb in complete silence. When she reached the floor above she sensed another vast empty space. She stepped cautiously forward. As she did so she could smell the dust rising from beneath her feet. She hoped it would not make her cough! It should be easy to tell if anyone had been here recently, though. She crouched down and, taking a small risk, shone the torch she had taken from the office around the floor close to the staircase. All that showed on the rough dust-covered wooden boards were her own footprints. She turned and, having hastily switched off the torch, started up the next flight of stairs. When she got to the top she found that there were no more stairs. This was the uppermost storey of the warehouse. Here too the floor was completely empty. The darkness was slightly less profound than on the lower floors. Christine, with increasing confidence, repeated her examination of the dusty floor near the top of the stairs. There were no footmarks. She shone the torch round briefly and was about to descend again when she saw that, close to the top of the stairs, there was a door on the outside wall of the building. It was a fire exit. The fastening was a metal bar which could easily be pushed to release the door from the inside. Christine detected a slight smell of oil mingled with the general background of dust. She felt the release bar and its mountings. There was an oiliness about the surface of the metal. Risking use of the torch once again she examined the door and saw that the hinges as well as the fastenings had been liberally oiled. Somebody must have wanted to use that door without making a noise!

It would be wise to explore further before investigating the barge, Christine thought. Quite possibly it was Max who used the stairs and emergency door when he wanted to slip out of the warehouse without being spotted. He might even have used it this evening on route for the station. Perhaps he had had an accident of some kind? Emergency escape routes of this sort often involved hazards like walking over roofs and down outside staircases. This warehouse was old and had probably not been maintained properly for years. Christine hesitated no longer. She pushed the bar. The door opened easily and silently. In case it should swing closed and trap her outside she took one of her shoes from her handbag and wedged it between the door and the lintel. Ahead of her was the flat roof of an adjoining building. In the darkness she could very easily have an accident herself. She would not be much use to Max with a sprained ankle or even a broken neck. She could easily miss her footing and fall three stories to the ground. Holding it as low as possible she shone the torch and saw duckboards leading away across the roof. They were old and had broken in places, however with discreet use of the torch, Christine made her careful way along the duckboard path. The duckboards led to the top of an outside fire escape staircase. It was made of cast iron and appeared to be in poorish repair. She could feel the handrail shake when she tried it. She was dubious of trusting herself to such an unsteady structure but she plucked up her courage and descended cautiously until she found herself, greatly to her relief, on firm ground.

She was in a narrow cobbled lane. It was pitch dark but she managed to feel her way along the high brick wall of the building whose roof she had just crossed. After fifty yards or so the lane bore to the right. She could now see that it joined the main road a short distance further on. There was no sign of anyone else and she decided that if Max had used this route he must have got as far as the main road without mishap. She would have to return the way she had come, close up the door she had wedged open, and set about investigating the barge. Her heart sank. She had tried to conceal it from herself up to now but she had a real dread of the barge and of the oily black canal, which was its habitat.

The cobbles were painful to walk on in bare feet and there were one or two puddles. The feet of her stockings were wet and she began to feel cold, and much less confident than she had when she had set out from the station. She was tempted to make her way out onto the main road, Bath Row, which she knew well. She could look for a policeman and ask his help. Then she reflected that, dishevelled and in stockinged feet, she would look a suspicious figure. At such a late hour the policeman would probably be pretty sceptical of her story. She might end up being taken in for questioning! There was nothing for it but to hobble back up the lane, over those awful cobbles again, then up the shaky fire escape and back over the rotting duckboards on the flat roof to the relative security of the warehouse.

The return journey did not actually seem as bad as Christine had expected. She retrieved the shoe she had used to wedge open the fire exit and closed the door as quietly as she could. Still in her stockinged feet she descended the iron staircase inside the warehouse till she got to the ground floor where the cars were stored. When she got to the bottom it suddenly struck her that the cars must have been brought in through some door which she had not yet located. Could that be the route her contact had used when he had set off for the station? The big door onto the wharf had obviously not been opened for ages and the entrance door beside the office was much too small for cars. Still in her damp stockings and carrying her shoes in her handbag she felt along the back wall, working away from the staircase. She reached a corner and, rounding it, soon felt the edge of a large door which must, she thought, be on the end of the warehouse, probably opening onto some yard connecting with the little lane she had just investigated. She shone the torch and saw that this was a large sliding door, quite wide enough for cars to negotiate. She could see tyre marks on the floor. She shone the torch on the fastenings and saw that the door was bolted and also secured by a large padlock - on the inside. Unless Max had had some accomplice to lock up after him, which seemed highly unlikely, he could not possibly have used this particular door as a route out of the warehouse. It seemed pretty certain now that he must be on the barge. Christine steeled herself to face what she had been dreading from the start. She knew it would be both difficult and risky to get on board.

By now the interior of the ground floor of the warehouse seemed almost familiar. It was not so difficult to find the way around now that she knew what to expect. Christine felt cold. She shivered a couple of times and guessed it was partly due to her fear of the unknown hazards of that dark, sinister-looking, barge. Cold wet feet did not help, though! It would be best to remove the damp stockings, dry her feet thoroughly and put her shoes on her bare feet. Once she had succeeded in getting onto the barge's deck she could remove the shoes again so that she would be able to move silently. Meanwhile, she would need her shoes to cross the wharf without injuring her feet on the rough surface or falling. She decided to go back to the office. It had been completely deserted and the light and chair would make the job a lot easier. She could even use Max's towel to dry her feet. She had seen it hanging near the sink. The idea of using something belonging to him was rather comforting.

The office door opened as smoothly as it had done before. Christine slipped in and closed it gently. She crossed to the sink, lifted the towel and, pulling a chair away from the desk to give herself room, she sat down and started to remove her stockings. She took off the right one first, from force of habit, and dropped it, limp and wet on the floor. Then, as she started to unfasten the button of the left stocking suspender, she thought she felt a slight draught. She looked up, puzzled, but saw nothing amiss. The draught, if there ever had been one, had gone. Perhaps it was her nerves! She knew she was strung up by all that had happened since Haw-Haw's broadcast. It had been unusual, to say the least, and up to the present her activities had had no satisfactory result. She returned to the job in hand and started to peel the damp stocking from her left leg. As she did so a large hand was placed firmly across her mouth. At the same moment a powerful arm gripped her tightly round the waist, pinning her rigidly to the chair! She desperately wanted to scream but even if she had not been so effectively gagged she knew that no sound would come. Her assailant had been so silent that she had been taken completely by surprise. He now spoke in a low harsh voice. "If you remain silent and don't struggle I will see that no harm comes to you."

Despite her horror Christine was intrigued. For a start she was surprised at her captor bothering to reassure her when she was so completely in his power. More puzzling still, she was sure she had heard that voice before - and not long ago either! "I should gag you and tie your hands behind your back, but if you are sensible you can save us both a lot of trouble." He spoke with a very correct and neutral accent. His English seemed perfect, yet she wondered? She knew the warehouse was the headquarters of the spy ring. This man must, of course, be one of them. He must be German. That would explain his English, which was almost too good for a native speaker. The man continued. "Nobody is likely to hear if you scream when I take my hand away. Now, do I have to apply a gag and secure your wrists or will you promise to co-operate? I hope you will. Screaming and struggling upset my equanimity - and this is most disagreeable for me." There was no doubting the menace in his voice. "Once you have given me your word we shall go to the barge moored outside there and join my colleagues. We will have to detain you for a while but if you co-operate with me no harm will come to you. Please do not attempt to struggle as we proceed to the barge. It would be very unpleasant for you and me to end up in that cold and very dirty canal!"

It struck her as ironic that she, who had been agonising about how to get on board the barge, was now to be taken there without any effort on her part. Perhaps she would find Max at last! She would not be of much use to him, though! Probably they would both be held prisoner. What their ultimate fate would be she dared not think. For a moment she contemplated trying to escape on the way across the wharf but then she realised that the man who had caught her so completely unawares would be more than capable of overpowering her. It would be best not to antagonise him. In any case, despite her fear, she was curious to see what was concealed on that dark hulk! She must keep alert and watchful. Perhaps there might still be a chance of getting away and summoning help. If she could get as far as the Accident Hospital, where she was well known, the staff would surely believe her story and act on it. With real luck she and Max might even be able to escape together and perhaps foil whatever plan it was that these German agents were hatching!

Chapter 14

The Inspector's mind was blurred but it came to him that he really should not be lying down on a settee at this time. He was supposed to be doing something important. He could not quite recall exactly what it was, but he was sure that it was important. The room he was lying in seemed peculiar, too, long and narrow and with such a low ceiling! He felt very sleepy and rather cold. This puzzled him because he was fully dressed and the air in the room did not feel particularly chilly. Then he realised that a conversation was going on at the other end of the room - an argument really. He could not see the speakers without moving, and he could not summon up sufficient energy to sit up and look at them. Instead he tried to listen. "You will be guided by me in this." The voice was sharp - dictatorial. "I don't like it at all," replied a deeper, worried, unhappy voice. "To put a drug in Mr Max's coffee was a wrong thing to do, let alone dragging him over here without his even being aware of what was happening." "We dare not take a risk on his loyalty," said the sharp voiced speaker. "If he is the man we have supposed him to be, no great harm has been done. The operation will proceed according to plan. I shall take over the role he had intended for himself. When he recovers I shall tell him that he was taken ill at the critical time and that, by good fortune, I happened to return to check a detail about my target and, finding him incapacitated, I took temporary charge until he was fit. I have a very reliable deputy on my team who will automatically take charge in my absence. If, on the other hand, it turns out that he is a traitor, as I now strongly suspect, then we have saved the whole operation from being wrecked and - If he IS a traitor - that would undoubtedly be his objective. In either event you personally have neither responsibility nor blame. You will merely have carried out my instructions." The other man sighed deeply but made no comment. At that point the Inspector lapsed once more into a deep sleep.

When he next awoke the Inspector heard a hoarse, anxious, whisper from the man with the deep voice. "Riddle, there's somebody coming down the steps onto the quay!" Straining his ears, Inspector Maxwell caught the sound of feet descending stone steps. The footsteps were unhurried and sounded quite leisurely. The sound changed as the footsteps reached the bottom of the flight of steps and the walker moved onto the level surface of the quay. All of a sudden the light in this odd room went out and there was the sound of a curtain being opened. Evidently the two men were looking out into the darkness; trying to see who might be approaching. The footsteps got nearer and then there came a knock, firm but discreet. "Go out and investigate," said the sharp voice. "Tell nothing and get rid of whoever is there as quickly as you can. "His voice sounded sharper than ever and very tense. Maxwell heard the sound of a door opening and then closing again. There was a muffled conversation outside. Maxwell could make out nothing of what was being said. By now he felt a little less drowsy. Very cautiously he lifted his wickedly aching head. At once he realised where he was. This was the cabin of a canal barge. He knew that he had been in this particular cabin before! In fact he had once eaten a meal in it! The "settee" on which he was lying was really a bunk near the front of the cabin. The deep voiced man must be Barnes! He should have recognised that voice from the start!

Maxwell heard the door open again. There was the sound of heavy feet; then the door was closed once more. The curtain was drawn and the light came on again. At the far end of the cabin he could see three men standing close to the door. One of them was Riddle the Gestapo man - he of the sharp tense voice. He recognised a very anxious looking Barnes. The third man seemed vaguely familiar, but Max could not place him. Now that the light was on again he lay completely flat and inert, pretending to be in a deep sleep, although, fortunately, none of the three seemed in the least interested in him at present. The worried Barnes spoke. "Mr Riddle, I thought it best to bring this gentleman inside. He asked for me by name and seemed to know all about me and my barge." When he replied, Riddle's voice was low and menacing. He was clearly very angry as well as tense. "Will you please explain who you are and what you want of Mr Barnes at this time of night. Mr Barnes and I are engaged on important private business. We have no wish to be interrupted." "Certainly," replied the newcomer, "but first perhaps Mr Barnes will confirm that you are a colleague of his and engaged on the same sort of work." "Mr Riddle and I have been associated for a long time," replied Barnes, "anything you want to tell me you can safely tell to Mr Riddle."

"Very well," replied the newcomer. By now Maxwell, lying still and quiet on the bunk, was feeling stronger and rather clearer in his mind, despite his throbbing head. The stranger continued, "My code name is Max. I was dropped by parachute some six months ago. Unfortunately the plane that brought me to England was attacked by a night-fighter. Our pilot took evasive action and I was thrown through the hatch and so missed my intended landing-place. As a result I was captured almost immediately. I have been imprisoned until this morning, when an opportunity arose and I managed to escape. I had been well briefed before leaving Germany and, as I have had little else to think about during the past six months, I remembered the details of my instructions very clearly. It was quite easy to locate the warehouse, opposite to which your barge is moored. When I saw the barge, I decided to contact Mr Barnes. I knew he was responsible for radio communications with the Kriegsmarine." He turned towards Barnes. "I hope, Mr Barnes, that you will now put me in touch with Mr Pattenson. I should have contacted him six months ago had I not been captured. Now that I am free it is my wish to help with his work in any way that I can. By the way, you need have no fear that I have been followed here. I have considerable experience of such matters and have covered my tracks in such a way as to make it impossible for me to be traced."

Riddle whistled softly through his teeth. Maxwell, who knew him well by now, guessed that Riddle's natural caution was struggling with his excitement at this apparent confirmation of his own suspicions. Maxwell knew only too well that he had been the object of Riddle's malign interest in recent weeks. He now realised, too late, that Riddle was more formidable and much more ruthless than he, Maxwell, had realised. How else could it be that he was lying on this bunk, as Riddle's prisoner, recovering from a heavy dose of some powerful sleeping drug? Caution and Gestapo training seemed to win the struggle in Riddle's mind - at least for the time being! Riddle looked towards the man on the bunk. He appeared to be completely inert: his breathing was slow and shallow, his face was pale, his eyes closed. Satisfied, Riddle turned to the new arrival and said, with a slight sneer, "That is a remarkable story, if I may say so! Have you any way of confirming that you are who you say you are?" The other man answered promptly and confidently. "This barge," he said, "is the communications unit for the German naval intelligence centre in Britain, which is located in Birmingham. Mr Pattenson is in charge of that unit. My mission was to join forces with him and set up Operation Chainbreak - by direct order of the Fuehrer. You, Riddle have been Mr Pattenson's managing clerk in the firm of Pattenson and Co., solicitors, for about ten years. You have also, at the same time, been his assistant in the intelligence service of the Reich. In 1914 you joined the Imperial German navy. You served in U-boats throughout that war. Does that satisfy you as to my authenticity?"

Inspector Maxwell sensed that Riddle was both impressed and pleased. Riddle's personal suspicions of Maxwell's bona fides would be confirmed if this new man turned out to be the real agent - the man that Pattenson and Riddle had been expecting six months ago! Maxwell recalled that ever since Riddle had related his evidence against Pattenson to him and he, Maxwell, had declined to take any immediate action against Pattenson, Riddle's attitude towards him had changed. Soon after that he had become aware that Riddle had started to watch him. He remembered the occasion when Riddle had followed him to the station. Riddle had tried and failed to get onto a train that Maxwell had just caught by the skin of his teeth! That had happened when Maxwell had gone to meet Avon, head of Air Intelligence's counter espionage unit. The two of them had had an impromptu discussion in the privacy of an otherwise empty first class compartment on the train from Birmingham to Chester. If Riddle had been able to get on board the train and had been able to eavesdrop, that meeting might have led to Maxwell's being unmasked weeks ago - with disastrous results for the British intelligence services.

It seemed that Riddle was still not entirely satisfied with the newcomer's story. "If what you say is correct," he asked, "how is it that the Britisher who took your place was able to locate our headquarters here so easily after you were captured? I have thoroughly examined the case that man," here he nodded towards the inert Maxwell, "brought with him when he first arrived here. There was nothing in it to indicate where our headquarters are situated." There was a pause, then Maxwell heard the other man reply. "That is indeed extraordinary. How he located your headquarters is a total mystery. You are quite correct about the case. The greatest care was taken to ensure that nothing in the case could betray your group if it fell into the hands of the British. The case contained much detailed information about radio-location stations and also a dummy explosive pack for demonstration purposes, but nothing else. It was thought that, if captured, the contents of the case might warn the British of an intended attack on their radio-location stations but would give them no hint of any of our other activities. Owing to the night-fighter attack I was thrown from the plane prematurely and without the case. A little while later that night the plane, which had been badly damaged in the attack, crashed not far from where I had landed. I went to retrieve the case, but found that someone else had taken it from the wrecked aircraft before I arrived. That person was trying to open it when I reached the scene. I was about to take the case from him - I had an automatic pistol with me - when I was attacked and overpowered by another man who had crept up behind me. Then I was taken away by car to a house where I was questioned. You will have to take my word for it that I remained completely silent. Eventually I was taken away by the British military police. I have been in one of their prisons ever since. This morning the vehicle in which they were transferring me to a different place was involved in a road accident and I escaped. While in captivity I have been questioned many times but have always refused to say anything at all. It appears that the British do not use physical means to extract information from uncooperative prisoners!"

Maxwell listened intently. He wanted to gauge Riddle's reaction to this account which, from his own knowledge, he realised, was probably entirely true. By now his headache was less severe and his brain was clearing a bit. He could recall that he should have gone to New Street station this evening. He should, in fact, be on his way at this moment to RAF Hamden Down! There was certainly no chance of managing that in present circumstances! The personnel there would just have to look after their station by themselves. Here on the barge was a much more immediate problem. Riddle had clearly taken charge. He would be receiving the messages from the various Chainbreak sabotage teams and would, before long, be passing that information on to Berlin. He and this new man and Barnes were all highly dangerous enemy agents. Somehow Maxwell would have to see to it that they did not escape. The net would close around the other German agents within hours. Equally, it was important that they did not pass on any useful information to Berlin. Soon every German secret agent in Britain should be "in the bag", together with a few other undesirables as well! It would be better if the Nazi

Intelligence Headquarters did not get to know anything of this! But how he could possibly overpower these three able-bodied men, at least one of whom was likely to be armed? He had no idea - yet! He thought things over and decided that his only advantage was that they thought he was still unconscious. Surprise, at least, would be on his side.

Riddle, who had listened to the story of the parachute landing, capture and eventual escape in silence, at first made no response. There was a pause during which Maxwell could hear the clock ticking on the bulkhead at the far end of the cabin and the gentle lapping of water against the side of the barge. Suddenly Riddle spoke. His voice was harsh and intense. Maxwell could sense Riddle's suppressed excitement. "I now believe that you are indeed the man sent to us from Berlin and that that man on the bunk over there is a British agent who has treacherously usurped your role. He will be dealt with shortly but first we have more urgent matters to occupy us. At present Mr Pattenson is with one of the sabotage units. There is no way of contacting him now. It is close to zero hour. He and his team will already be moving into position, ready to attack their target. I request therefore that you will join Mr Barnes and myself here at the centre of operations." The newcomer murmured his agreement. "We shall be glad of your assistance," continued Riddle. "By 3am one of us will have to be in the warehouse office to await telephone calls from the teams. They have been told they must adhere to a very precise timetable. This is so that as soon as one call is over the line is immediately clear for the next. I myself will take charge of the phone at that stage. I am familiar with both the timetable and the coded messages which will be coming in. I would like to have the phone manned well before 3am, however, in case of any unexpected call. Will you take on that job? From 3am on it will be very useful to have you with me in the office so that, using you as a messenger, I can maintain contact with Barnes. He will, of course, be unable to leave his post at the radio here on the barge.

The three men seemed to have completely forgotten Inspector Maxwell's existence for the present. He heard the opening of a cupboard and the sound of crockery and cutlery being set out. Shortly afterwards there was a faint aroma of cheese. Soon he heard the cheerful noise of a briskly boiling kettle followed by the distinctive smell of coffee. Riddle seemed to have relaxed all at once. He had evidently made his decision about the man who claimed to have escaped from prison that morning. He was evidently happy with that decision. "Well done, Barnes," Maxwell heard him say. "It's an excellent idea for us to have something to eat and drink while we are waiting to go into action. It will be a long night. It is essential that we are all fully alert throughout." Then he seemingly turned to the newcomer. "I suppose we had better call you "Max" as that was your designated code name. It will be an effort though. We have been using the same name for that creature lying drugged on the bunk over there. He will not get away with the deception lightly! Even though you have been out of touch with events for many months you may guess that by this time tomorrow the German invasion fleet will probably be crossing the Channel! In a few weeks most of Britain will be under German control. We shall have a few scores to settle then!"

There was no more conversation for a while, but the sound of eating and drinking continued. Eventually Maxwell heard Barnes' voice, still a little unhappy, he thought. "Mr Riddle time is getting on. I would like to make a final check on the extended aerial and then clear everything in here away ready for transmitting our "all clear" message for the Luftwaffe when the phone calls are in. I think also that it will be very important for us to continue in contact with Berlin after that. Then we will be able to assist once the invasion begins." "Agreed," said Riddle shortly. Then he addressed the other man at the table. "Barnes will attend to things here on the barge. You would do well to go over to the warehouse now to familiarise yourself with the surroundings and make sure that the phone is clear and working. We must be certain that everything in the office is ready for

3am when the phone messages will start to come in. It will also be a chance for you to get your bearings generally." There was the sound of chairs being pushed back and of crockery being collected up. All this time Maxwell lay absolutely still, eyes closed and breathing as slowly and quietly as he could. He heard the sound of Barnes and the newcomer leaving the cabin and then the tread of Barnes' footsteps on the roof above. "The aerial is in order," Barnes reported on his return. "Right," replied Riddle, "I have something to do before we proceed." Suddenly Maxwell heard someone moving towards him. Next moment he was seized by the hair and shaken violently. With a supreme effort he managed to remain flaccid and to give no indication of the pain he felt. His head was dropped unceremoniously back onto the bunk and he heard Riddle say, with a laugh, "I must have given him a good dose of that stuff I put in his coffee. He's still flat out. He'll give us no trouble. We can deal with him properly later on." Shortly afterwards there came the noise of Barnes clearing the table of the remains of the meal. Then he heard a cupboard being opened and some sort of equipment being moved about. Riddle's voice, now sharp and anxious enquired, "Is it all in order? I want no last minute hitches!"

Despite, or perhaps because of, the shaking he had received Maxwell's thoughts were becoming much more coherent. If he was to have any chance at all of foiling these three enemy agents who were holding him his only hope was to use surprise to get the better of them! He could see no other possible way of overpowering them. They were all fit active men. Riddle was almost certain to have a pistol. Barnes never carried a weapon and the new man wouldn't have a gun if he had only just escaped from a military prison. The thought of Riddle's gun reminded him that his own automatic pistol should be slung under his left armpit. By squeezing his left arm very cautiously against his side he discovered that it was no longer there! It really seemed very unlikely that he would be able to capture the enemy agents and prevent them from sending messages to Germany! He remembered that he and Avon had agreed some time ago that it would be best to keep enemy headquarters in Berlin guessing on the night of Operation Chainbreak. According to plan, of course, both Pattenson and Riddle should, by now, have been far away at the sites they had been detailed to sabotage. Earlier in the day Maxwell had instructed Barnes not to communicate with Berlin until given the order to do so by Maxwell personally. As, by 3am, Maxwell had intended to be at Hamden Down, arresting Hector Sedler and his accomplices, Barnes would never have received that order! The enemy would never have known whether the attacks on the radio-location sites had succeeded or failed or whether there had simply been a breakdown of the radio-communication. Uncertainty was, Avon and Maxwell had thought, likely to give the enemy more problems than any definite information - whatever that might be! As these thoughts flitted through his head, Maxwell reflected that Riddle and the others imagined him to be ignorant of what they were about and that they believed him to be physically helpless. Their ignorance was his sole advantage.

Chapter 15

Maxwell was surprised to hear footsteps approaching along the wharf within minutes of von Straussen's departure. Even more surprisingly, there seemed to be two people approaching! Barnes, busy assembling his rather complex radio equipment, did not appear to notice the approaching footsteps. Next moment came the sound of the cabin door being opened. He heard Riddle exclaim, "What the hell's going on? Who is this young woman? What on earth is she doing here?". "I chanced upon this young lady changing her stockings in the warehouse office," said von Straussen, deliberately calm - almost languid. Turning to the girl he said, "Kindly sit on that bunk over there, opposite the one that's already occupied, and prepare to explain to us what you were doing in our warehouse!" Maxwell realised at once that this totally unexpected development might give him the only chance he was likely to have of turning the tables on his captors. He guessed immediately that the young woman must be his faithful "contact", Christine. For a moment he was thrilled. Here was a staunch, quick-witted and reliable ally! A moment later, however, he felt a sinking sensation in the pit of his stomach. How appalling that she had been brought into such a hideously dangerous situation - and all because he had been fool enough to allow himself to be drugged! These thoughts passed through his head in quick succession. Meanwhile his body was already carrying out the plan he had thought up minutes earlier. Suddenly he leapt to his feet. He would make a dive straight for Riddle's weapon. Once that was in his hand he would be master of the situation!

Unfortunately Maxwell had gravely underestimated the power of the drug that had been added to the bottle of "Camp" coffee he had used to make his hot drink just prior to setting off for the station. His evening cup of coffee was a habit that his associates knew well - too well! The sudden leap from prolonged recumbence to an upright position triggered an immediate attack of the most horrible vertigo! He lost all perception of where he was in space. The cabin spun crazily. Its occupants whirled around him in a frantic dance. Christine, watching in horror, saw him sway. Then, with a supreme effort, he lurched in the vague direction of

Riddle. It was hopeless. Riddle whipped out his pistol in an instant. In another he had fired. Maxwell slumped back, half on the bunk, half on the floor, blood spurting from a long deep wound on the side of his head. Christine instinctively started forwards to help him. She was restrained by Barnes, who happened to be closest to her. She saw Riddle aim the pistol at Maxwell again. She cried out in horror, but at the same moment she heard a sharp order in harsh German. Riddle instinctively lowered his pistol and looked round in astonishment. It was the newcomer, Maximillian von Straussen, the man who had captured Christine only a few minutes earlier, who had spoken. Riddle addressed him in an indignant, protesting tone. "We must deal at once with this man", he said. "He has betrayed us and has now tried to attack me. I intend to shoot this young woman also. She has been caught red-handed - spying on us." "You will do no such thing," came the response in a firm authoritative voice. We are Germans - civilised people - not barbarians. We don't shoot wounded men, nor prisoners. In any case I gave this young lady my word that if she came to the barge without struggling she would come to no harm." He signed to Barnes to release Christine. She glanced at Riddle. He was white with fury. Nevertheless, the instinct to obey the orders of a superior officer, instilled into him from his very first days as a boy-entrant in the Imperial German navy, was so powerful that he made no further protest.

Maximillian von Straussen turned to Barnes. "Do you have a first aid box on board," he asked. Barnes, opening a drawer, produced a small black metal box with a grubby red cross on the lid. "Can you attend to your colleague?" Von Straussen asked Christine in a not unkindly voice. She nodded and then asked, "Will one of you help me get him up onto the bunk so that I can see to him properly." Von Straussen turned to Barnes, who lifted Maxwell onto the bunk with ease and then straightened out his inert body and put a pillow under his head. Riddle watched in silence, his pistol still in his hand, as if he was expecting some further attack from the now unconscious man or the young woman attending him! At last he spoke, his voice tinged with sarcasm as he addressed von Straussen. "As you are so concerned about the welfare of our enemies I suggest that you stay here to guard them! Barnes and I have serious work to do," he added with a sneer. He turned to Barnes. "Please continue your preparation of the radio equipment, and make sure," he said, with a hint of menace, "That everything is in perfect order by 3.30am. - despite the interruptions to which we have been subjected." He seemed to Christine to be regaining his confidence and recovering from the shock of von Straussen's outburst. He turned to the latter. "Kindly take care that these people do not escape nor interfere any further in our work on behalf of the Third Reich! May I remind you that tonight is the climax of six months of hard work and preparation - which you have missed due to your capture! I will now go back to the warehouse to prepare for the final phase of Operation Chainbreak. Heil Hitler!" he gave an attenuated Nazi salute, cramped by the low cabin roof, turned on his heel and left. The others listened in silence to his footsteps tramping across the wharf towards the warehouse.

After Riddle's departure there was an unspoken sense of relief in the little cabin which, to Christine, seemed almost physical. Immediately she was on her knees beside Ian Maxwell as he lay inert on the low bunk. She felt his pulse. It was rather slow, but quite strong. His airway was clear and, though shallow, his breathing was regular. She examined the head wound. It was deep and long and bleeding freely. She heard Von Straussen say, "Mr Barnes, we don't want any more unexpected visitors. Do you think you could fix the door at the top of those steps down onto the wharf so that it can't be opened from the other side." "Easy!" said Barnes, "There are good strong bolts. They haven't been used lately but they're still in good order. I happened to notice that a few days ago." Christine suddenly interrupted. "Before Mr Barnes goes anywhere, can I have a bowl of water that has been boiled and some scissors." The two men seemed surprised by her firm request but made no objection. Barnes got a bowl and filled it with water from the kettle and produced a large pair of scissors from a cupboard. Christine thanked him briefly. After that she paid the two men no further attention. Carefully she cut her patient's hair away for about two inches all-round the gaping head wound. Remembering her Red Cross training, she cleaned the skin around the wound and cut away the hair. Then she unfolded a clean handkerchief to use as a dressing on the wound itself. Her instructor had explained to the class that the inside part of a handkerchief that has been ironed and then folded is likely to be as near sterile as anything that one might hope to have available in an emergency. The bleeding from the wound edges eased and she gently felt the wound through the handkerchief. It was shallowest at the front and deepest at the back, where she could feel something hard. Probably bone, she thought, or perhaps the bullet itself. It might be lodged against the skull. She decided to dress the wound. This would help to stop any further bleeding and perhaps keep germs out. There must be no pressure though on the place where the bone was projecting or the bullet lodged. Christine opened Barnes' first aid box. There were a number of little Elastoplast dressings and a roll of white adhesive tape: no use in the present situation! Then she found some paper packets. One of these contained a large piece of lint. She rolled this carefully to make a ring pad and then, using a decent sized cotton bandage that she found in the bottom of the box, she gently but firmly secured her dressing in place. She knew well that this man needed the attention of a surgeon as soon as possible but, for now, he was breathing regularly, had a good pulse and should not lose much more blood.

While she was at work on Ian Maxwell's wound, apparently oblivious of her surroundings, Christine was actually listening carefully to see if she could learn anything useful. Once Barnes had produced the things she needed, she heard von Straussen say to him, "Better go up now and bolt that door. Be careful, though. We don't want our trigger-happy colleague loosing off at you!" For the first time that evening Barnes gave a little laugh. "Don't worry. I'll take no chances. I know Mr Riddle too well. Once he gets the bit between his teeth he'll stop at nothing. I've sometimes thought there's a streak of madness about him!" Christine heard the door open and close very softly. She heard von Straussen who, she guessed must be pretty tired, pull over a chair.

He sat himself down stationed where he could watch both the cabin door and his prisoners. Christine heard him yawn. She knew she had to try and keep on good terms with him if there was to be any hope of getting surgical help for Ian Maxwell. "Thank you for stopping that fanatic killing this poor chap and me," she said. "I gave my word, "replied Von Straussen, "That you would come to no harm if you came over to the barge quietly. You kept your part of the bargain and I always keep my word. Nothing less would be expected of me as a

German officer." "In which service are you an officer?" Christine enquired innocently. Her weary captor was off his guard in the cosy little cabin alone, but for the unconscious Maxwell, with this self-possessed young woman. He realised suddenly that she had been the pleasant waitress who had served his evening meal. He remembered admiring her as she walked down the street at the end of her day's work. In any case what harm could she do now? Operation Chainbreak would be under way within the hour. Nothing could stop it now! "I have the honour to serve in the Luftwaffe," he replied. Then he gave a little laugh. "I rather think that the man you are attending to so assiduously helped to capture me some months ago! I bear him no personal malice. I should have done exactly the same had our positions been reversed. Curiously our paths crossed briefly in the last war also. On that occasion, too, I was a prisoner. However I managed to escape much more quickly that time!"

There was a slight movement and the door opened softly. Barnes re-entered. "The gate at the top of the steps is securely bolted now. Anyone trying to get down to the canal from the road will have quite a job to break it open! The noise should give us a bit of warning! Anyway, I'd better get that radio finally tuned in and ready to transmit at 3.30am. Berlin should be sending out the tuning signal by now so that I can find the right wavelength."

He crossed the little cabin, sat down, and was soon busy with his equipment. Christine decided to try and continue her conversation with von Straussen. She felt she had made a good start. If she encouraged him he might give something useful away. "What about moving my patient?" she asked suddenly. "He needs to have proper surgical treatment as soon as possible. There's a hospital just the other side of the canal. He ought to be taken there without delay!" "I am afraid that will not be possible for some time," was the reply. "We are in the middle of a most delicate espionage operation which is vital to my country's interests. You will have to do the best you can for him for the next few hours. After all, if he had been wounded on a battlefield he would probably have to wait much longer than that to get to a field hospital! What is happening here at the moment is really the opening part of a great battle which is just about to begin." This confirmed Christine's suspicion that she had stumbled on some major enemy operation. This German officer was being surprisingly reasonable. When he had caught her in the warehouse office he had seemed very sinister. She had been very afraid of him then but now he was mellowing. If she could talk him round there might be a slim chance she could slip away and get help to put a stop to whatever these men were up to. "Would you not allow me to go over to the hospital and get some expert advice on how to deal with this severe head injury?" she enquired. Von Straussen laughed, not unpleasantly. He had taken a liking to this cool, good-looking young woman. "You must think me very innocent. I guess you must be connected with the British security services yourself. Why else would somebody like you be exploring an old warehouse late at night. Incidentally, the way you were using that torch was a flagrant breach of the blackout regulations! Lucky for you it was I who noticed the light and not some nosey air raid warden! No, in answer to your question. I am afraid that your patient must wait here until our work is done!"

Barnes, who had been absorbed in tuning his elaborate radio equipment, interrupted the silence which had followed. "What time do you make it, sir?" he asked von Straussen. "I don't want to take my eye off these dials." "3.25am," came the reply. "Riddle should be over in five minutes. Are you ready to transmit?" "Yes, everything seems to be working perfectly," Barnes confirmed. Christine realised that there was no chance of her being able to stop what was going on - unless? - she had a sudden thought. It would be suicidal, but it was just possible that she might be able to wreck their transmitter at the vital moment! In her possession were the large, rather clumsy, scissors that Barnes had given her to trim Ian's hair around the head wound. If she moved very fast and very suddenly she might just do it! Their enemies would most probably kill both Ian and herself afterwards, but she realised it was absolutely vital to stop this "Operation Chainbreak", even though she knew little about its objective. As she looked surreptitiously around, trying to figure out the best way of sabotaging the radio equipment, the cabin door opened and Riddle entered. Christine looked round. Riddle was deathly pale. "Something terrible has gone wrong," he said, in a voice charged with emotion. Von Straussen looked at him with cool appraisal. Barnes never took his eyes off the dials he was watching. "Well?" said von Straussen. "Only one of our observers has made contact. Hamden Down is out of action, in accordance with our plan, but there has not been a single message from any other site. I believe that traitor over there has wrecked everything, though how he's done it I can't understand." His right hand started to move towards his left armpit - for the pistol concealed in its holster there. "Don't be a fool," said von Straussen sharply. "We need cool heads. This is no time for emotional revenge. It is possible that the co-ordination of the operation has gone wrong in some way. We must give the observers a little more time. Go back at once. First ensure that the phone is still working properly. After that wait for a further fifteen minutes and then report to me." Christine was astonished at the way in which this man, the newcomer to the group, had instinctively taken charge at the moment of crisis.

Riddle flung out of the cabin without another word and disappeared into the night. When he had gone von Straussen turned to Barnes and said, "Well Mr Barnes, what do you make of all this. You've worked for German Intelligence longer than any of us." Barnes did not look up but remained intent on his control panel. There was a pause before he replied. Christine could almost hear him thinking. Eventually he said, "The man we called Max, who is lying over there, told me not to contact Berlin, whatever happened, until he gave the word. If he's on the other side, as Mr Riddle seems convinced - and your story bears that out - we probably ought to do the opposite to what he said. If you want my opinion, sir, I think we should signal Berlin that the operation has failed!" "Right," replied Von Straussen. "I will go over to the warehouse for a final check in case there has been any further development. If there has been none we will do as you say. I agree with your assessment. In view of what you say about your instructions from the impostor there, notifying Berlin that the operation has failed seems the logical thing to do." He looked at Christine and Ian Maxwell, then turned back to Barnes. "I don't think these two will give you any trouble." Von Straussen then left the cabin and soon Christine heard his footsteps receding across the wharf.

Christine tried to weigh up the situation. Was it worth trying to stop a signal of failure being transmitted?

Barnes looked very strong and could easily stop her getting at the radio. Unless there was some sort of distraction she wouldn't have a chance! She listened to the hissing and bleeping noises escaping from Barnes' headphones into the silent cabin and covertly studied the apparatus he was using. It had been designed to slide out from a concealed recess in the wall of the cabin. She realised that there was unlikely to be mains electricity on the boat. The cabin was lit by a powerful paraffin lamp - the type with a mantle. It glowed with an intense white light and gave pretty good illumination. She could see the layout of the radio quite well. There were valves glowing on a panel and a number of dials and several control knobs which Barnes was constantly adjusting. She remembered the radio set at her parents' home: a simple domestic wireless receiver, but of good quality and fairly modern. It worked off a battery but, she recalled, it also needed an accumulator which had to be charged regularly. Barnes' was a much more elaborate apparatus. It must have a power source. Christine saw that there were two electric wires running from the side of the equipment back into the depths of the cabin wall. One was thick and one quite thin. The batteries or accumulators or whatever supplied the power must be concealed in the space between the cabin wall and the hull of the barge. If there was a chance she would try to cut the smaller wire. She guessed that would be well within the capability of her scissors. It might actually be quite easy provided nobody was paying attention to her at the time.

Suddenly there was an outburst of loud hammering - not far away! A stern voice shouted, "Police here! Unfasten this gate at once!" Barnes started up. Then Christine heard the sound of running footsteps. A moment later the cabin door was flung open. "The police are trying to break down that gate and get onto the wharf," called von Straussen. As he entered the cabin he added in the slightly sardonic manner, which never quite deserted him even at moments of crisis, "I am particularly anxious not to meet them! Have you any suggestions?" Barnes wasted no time. "If we run along the tow path in the opposite direction to the gate we will get to the railway shunting yard. It's only about quarter of a mile away. A mixed goods train usually leaves there for the north about this time. We might just have a chance of escaping if we hide on one of the wagons. I have a sister in Cheshire who could help us after that. I'll get that message off to Berlin, then we must go. You collect Mr Riddle." Barnes turned to the radio transmitter and tapped out his brief coded message. In his haste he did not notice that, while he and von Straussen were hurriedly planning their escape, Christine had quietly cut the smaller of the two wires leading to his set.

The noise outside increased. Christine could hear repeated heavy blows as the bolted door leading from the road down onto the wharf was attacked resolutely with some heavy tool. She heard von Straussen's voice, urgent and exasperated. He was calling to Riddle. "For heaven's sake, man! Never mind going back to shoot the girl and the prisoner now. Our first duty is to escape. We must continue our work from somewhere else. By now we may be the only German agents in England still free!" Riddle seemed to completely ignore the urging of his colleague. She could hear his footsteps getting nearer and nearer the barge. He must be coming back to finish them off after all! Suddenly there was a splintering crash as the door started to give way under the assault of the policemen out on the roadway. She heard a final protesting shout from Von Straussen followed by a curse from Barnes, then the sound of running footsteps which got rapidly fainter as the two men made their escape. Riddle's footsteps, however, came nearer and nearer, horribly menacing, as he got closer to the barge. He seemed completely oblivious to the risk of capture. Christine ran to the cabin door, bolted it, and jammed the table against it.

Ian Maxwell opened his eyes. It was daylight. His head felt heavy and swollen and ached like the devil. Then he saw that he was not alone. Somebody with brown eyes was watching him intently. He knew immediately who it was. He reached out his right hand. He felt Christine's fingertips gently touch his own. They grasped hands, lightly at first, then firmly and confidently. They were silent and content. Five minutes later there was a knock at the door of the little hospital room. A nurse entered. She was followed by a man with his left arm in a sling. Group Captain Avon regarded them with a slightly quizzical air. "What are you two up to now?" he asked. "Don't you think you've given me enough trouble and anxiety already?" Christine jumped up. "How are you, sir?" she asked. "Is your arm going to be all right?" She pulled her now vacant chair forward. "Please sit down. You must be exhausted after all that happened last night - and ending up in the operating room, too, while they dealt with to your injured arm!"

The Group Captain accepted the proffered chair gratefully. He steadied himself by resting his uninjured right hand on the locker beside the bed and then lowered himself cautiously into the seat. "Thank you, Christine," he said. "By the way after our adventures last night I hope you don't mind me calling you by your Christian name. Officially though, as of this morning, I should be addressing you as Sergeant. You've had the home front's equivalent of promotion in the field!" Ian Maxwell was, by now, beginning to feel better. He was desperately anxious to know what had happened in the previous twelve hours or so. He could remember absolutely nothing! He looked at his senior officer, now sitting back in the chair, and said, "I owe you and Christine a profound apology, sir. I am afraid I must have caused you both a great deal of grief. Has my being out of action at the crucial time wrecked our whole operation?"

Avon smiled. "Thankfully we have not done at all badly. The saboteurs, except for Hector Sedler, who is dead, and his young woman accomplice, who has disappeared, were all arrested as they moved in to attack the radio-location sites. The "observers" you told me about have mostly escaped - for the moment. However, they're a relatively feeble lot and pose no immediate danger to national security. We'll mop them up at leisure! Hamden Down is out of action temporarily, but all the other radio-location stations are intact. The Huns never attempted their dawn attack on our fighter stations, thank God! Due to Christine quietly immobilising Barnes' radio apparatus no message ever got through to Berlin! We were monitoring the transmitter on the barge throughout the night. Obviously the Luftwaffe decided not to risk an attack. They must have been completely in the dark as to what was happening over here! By an extraordinary coincidence von Straussen, the man you impersonated, escaped from his military escort yesterday morning and turned up at the warehouse in the evening. Christine has been able to give us a detailed account of his activities last night. Unfortunately both he and Barnes escaped. The police are mounting a major search for them. Von Straussen seems to be an exceptionally enterprising sort of chap. He could be a considerable nuisance to us in the future if he isn't recaptured. As to what happened to you last night, we think that Riddle came back to the warehouse secretly yesterday and managed to drug your evening coffee. Later, when you came round, you tried to attack Riddle but he shot you. Christine was a prisoner on the barge by then and saw the whole thing. Surprisingly, she managed to persuade them to let her attend to your head wound. Luckily for you Riddle's bullet only grazed the outer part of your skull but, of course, you were pretty badly concussed."

Ian sighed a deep sigh of relief. At least he was not responsible for a total failure of the counter-espionage operation he and Avon had planned so carefully. If the Nazis had succeeded with the whole ghastly plan envisaged in their "Operation Chainbreak" Britain might, by this morning, have been without fighter defences and wide open for invasion! Now that horrifying prospect was laid to rest, he was anxious to hear the full details of what had happened since he had drunk the fateful cup of coffee last evening. "Thank God the rest of your team performed so well," he said. "Now that weight is off my mind, can you satisfy my curiosity as to what happened after Riddle's drug began to work and I passed out. You see I can't remember a thing from the early evening onwards." "You can thank Christine that you're still alive," said Avon, "although she deserves, and will get, a reprimand for hanging up the phone on a superior officer - once I feel up to the task! Mind you if she had carried out the order that I would most certainly have given, had she not cut me off, I doubt if you would have survived the night!" When you failed to turn up at New Street to catch your train she phoned me. Then, as I said, she hung up immediately. After that she came straight up to the warehouse to look for you. Your "friends" captured her, but she kept her wits about her and eventually got her chance to sabotage their radio. Before that she dealt with the head injury you got when you tried to tackle Riddle and he so inconsiderately shot you! Without her skilled attention you would most probably have bled to death!"

"When I got Christine's phone call," proceeded Avon, "I guessed that somebody on the other side had at last realised that you weren't a senior German intelligence officer after all. I knew things were likely to get pretty sticky and that there was no time to lose! I left my 2i/c,

Wing Commander Beveridge, in charge of co-ordinating our own operation from headquarters in London then grabbed young Anderson, who was duty officer at HQ. last night. We got a taxi and caught the fast night mail train to Birmingham by the skin of our teeth. Meanwhile Beveridge had contacted the Birmingham police. When we arrived at New Street a Superintendent and driver were there to meet us. A squad car was waiting and half a dozen officers followed in a van. We raced for the warehouse but found the door down to the towpath had been securely fastened. Breaking it down was quite a job! The noise obviously disturbed your friends. When the door finally gave way the first two constables started down the steps to the warehouse. To our horror they were immediately shot down by Riddle. Apparently he was on his way to settle with you and Christine in revenge for your having wrecked the German plan. One constable died on the spot. The other is in the hospital here with chest wounds. The surgeon says he will live."

Avon continued his account. "The police weren't armed but Anderson and I had our service revolvers so I made the Superintendent hold his men back and we had a go. Riddle got me in the arm, as you see. Fortunately Anderson is a first- class shot and has cat's eyes! He put a couple of shots into Riddle and killed him instantly. In the melee we did not realise there were two other

German agents involved. Once we had attended to the dead and injured we checked out the warehouse. It was only after that, that we investigated the barge. We found Christine, who had wisely kept her head down while all the disturbance was going on. She told us the whole story. We immediately organised a search for Von Straussen and Barnes, and had you carted over here to the Accident Hospital, where they took the bullet out of your skull. The surgeon says you were damned lucky! You have a thickish skull and the bullet went through the outer table of the bone at an angle. It never penetrated the inner table. Such brains as you have are still in one piece!"

Avon got to his feet. He yawned. "I'm off to get some sleep. See that you two behave! Tomorrow we'll have a proper debriefing. I want you both fit - and on your best behaviour - for that!" He struggled to his feet turned and left the room. The nurse, who had been waiting, silent, on the far side of the bed, looked at Christine, gave her a little smile, and then followed Avon, closing the door gently behind her.

On 22 June 1941, a few weeks after the collapse of Operation Chainbreak, Hitler abandoned his previous cordial relationship with Stalin, and the German army, backed by the Luftwaffe, swept Eastwards in an all-out attack on the USSR.

THE END